other books in this series, you'll get a good chuckle and shed a few tears."

—Fresh Fiction

"Holby writes an enjoyable romance."

—*RT Book Reviews*

WINDFALL

"A great story with warm, likable characters."

—The Best Reviews

"If you're fascinated with the Civil War, Holby gives you everything you want and more."

—*RT Book Reviews*

CROSSWINDS

"Cindy Holby proves she is quite talented with an enjoyable saga that fans will relish."

—*Midwest Book Review*

"A reader who is enchanted by history and the U.S. Civil War will be sure to enjoy this read."

—Roundtable Reviews

WIND OF THE WOLF

"A wonderful story! It captured my attention, pulled me in and made me feel like I was there with the characters."

—*Old Book Barn Gazette*

"Cindy Holby displays her talent with an insightful look at tragedy."

—*Midwest Book Review*

CHASE THE WIND

"Cindy Holby takes us on an incredible journey of love, betrayal, and the will to survive. Ms. Holby is definitely a star on the rise!"

—The Best Reviews

"*Chase the Wind* is like no other book you'll read, and you owe it to yourself to experience it."

—EscapetoRomance.com

"MINE."

His lips claimed her. They branded her. His hand was splayed across the back of her skull so she could not move. She felt the steel of his blade and the heft of the hilt at her back as he wrapped his sword arm around her. Her arms were trapped between them. The leather of his hauberk pressed through her clothes. And she knew there would be bruises where the buckles touched. She felt the ridge of his erection as it pressed against her stomach, and her body lurched at the brazenness of his claim.

No man had ever kissed her. No man had dared to touch her, yet this man laid claim to her with the blood of his victims smearing his face as if he were a Viking chieftain of old. Ancient Viking blood ran in her veins, she felt the stir of it deep inside her like a wolf calling to its mate. Indeed she heard Llyr's rumbling growl beside her as Rhys made his claim. She could not breathe, she could not move, but she did not want to protest. It was his right to claim her.

Other *Leisure* books by Cindy Holby:

FALLEN
RISING WIND
WHIRLWIND
FORGIVE THE WIND
WINDFALL
CROSSWINDS
WIND OF THE WOLF
CHASE THE WIND

Writing as Colby Hodge:

TWIST
STAR SHADOWS
SHOOTING STAR
STARGAZER

Cindy Holby

Breath of Heaven

LEISURE BOOKS NEW YORK CITY

A LEISURE BOOK®

June 2010

Published by

Dorchester Publishing Co., Inc.
200 Madison Avenue
New York, NY 10016

ISBN 10: 0-8439-6404-9
ISBN 13: 978-0-8439-6404-2
E-ISBN: 1-4285-0875-0

Visit us online at www.dorchesterpub.com.

For Rob, who always believes in me.

*And as always, I could not write a word
without the constant support of my friends,
Alesia, Barb, Eileen, Michelle, and Serena.
Thanks, guys. I'd be lost without you.*

Breath of
Heaven

Chapter One

Rhys de Remy was not surprised when a hand snaked out from behind the velvet curtain and pulled him into an alcove within the upper hallway of the king's residence in London.

"Marcella," he said to the pale and willowy blonde clutching his sleeve. "Do you make it a habit of snaring unsuspecting men in dark hallways?"

"Sir," she gasped. "You wrong me." Her pale lashes fluttered over her light blue eyes as she turned her head away as if frightened by his proximity. Her body trembled as he moved his hands up the long sleeves of her bliaut until he could grasp her upper arms.

He knew her game and was more than willing to play it. He captured her jaw and covered her mouth with a kiss. Marcella enjoyed the chase as much as she enjoyed the conclusion. She swayed against him with her hands clutching at the thick leather of his practice tunic while his mouth moved down the exquisite line of her jaw to her gracefully arched neck. Her small breasts pushed against his chest when she sighed her surrender. As if he had been the one to chase her.

It was always so easy for him. It had been ever since the first time the lovely, generous, and most conveniently widowed Lady Sybille invited him to her chambers and showed him the wonders to be found in lying with a woman. He was just sixteen at the time

and a most eager student. Now Lady Sybille was once
more married and no longer as lovely or as slender as
she had been in her youth, but the things she'd taught
the young squire still served him well. He remembered her fondly at times. Or as fondly as he would
allow himself to feel toward anyone. He did not waste
time with feelings. Rhys found it more practical to concentrate on physical things, such as the willing woman
before him.

Rhys pushed Marcella against the heavy stone of
the castle wall. Freezing rain pounded against the
thick glass of the window beside them. The rattle was
loud enough to cover any sound they might make. It
would not do for one of the king's wards to be caught
in a tryst, even if she was a widow. Marcella would,
along with all her property, eventually be given in marriage to some deserving servant of King Henry.

Rhys was not interested in marriage. Not in the
least. Why buy a cow, he asked, when you could have
the milk for free? And it seemed he was always sup-
plied with plenty of milk no matter where he went. He
had no desire for more land or riches, because with
both came more responsibility. He had no heirs that
he knew of, and no bastard had yet claimed him as
sire. He was young enough and open-minded enough
to think that someday he might change his mind about
marriage, but for now he was content with his life. He
served his own needs and those of the king and once a
year he offered his right arm to the one man he owed
a great debt. The man who'd saved his life. Lord Edward Chandler of Aubregate.

"You do love me," Marcella whispered as Rhys
raised her skirts and she wrapped her thin legs around

his waist. The heat from her pale thighs warmed his hips as he slipped his chausses down.

"Do I not constantly show you?" Rhys replied as he pushed inside her without ceremony. He caught her gasp as he covered her mouth with his. He was not worried about hurting her. She might appear to be delicate and fragile, but Marcella liked her sex play to be rough. She responded by trying to bite his lip, but Rhys pulled his head back before she could capture it and instead buried his face in her neck so that he would not have to look at her.

So he would not have to respond to her words of love.

Rhys lost himself in the moment. In the rhythm of their bodies. In the building cataclysm that he hoped would fill the emptiness inside him.

Despite the damp and the aching cold that leached through the window, their bodies grew slick with sweat. Rhys felt the pressure build and he held Marcella up with one arm so he could brace the other against the wall as he prepared for the tide of his release to wash over him. She clung to him in her own fervor but then let out a gasp as a blast of cold air caressed his naked backside.

The timing of their exposure could not have been worse, but at the moment he did not care. He let the tide come, let it blast through his body as he clenched and bucked against Marcella, who pushed against him in haste. He didn't care. The damage was already done and he could not change it. It wasn't until he heard a shriek and felt a hand grasp his hair that he realized who had discovered them.

"Jane," he said calmly as she turned his head toward

her. He jerked his chausses up and dropped his chainse and jerkin back into place as Marcella's skirts dropped down around her ankles. She staggered a step when he released her, and clutched greedily at his arm. Rhys shook her off and instead grabbed Jane's arm as the lushly dark brunette swung an open palm toward his cheek.

"Cheat!" she shrieked. "Liar!" she added at a higher decibel. Rhys grabbed her about the waist and lifted her from the floor to keep her flying feet from connecting with his shins. Another woman stood in the hallway, along with Jane's maid, who watched her lady struggle with something akin to glee on her face. "You said you loved me!" she added as she dissolved into tears.

"I never said I loved you," Rhys stated clearly. He released Jane, confident that she would not attack him, only to receive a stinging slap from Marcella.

"Bastard," she hissed. "You never said you loved me either."

Rhys arched an eyebrow in admiration. Of the two he dallied with, he'd always thought Marcella the more intelligent. They both had qualities he admired—their willingness to enter into an affair with him being one and the fact that they were not virgins another.

"I never lied to either of you," Rhys said. "You both heard what you wanted to hear, and you both got what you wanted." He crossed his arms and leaned casually against the wall as if he were observing the drama before him, instead of the cause of it.

Jane sobbed in the arms of the woman who accompanied her while Marcella straightened her gown and adjusted her headpiece with several dramatic sighs. The fashions of women. Rhys found them arduous and inconvenient. Especially the things that covered their heads.

"The king will not be pleased that you have used his wards so lightly, Lord de Remy," she said. She patted the sobbing Jane, who had her head buried in her companion's ample breasts. Indeed, they were so ample, Rhys feared Jane would disappear between them.

"I took nothing that was not willingly given." Rhys tried to recall the woman's name and position at court. She seemed vaguely familiar to him. "Nor am I the first to do so," he said with a pointed look at Marcella.

Marcella gasped at the affront, gathered up her skirts, and marched off in one direction while Jane dashed off in the other.

"I shall speak to the king of your despicable behavior," the lady assured him.

Rhys gave her his most courtly bow as she turned and followed Jane. Jane's maid gave him a devilish grin as she dropped a curtsey and sauntered off. Rhys watched her go and wondered if he might seduce the wench. He was certain the mistress would no longer be bestowing her favors upon him.

He was not concerned about the woman's threat to speak to the king. Since Eleanor had gone back to France some five years earlier, there was no queen overseeing the morals of the court. And Henry's mind was occupied with the troubles of one Thomas Beckett, not the silly gossip of the women at court. Still, someone must supervise the wards, and Rhys suddenly realized that the woman who'd threatened him was indeed the one who did so.

There was no reason to worry. He would absent

himself from court until the talk died down. Mayhap he should pay a visit to his lands, if the king would permit it.

He would leave before the women had a chance to complain about his "mistreatment." Rhys grinned ruefully as he made his way to the winding staircase that led to the lower levels and eventually the stables. Yes. He was running away. The subtleties and politics of court life tried on his patience mightily.

All this talk of love . . . Why did women need to hear it? Did they think that it made the deed any less a sin if pretty words were attached? Love was a lie made up by the troubadours and balladeers and that was all it ever would be.

He had been on his way to meet his squire, Mathias, when Marcella had interrupted him. He knew Mathias would wait for him since Rhys intended to continue his lessons in swordsmanship. When he entered the main hall, he saw several pages standing about, waiting until they were summoned to run an errand for the lords and ladies of the court. Two of them were engaged in a mock sword fight with rolled parchments as some of the others cheered them on.

Interested, Rhys leaned against a table and watched the game for a moment. The play of children always fascinated him. There had been no such luxury for him in childhood. First, his grandmother had been intent on teaching him his obligation to his Lord and Savior who resided in the heavens above, his duty to the king, and his responsibility to his lands and vassals. He must be fit to rule Myrddin when he became a man. Time spent in frivolous play was time taken away from his prayers and his studies. Then he'd been sent to his grandmother's cousin Lord Allan, who immediately packed up his men-at-arms and went off to help the king secure his crown.

At a very young age, Rhys had seen the horrors of battle and the desperation of men. He'd often wondered how the God of peace that his grandmother prayed to could allow such things to happen. There was no one to explain such things to him. He was an unimportant lad who was not allowed to ask questions of men and squires who had important duties to attend. Lord Allan taught him to fight and not much more. Rhys soon learned from his experiences that no one cared if he lived. No one except one kind lord, Edward Chandler of Aubregate. If not for the generous nature of Lord Edward and his squire, Peter, who'd taught Rhys how to fight with his fists, he never would have survived those years, especially with the likes of Renauld Vannoy around.

As if conjured up by Rhys's thoughts, Renauld entered the chamber from the opposite door and grabbed the arm of a page who was engrossed in watching the mock battle. He was not gentle with the boy; instead he seemed intent upon wringing the page's arm from his shoulder. There was much gesturing upon the boy's part as if he was offering some sort of explanation.

Rhys resisted the urge to cross the room and slam Renauld against the wall. Indeed, if he had his preference, he'd pitch the man from the top of the battlements. His resentment at the years of abuse he'd suffered at the older squire's hands had not lessened in the years since Renauld had left Lord Allan's care. Whatever the page said must have appeased Renauld, for he left quickly and the page returned to watch the game, holding his arm as if it pained him.

Rhys remembered the pain in his own arm when Renauld would jerk him about, along with the bruises left by his tormentor's pinching. He remembered shivering from cold and the empty hollowness in his stomach when Renauld either withheld blankets or made it impossible for him to eat. There wasn't a deep enough hole in hell for Renauld Vannoy as far as Rhys was concerned.

"Milord," Mathias said as he suddenly appeared beside Rhys. The boy had a knack for moving silently. He seemed to walk without placing his feet upon the floor and there was never any sound of his passage. It was a gift. One that actually might serve Rhys well. Mathias was his first squire, the son of the knight who held Myrddin for him. Mathias had only been with him a few months, and Rhys was already appreciating the boy's talents. Discretion was one of them.

"Did you tire of waiting for me?" Rhys asked the boy.

"You bid me wait," Mathias said. "But a messenger has come with a letter for you. He awaits you now in the stables."

"Why did he not pass the message to you?" Rhys asked. "Is it not from your father and my holdings?"

"Nay," Mathias said. "The man said he is from Aubregate. He brings you word from his master. His name is Han."

"I know this man," Rhys said. Every year since he was a boy, Rhys had written to Lord Edward, offering to repay the debt of gratitude he owed the man. And each year, Han had come to him and delivered a personal response to Rhys's letter. "Milord is happy to know you are doing well and will await news from you next year. He bids you to stay strong and true to yourself." He always ended the message with "At this time milord does not require payment of your debt to him." Fourteen years of the same response had come and gone.

In all that time, Han had not aged one bit. The passage of years had transformed Rhys from a skinny boy to a man full grown, but for Han it was as if time had stopped.

He had not changed since that memorable day fourteen years earlier when Lord Edward had saved Rhys's life on the battlefield. The young squire had fallen from a bridge over a muddy torrent, and no one but Lord Edward had cared enough to save him. Rhys would never forget that one act of kindness, but he had not seen his benefactor since. He only knew of Lord Edward what he had heard through the years.

The king held the Lord of Aubregate in high regard. Edward had come home from France after the battle for Anjou to find his wife dead and his daughter motherless at the hand of Renauld Vannoy's father. The king forgave Edward for killing the man, and bade him remain in peace upon his land to raise his daughter.

Lord Edward had not made an appearance in court for over fourteen years. Most of the younger nobles had no idea who the man was except that he was a great warrior who had once been called the Flaming Sword because of his bright red hair.

"Mathias," Rhys said. "Do you know of Renauld Vannoy?"

"Only what I have heard," Mathias replied. "None of it good."

Rhys nodded. "See what you can learn of his purpose for being at court," he said. "While I go see to the messenger."

"Should I be discreet, milord?" Mathias asked.

"Always where I am concerned," Rhys replied. "Find me as soon as possible," he added. "I am not sure how much longer we will be staying at court."

"Will we return home?" Mathias asked.

Home . . . When Mathias said home he meant Myrddin, where his father, mother, and sister resided. It was the place where Rhys was born, the place where his mother and then his father threw themselves from the battlements and died on the rocks before the sea carried their bodies away. It was the place where his grandmother taught him about the responsibilities that would be his when he achieved knighthood.

It was not his home. There was no such place.

"Yes," Rhys said. "Home. If the king allows it."

Mathias grinned.

"Go," Rhys said. He resisted the urge to ruffle the boy's hair. It would not do to encourage the lad or show him any weakness. Mathias was given into his care to become a knight, not to be indulged.

Mathias went off to do as he was bid. Rhys could not help noticing the jaunty hop in his step. Mathias had yet to learn that a subject's desires counted for naught without the blessing of the king. They could very well be stuck here for weeks upon end if the king chose to keep them.

The ice clung to Rhys's hair and covered his leather-clad shoulders as he dashed across the bailey to the stable. He slipped and caught himself as he came under the eaves. The shelter was crowed with servants huddling around a small fire in the hope that they would not be called out to perform some menial task in the miserable weather.

The interior of the stable was warmer. A fat orange cat washed its hip upon the top of a barrel beside a small brazier of coals. Soft brown eyes peered at him from heads of every color. Rhys walked down the row of stalls to where his black stallion, Yorath, was stabled. The great horse tossed his head and clomped a plate-sized hoof against the front of his stall as if he could knock it loose and escape.

Rhys rubbed his hand up the animal's straight nose and beneath his forelock. Yorath's ears swiveled back and forth and Rhys murmured words of comfort to the restless beast. "Soon," he promised. "Soon we will leave this place."

"Milord," a voice said. It was Han, unchanged as always.

Rhys had never seen Han without a tight wool hat on his head. In the summer it was uncomfortably out of place, but now it served to protect him from the cold and freezing rain. As always, it covered his eyebrows and came over his ears. A long braid hung down his back, and his skin was strangely pale. He showed no hint of a beard; indeed his skin was as unblemished as a child's. His eyes were a pale shade of blue, and oddly translucent. Han's brows, straight and slanted slightly upward instead of curving over his eyes, only added to the mystery surrounding the messenger.

When Rhys was younger, Han had frightened him,

although the servant had never given him any reason to fear.

"I hope all is well with your master," Rhys said as he took from Han the leather case that held the missive. "This is not the usual time for our exchange."

"My master bade me wait for your reply," Han said.

His response was not what Rhys expected. Usually Han relayed word for word what Lord Edward wrote upon the parchment. Now he just stepped back as if to wait. Rhys slid the parchment from the case. Lord Edward's seal was upon it and he stepped into the dim light cast from a high window as he broke it.

I have need of you to repay in kind a deed well done.

There was nothing else except the date. He looked at Han, who remained in the shadows. "Are there any words to go with this message?" he asked.

"One," Han said. "Hurry."

"I must get permission from the king," Rhys reminded him.

"My master always says God will help those who help themselves."

Rhys had not talked to God since he was a child, when his grandmother insisted he spend several hours on his knees each day. Most of that time he'd used praying for the time to end.

"Milord," Mathias said as he rushed into the stable. "The king requests your presence immediately."

One problem solved. He would not have to request an audience. Yet the abruptness of his summoning did not bode well. It must be because of the women.

"Wait here," he said to Han. "You can sleep in the

stall if you are not afraid," he added. "I will send Mathias with word when I am able to depart."

Han bowed quickly and Rhys was amazed to see him slip into the stall without fear. He was still more amazed when he realized that Yorath, who was very particular about who entered his stall, did not seem to mind his presence there in the least. He did not have time to dwell on his surprise, however. He had more important things on his mind. As he walked out of the stable and into the freezing rain, he felt as if he were up to his neck in a very deep cauldron and the king was not above stirring the stew for his own enjoyment.

Chapter Two

Rhys changed into his best clothing: a finely sewn white linen chainse, a velvet tunic of a rich burgundy over gray chausses, and his finest black leather boots. He splashed water on his face and ran his fingers through his thick dark hair. He strapped his sword and scabbard to his side and took a moment to peer into the silver-painted glass at his reflection. Eyes as dark as night stared back at him. Eyes that were, for once, full of worry.

What did Edward expect of him? Why had the king summoned him? He had a sinking feeling that it had something to do with Marcella, Jane, and the earlier events of the day. What else could it be?

Mathias, hastily scrubbed, was also wearing his finest, a tunic of sapphire blue over brown chausses. The color matched his bright blue eyes and complemented the golden hair that curled about his ears. He held Rhys's mantle, a deep midnight blue with a silver fur lining. If he was about to be cast into the pit, at least he would be warm.

"I will look like a peacock," Rhys said as he flung the mantle over his shoulder and raised his chin while Mathias attached a huge ruby brooch that had been his father's.

"Better a peacock than a pea, milord," Mathias said.

Rhys arched his brow. "Is there supposed to be a meaning to those words?" he asked.

Mathias's cheeks turned pink as he grinned ruefully. "I thought the occasion called for something profound." He shrugged. "It was the best I could come up with."

"Let us hope that you are better with a sword than with your wits," Rhys replied.

"Is it not your duty to instruct me in both?" Mathias asked.

"You presume much," Rhys said as he resisted the urge to laugh out loud. "And fortunately for you, I have not the time to beat you for impudence."

"Yes, milord," Mathias said humbly.

Rhys adopted Mathias's attitude of humbleness as they entered Henry's throne room. He was not encouraged when he saw Marcella and Jane, both dressed in their most flattering gowns and both flanking the woman who had accompanied Jane earlier. Her name came to him now. Estella, a distant cousin of the queen and stewardess of the ladies who were under Henry's protection. Several of Henry's advisers stood about also. Of them all, Rhys only saw one friendly face. Peter of Salisbury, Lord Edward's former squire and Rhys's longtime friend. That was good. He needed to speak to Peter of Edward's summons. He needed to know what Edward's message meant.

Rhys bowed low before Henry when he was announced.

"I have heard that a fox has been loose among the hens," Henry said. His face was serious, but the eyes above his reddish beard twinkled merrily.

At that moment, Rhys knew he was in deep trouble. Henry needed a distraction from his long-standing battle with Thomas Beckett and the Church, and Rhys had a feeling he was about to become the king's amusement.

"Have you been generous with your . . . affections . . . Lord de Remy?" Henry asked.

"My grandmother always taught me that it is better to give than to receive," Rhys declared loudly enough for all to hear. He must tread lightly. It would do him no good to insult the character of either woman.

"Then we must thank the good lady for teaching you charity in all areas of your life," Henry replied, quickly joining into the game. Polite laughter went through the throng as Henry acknowledged Rhys's bawdy attempt at humor. "As we all know, you have always shown yourself to be generous in every undertaking, whether on the battlefield, here at court, upon your lands . . . and now with these new"—the king cleared his throat meaningfully—"conquests."

Rhys bowed at the compliment, yet kept his eyes upon the king.

"It has been lonely for you all these years, has it not, Lord de Remy?" the king asked. "A life without the comfort of family is not an easy thing to bear."

"I have grown accustomed to my solitude," Rhys answered cautiously. "My country and king have taken the place of family in my heart."

"A fine sentiment indeed," Henry said. "I have found you to be ever faithful in all that you do and therefore most deserving."

Rhys's stomach sank. He was fairly certain he did not want to hear what it was the king felt he deserved.

"It is time, nay, past time, for you to marry, my very deserving and devoted Lord de Remy."

Rhys swallowed hard as the king casually lifted a hand. Marcella stepped forward and Estella prodded Jane in the back so that she jumped forward with a small squeal. Both women kept their eyes demurely downcast and their hands folded before them. Marcella's shoulders and back seemed rigid, while Jane's trembled, whether from fear or shame, Rhys could not tell which.

"I will give you the chance to choose a bride," Henry said. "I gladly submit two of my wards for your consideration. The lovely Lady Marcella, and the equally lovely Lady Jane. Both untimely widowed and in possession of substantial lands and riches. Each a fitting prize for a devoted servant." Henry looked at Rhys, who tried his best to suppress the shiver that went down his spine. He was caught in a neat little trap. He cared for neither of the women, nor did he care to be saddled with a wife. Yet he must obey the king. Still, he would not be a willing victim. Not if he could help it.

"I am not deserving of so fine a gift," Rhys said. "And I find I cannot choose between two equally perfect ladies."

"But I insist," Henry replied calmly. "It is time for you to wed, Rhys. I will give you leave to choose your bride where you will. But mark my words, you will choose a bride, or I will choose one for you."

"If I may, milord," Rhys said as an idea suddenly came to him. "I have just this morning received word from a faithful servant of yours, Lord Edward Chandler. He has need of me. I owe him a great debt and it is time for me to pay."

"What debt is this?" Henry asked.

"He saved my life," Rhys said.

"Ah yes," Henry replied. "At Anjou. He snatched you from a pit of mud."

Rhys took a moment to wonder if Renauld was present at the gathering. It was due to his push that Rhys had found himself drowning in that pit of mud. He'd never said anything to anyone about the circumstances of how he'd found himself in such desperate straits, and he was not about to now. It would become common knowledge in God's due time.

"Yes, milord," Rhys replied. "I beg your permission to go to Lord Edward, for he bade me come quickly."

"I have always held Lord Edward in the highest esteem," Henry said. "And have long missed seeing him. I bid you go and see to his needs at once and report back to me on his well-being."

Rhys bowed.

"And when you return, you will have made your choice," Henry reminded him. "A bride for Lord de Remy. By the first day in February," he added.

"As you wish," Rhys said, and once again bowed. He cast a glance toward the women. Both seemed displeased with him. He must choose one of them, and soon. Which would it be? He would think upon it while undertaking the journey to Aubregate.

What was it exactly that Lord Edward expected of him? Rhys wondered. As he backed away from the king and made his exit, he saw Peter making his way behind the onlookers to meet him. Mayhap his friend could shed some light upon the mystery of Lord Edward's summons.

"It seems you are ever falling into the morass, my

friend," Peter said when they were both free of the king's chamber and Rhys had bid Mathias to prepare for their journey.

"Neither time was intentional, I assure you," Rhys replied.

"So you accidentally fell and slipped inside two of the king's wards?" Peter asked with a grin.

"Nay," Rhys replied with his own sheepish grin. "Those slips were quite intentional and most enjoyable. The problem arose when one caught me with the other."

"I am surprised you are still standing," Peter said. "My own wife has assured me that I would be missing a part I hold most dear should I be caught in similar circumstance."

"Which is why I have avoided the married state so far," Rhys said. "I have no desire to be trapped by feminine whim."

"There are many benefits to be had also," Peter said. "Do not dismiss marriage until you have at least attempted it."

"I shall keep that in mind as it seems I will be wed very soon," Rhys said dryly. "Have you news from Lord Edward?"

Peter shook his head. "Not since a month past. You know his health is not good," he added.

"I did not. In truth, he has not shared anything with me through the years beyond his wishes for my continued good health and his hopes to hear from me again the following year. What I've learned of him I have gleaned from those who know him. All speak highly of Lord Edward." Rhys watched Peter's eyes closely as he asked the next question. "But is it true what is said of his daughter? That she is disfigured in some way?"

Peter shrugged eloquently. "There are those who talk nonsense of things they do not understand." After giving that mysterious answer, he quickly changed the subject before Rhys could question him further. "Did Edward offer a reason for his summons?"

"He said, 'I have need of you to repay a deed well done.'"

"He means to collect the debt you owe him," Peter said. "Do you have any idea of how you are to repay him?"

"I do not, and I must admit it troubles me," Rhys said. "There is only one way to find out what it is Lord Edward desires of me—answer his summons. I must be off, and quickly, as milord has requested."

"Good journey to you," Peter said as he clasped his hand on Rhys's shoulder. "Please tell milord that I am ever his faithful servant."

"As am I."

"You will invite me to the wedding," Peter added with a wry grin as they shook hands.

"In honest truth, I hope by the time I return, it will be forgotten."

Peter's eyes darted over Rhys's shoulder. "In honest truth, I will remind you that some will not let it be forgotten."

Rhys glanced over his shoulder and saw Jane watching him.

"Go," Peter said. "I will keep the lady from distracting you from your purpose this day."

"Thank you." Rhys tried his best not to run from the hall as he heard Peter greet Jane behind his back.

He felt somewhat a coward, but he was also wise enough to know when to retreat.

If he'd been so careful in all his dealings, he would not now be in this fine mess. As it was, he would be grateful for his escape and hope that fate would lead him to a solution. Perhaps he would find one in Aubregate. Rhys nearly stopped and returned to Peter when he realized his friend had not answered his question about Edward's daughter. "It seems I will have to find out firsthand when I get there."

Chapter Three

*E*liane Chandler, daughter of Lord Edward and the long departed Lady Arden, stood at the door of her father's chamber and watched as his man, Cedric, helped him sit up and plumped the pillows behind him. Her dog, Llyr, stood at her side and Eliane twirled the thick dark hairs at the dog's neck through her fingers without giving any thought to the action. She heard the soft murmur of Cedric's voice and her father's raspy reply. Then in a weak voice her father called her and she stepped into the room with Llyr, as always, on her heels.

Her father, once strong, grew weaker with every passing day. His grasp, once mighty enough to hold a broadsword with ease, shook with tremors as she took his hand in hers and sat upon the bed beside him. The days, which had once been bright with his steady gaze, now were as gray as his pallor. Indeed the very land seemed to wither with the lord who no longer had the strength to rise from his bed.

Eliane knew the land was at rest for the winter and would come to life once again with the promise of spring. There was no such promise for her father. His life, which once seemed endless, would now only last for a handful of days.

Then responsibility for the people of Aubregate and

its land would be hers. She would become its guardian, from the deep wood, over the fields and town, to the high cliffs that stood sentinel over the sea. All that inhabited the land would look to her for their protection as they had her father for so many years. She was not sure she was up to the task.

"Tell me of your morning, daughter," Edward said.

Every day before the noon meal, she came to him after seeing to the keep and townsfolk. Each day he asked and she went over the happenings of life at Aubregate. The simple things of everyday living went on even as the lord lay dying. It was the way of things, the way it was supposed to be. But knowing it should be so did not make the pain any easier to bear.

"It snowed again last night and the well was covered with ice so thick that Goran had to drop an anvil attached to a rope to break it." She watched his face as she imparted the news. "It took three men to pull it up. I was most relieved to see that the rope did not break on the way down." She knew, and Goran now knew after the lashing she'd given him with her tongue, that he should have used a chain instead of a rope. She waited to see if her father would offer an opinion upon the matter. Instead a smile flitted across his face, more evident in his eyes than his mouth.

"I was prepared to tie a rope to Ammon and send him down after the anvil," she added. Her father's smile grew broader at the thought of the gangly stable boy dangling from the end of a rope over the well.

"I am sure Matilde would be more than willing to hold the rope," he said.

Eliane smiled at his joke. There was a long-going

war between Matilde, who ruled the kitchens, and Ammon, who was always lurking about, looking for a tidbit to fill the bottomless pit that was his stomach.

"How fare the townsfolk?" Edward asked.

"They fare most well," Eliane said. "There are stores aplenty. I saw Gryffyn's new son and he is hale and hearty," she added. She chose not to mention that the blacksmith had asked to bring the babe to the keep for the lord's blessing or that she had put the young man off, bidding him keep the babe close to home until it warmed a bit and the snow was not so deep. She did not want the people to see her father like this. They should remember him as the lord he had been, not the wasted man he had become.

"Ferris saw a boar at the edge of the wood yester-eve," she continued. "There will be a hunt later today."

"And you will ride?" Edward asked. His hand grasped weakly at the hem of her tunic, then moved down to flip the ends of the cross garters that held her chausses firmly in place around her thighs.

She shifted her seat. She knew her position was most unseemly: she had one leg curled on the bed and the other poised against the rug that covered the oaken floor. "I always ride, Papa," she reminded him. "You taught me well."

"I fear I have taught you too well the ways of a man and not enough the ways of a lady," he said. His glance took in her state of dress, which made her look more like a woodsman than mistress of Aubregate. It made sense to dress that way. How could she climb a tree or pull a lamb from a frozen stream if she wore skirts?

Eliane could not tell if he was sad or just weak. She could not stand to think he felt regret, so she hastened to assure him. "I have found your teachings to be most wondrous, Papa. Indeed I feel that I have fared better than most daughters of lords who are kept as secret treasures and then bartered off in marriage at a very young age. Most of them before they can even comprehend what it means to be a woman."

A wry smile twisted Edward's face. "And do you comprehend these things, my daughter?"

Heat flamed her neck and cheeks, almost matching the fiery hue of her hair. "Madwyn has taught me the way of things," she said softly. "I know what happens between a man and a woman." She could not meet her father's gaze. Instead she looked at Llyr, who laid his head upon her lap at her sudden discomfort and rumbled questioningly while he stared up at her with his deep brown eyes.

The silence stretched uncomfortably between them until Eliane could not bear it any longer and looked up from beneath her lashes to make sure her father was still with her. She found him studying her carefully as if something weighed heavy on his mind. Since she did not like the direction the conversation had turned, she gratefully changed the subject.

"Something troubles you, Papa?"

"I will be leaving you soon, Eliane."

Her throat swelled and she forbade the tears to spring forth. It was hard enough to think of her father's death without his speaking of it. She liked it better when they both pretended that he was merely ill.

"Do not say such things," she urged. "You will be better come spring. You are as strong as the earth and merely need the sun to bring you back to life. Indeed, I feel much as you do, and would love to pass the days lying beneath soft blankets and furs." Usually her teasing pleased him and she looked at him in anticipation of a quick rejoinder about having worked long and hard for many years and being deserving of a few days of rest. Today her teasing did not please him.

"The time has long gone past for you to marry," he said. "Are you certain there is no one you would choose for husband?"

"There is no one, Papa," she assured him.

"No man of the forest or town interests you?"

"Is it not my duty to marry someone of title?"

"Yes, daughter, it is, but I would know if there is someone you care for . . . someone you could love."

The heat rose in her cheeks again and she looked away. "There is no one, Papa, I promise you." How could there be when every man she knew felt as if he were her brother or uncle or grandfather? They were all her people, from the huntsmen of the forest to the fishermen by the sea. There was none who would look at her in any manner other than with sweet caring and respect for her role as Aubregate's future protector. There was no one she would consider for husband.

"It is my fault for keeping you close at hand," Edward said. "How can you choose a husband when I have not given you anyone to choose from?"

"I trust you to make the right decision for me," Eliane assured him once more, yet she could not help the shiver of fear that crept up her spine.

It seemed her father was determined to have her married before he died, yet whom did he expect her to marry? It was her duty to choose a husband who would protect Aubregate and the secrets that lay deep in the forest.

If he were available, she would choose Peter, for she knew him to be kind. But Peter had had a wife chosen for him at infancy, as most lords and ladies of the realm did. If only her father had chosen someone for her when she was a child, then the problem would be resolved. She would most likely be long married with a daughter of her own.

Yet he had given her the gift of choosing as her mother had chosen him and she'd neglected it all these years. She'd stayed close to Aubregate, as if her very life depended upon it. Many times she felt as if it did, as if she would suffocate or die of a broken heart if she set foot outside its borders.

There was only one other lord she knew, and he was not one she would choose, even if he were the last man on earth. She would never marry Renauld Vannoy. She had witnessed his cruelty as a boy and knew that a black heart like his only worsened with time.

Surely her father would not choose Renauld? It would be most practical for her to marry him, as her lands bordered his along the deep forest. Their union would bring peace to both their lands, healing the enmity that had arisen when Renauld's father had killed her mother, and Edward had taken his revenge on his wife's murderer.

To this day the border they shared was not safe. Any of Renauld's men who dared venture into the forest never returned, and a similar fate awaited the few unfortunate souls of Aubregate who happened to be caught away from its protection.

Her words echoed in her ears as she watched her father's face. She trusted him to make the right decision for her. Surely the right decision did not include Renauld?

What if it did?

"Ride with the hunt this day, Eliane," Edward said. "But upon the morrow, I would have you dress as befitting your station." He tugged on the end of her braid, and his eyes moved up to the wool cap that covered her head.

"Yes, Papa," Eliane said. She stood and Llyr moved beside her, anxious to be off. He knew there would be a hunt today. He'd seen the preparations.

She bent to kiss her father and he took her hand. "I love you, dearest daughter. You have forever been a blessing to me."

"I love you too." She turned quickly so he would not the see the tears that once more threatened to spill forth. Carefully, she walked away with Llyr at her heels. As soon as she was through the door, she fled as if her father's pending death could somehow snare her also.

Eliane ran down the curved stone steps and into the main hallway. She heard a maid squeal in surprise as she pounded by and recognized the cook's voice calling out after her. She ignored them both and did not stop until she reached the inner bailey.

Weak sunshine greeted her, along with a wall of frigid air that made her lungs ache. Her childhood friend Ammon stood with her mare, Aletha. Llyr bounded to the mare's side and greeted her joyfully. Her bow and quiver hung from the saddle, along with a short sword and belt. No one hunted boar without weapons. To do so would be foolish. A bow such as hers would not stop a wild boar, but it might give the beast pause until her men could bring it down with their spears.

"Are the men ready?" she asked Ammon as she took the reins and checked the girth on the saddle.

"Yes, milday," Ammon replied. "They await you outside the gate."

"Milady!" The cook stood in the door, her ample sides heaving with exertion. "Is anything amiss?" Matilde held Eliane's cloak in her arms.

"Nay," Eliane said when she saw the concern on the cook's face. "I am just anxious to be off." She smiled gratefully at Matilde as she placed the fur-lined cloak over her shoulders.

Did Matilde hide her fear for the future as Eliane hoped she hid hers? Did she, along with the other people of Aubregate, worry that their lady would not care for them as well as their lord? There was no fear evident in the brown eyes of the cook who had been as much a mother to her as Madwyn. Both had offered comfort to the small girl who'd watched as an arrow pierced her mother's heart. Impulsively, Eliane gave the cook a quick hug. It was not the proper thing for the lady of the keep to do, but Eliane had never been one to worry about propriety.

Mayhap it was time she started. It seemed as if that was her father's greatest wish and she could not deny him. Not when he was dying.

"Will you ride with us, Ammon?" He cupped his hands to boost her into the saddle. It was more of a polite gesture than anything, as Eliane's legs were long enough to meet the stirrup on her own. A gesture born of long habit. Ammon was only a year younger than

Eliane. They'd grown up together. Others might think her chausses and tunic inappropriate, along with her seat astride the horse. Ammon would have been more surprised if she wore skirts and rode sidesaddle. Would he look upon her differently when she became his protector?

He grinned up at her. "I only await your permission."

"'Tis given," she replied with a smile. He ran across the courtyard and vaulted upon the back of his mount. It was one of the younger mounts, born of her mare's dam and her father's destrier, who now awaited her father in heaven so that they might once more ride together. That was her version of heaven, not the one described by the priests. Eliane could not conceive of paradise without the love of a trusted animal such as Hector, Aletha, or Llyr.

They rode through the raised portcullis and into the outer bailey, where the huntsmen waited. The hounds were held tightly in check by Ferris, the hunt master, and they bayed in earnest when they saw Llyr trotting by her side. He ignored them as always. Eliane knew he felt vastly superior to the hounds because he was allowed full run of the keep instead of being chained at night. What other dog slept at the foot of a soft bed but Llyr?

Eliane and Ammon rode through the gate and across the drawbridge that was the final defense of Aubregate Keep. Stags, carved from stone, their features long ago faded from wind and weather, kept watch over the towers on either side of the gate. She should make sure the hinges were oiled and have the chains checked on both bridge and portcullis. It had been so long since they'd been lowered that she was not sure if they were in working order. It was quite possible she would have need of their protection soon. If her father died before she married, there would be suitors who would come, suitors such as Renauld Vannoy, whose desire to possess Aubregate was bred into him, along with his hawkish looks and indifferent cruelty.

She would come under the king's protection. The sudden thought nearly caused her to pull up on Aletha's reins. As it was, the mare danced sideways and bumped into Ammon's mount. The young stallion reared and fought the bit as Ammon struggled to retain his seat.

"Milady?" he asked when he had his mount once more under control.

"I feel I am too distracted today for the hunt," Eliane declared loudly enough for all to hear. "I will visit with Madwyn today and look forward to your tales of conquest at dinner this eve." Without waiting for their response, she kicked her heels into Aletha's sides and took off across the field to the forest with Llyr bounding through the knee-deep snow at her side.

Eliane felt the peace of the forest come over her as Aletha wound her way through the trees and onto the path cut by the innumerable deer that came to the field to graze at night beneath the safety of Aubregate's towers. She let the mare have her head.

The air fairly crackled with cold and their breath emerged as puffs of fog that seemed to freeze in midair. Aletha's hooves beat a steady rhythm that accompanied the beating of Eliane's heart. Branches popped

overhead as squirrels scampered above in their haste
to make sure the intruders were not after their treasure trove of food hidden away for the winter. A robin
flew ahead, skimming just ahead of them with its red
breast glowing bright against the dim grayness of the
forest.

Llyr turned to look at her with his mouth open
wide in a semblance of a smile, and Eliane smiled back
in return, snatching the wool cap from her head and
stuffing it into her cloak. Without it, she felt a sudden
sense of freedom. In the distance, she heard the crash-
ing of heavy bodies through the wood, along with the
cries of the hounds. They were on the trail of the boar
and headed away from her, to the north.

The trail began to slope downhill, and the tinkling
sound of water moving beneath ice greeted her ears.
Even though the air was frigid, the stream moved
quickly enough to keep it from freezing entirely. The
trail paralleled the stream, and both Llyr and Aletha
quickened their steps, knowing their destination was
close by.

Suddenly Llyr stopped and Eliane quickly pulled up
on Aletha's reins so she would not run into the dog,
which stood in the middle of the trail with his ears
pitched forward. Eliane listened, her ears trained by
Madwyn to differentiate between the sounds that belonged in the forest and those that did not. A weak
bleating noise filtered through the normal sounds of
birds chirping, trees creaking, and small animals scur-
rying about the undergrowth. Eliane urged Aletha
forward.

The path opened into a snow-covered glade with a
large pond in the middle. The pond was covered with

a sheet of ice, and a snow-trodden path led down to its banks. A doe raised her head at their appearance and trotted cautiously away a few steps. As Llyr bounded forward, she ran into the woods.

Eliane heard the bleating again and saw something move close to the bank. She dismounted and followed the path to the pond's edge, where a fawn struggled to escape the broken ice. As Eliane approached, the little creature stopped its struggles and stood trembling in the icy water with only its head showing above the crusting of ice.

"Poor thing," she cooed. Quickly she removed her cloak and gloves and commanded Llyr to stand back. Her first step into the pond brought a gasp as the icy water poured into her boots. Still, she moved onward and the fawn bucked desperately. Fear drove it farther out into the water. Eliane lunged and caught the creature just as it slid beneath the ice.

She shivered violently as she pulled the baby against her breast, capturing its thin legs beneath her arm to keep it from striking her. It bleated once more, then sagged against her as she struggled to climb up the steep bank of the pond. She felt it shaking with cold and realized it was likely to freeze to death.

She struggled upward and onward. The fawn, while gangly, was also light, so Eliane shifted it to her side as she snatched up her cloak. She cleared the snow from the ground with a swipe of her foot and wrapped both of them up in the fur lining as she sank to the ground.

"Llyr," she commanded. "Come."

Llyr obediently trotted to her side and sank down beside her. Eliane leaned against his side for warmth and spoke soothingly to the fawn, which could not be more than a few days old. Born in the dead of winter, its chances for survival were bleak, yet she was determined to do what she could for it.

"Poor thing," she said. "Trapped in the ice. I sympathize, my sweet, for I feel that I may soon be trapped also." She rocked as she petted the fawn's spotted neck and felt it calm beneath her hands. "Trapped in responsibility, trapped in marriage, trapped by the people and the place I love most."

Aletha snuffed at the snow and then raked a hoof across it until the tips of some sweet grass peaked through. Llyr watched from her side, and the heat of his body seeped through her cloak. Her feet felt like ice, so she slipped off her boots with some difficulty. She poured the water out onto the ground and set them aside. She wrapped her feet in the cloak and slid them up beneath Llyr's front legs to warm them, then leaned against his hindquarters with the fawn in her arms.

The fawn's breathing slowed and it snuggled deep into her arms and the warm fur of her cloak. Eliane realized it was sleeping. Its fight for life had left it exhausted. She was unwilling to disturb the little animal, so she relaxed a bit and let Llyr support both of them. As peace settled over the glade, Eliane watched the doe timidly step forward and browse among the tufts of grass that Aletha had revealed.

If only my life could continue to be this simple. . . .

What would happen come the morrow? Her father had asked her to put away her usual clothing, and dress as befitting her station. Was there a reason for his request? Why did he ask her if there was someone she wished to marry? Was he now prepared to choose for her? She had said she would leave it to him; now that the time had drawn nigh, she must stand by her word.

What if he died before he made his choice? What then? Would the king send for her? Take her away from Aubregate? Use her as a pawn or give her as a reward? Eliane well knew what became of unmarried heiresses.

There was no need to dwell on things she could not change. She trusted her father to choose well, and she would live with his choice.

And if her marriage was not accomplished before her father died, then she would close up the gates and defend herself against unwanted suitors.

I cannot . . . the people will suffer. Aubregate will be lost. . . .

If only she could disappear into the forest. Fade into the trees and lose herself in the world that remained hidden there. She could go with Han. He would show her the way.

Where is Han?

He had not participated in the hunt, and now that she thought on it, it had been several days since she'd seen him. It was not unusual for him to disappear for long periods. Han usually stayed in the deep woods, only coming out occasionally, or when her father had need of him.

"Father has sent Han to find me a husband," Eliane said aloud. Aletha and Llyr both looked her way. The doe raised her head and the fawn stirred in her arms.

"Be gone, little one," she said as she stood the fawn up in the snow. It cried out and moved to its mother with its tail raised like a flag in greeting. The doe sniffed it carefully, then looked at Eliane with its soft brown eyes full of gratitude.

"You are most welcome," Eliane said as the two faded into the forest. "Now see if you can avoid the huntsmen's arrows and all will be well."

Llyr stood and stretched and Eliane pulled her boots on, even though her woolen stockings were still wet and the leather of her boots was stiff with ice. She must be off. She must find Madwyn and learn what the wise woman knew about her father's plans.

Only the foolish were unprepared. Whatever was to come, she would meet it head-on. Her people were depending upon her.

Chapter Four

*R*hys was not pleased. Not at all. The journey had been miserable right from the beginning. First freezing rain and impossible roads, now snow that drifted and made the roads impassable. To complete his frustration, Han had disappeared into the forest this morning, leaving Rhys only a brief set of instructions.

"Stay on the road and you will be at Aubregate before the sun sets," he'd said. "Do not wander into the forest lest you lose your way." Then he was gone without a backward glance. Into the very forest he warned them against.

Mathias was not much help with anything. His sad face, heavy sighs, and resentful attitude tested Rhys's patience. He well understood what made Mathias so miserable. The boy wanted to be on his way home to Myrddin, not traipsing about the northern country in the snow.

They were cold, they were wet, they were tired and hungry, and now they were without a guide. The road was poorly marked, if there even was a road. No one had passed this way in several days. The path was nothing more than a snow-covered depression between the forest and the fields that seemed wide enough to hold a wagon. Rhys could only hope that they'd make Aubregate before the sun set. The prospect of spending another night freezing beneath his furs by a puny fire was not welcoming. The sun, weak and distant as it was, did little to warm them, yet it was better than the dark and endless nights.

"Damn!" Mathias cursed, and Rhys brought Yorath to a stop. The stallion tossed his dark head in frustration. He was as anxious to reach warmth and shelter as his master. Rhys turned about and saw their supplies lying in the middle of the path. The packhorse stood with his saddle twisted about his belly.

"The girth broke," Mathias exclaimed as he dismounted.

"I suggest you fix it," Rhys ground out between his clenched teeth. He was ready to strangle his squire and was long past the end of his patience. "And quickly, lest I be tempted to beat you," he added. He'd been threatening to beat Mathias the entire trip but to no avail. Mathias knew he was lying just as Rhys did. He'd been beaten often enough himself as a child and as a squire to know it was a poor form of correction. His grandmother had beaten him regularly in an attempt to drive the devil from his soul. The only thing that accomplished was teaching Rhys to hide his true feelings from the world lest the devil be known.

The best way for Mathias to learn from his mistakes was by having to suffer the consequences of them. He'd been neglectful in his care of the saddle; now he would have to repair it and repack their things. It would take him a while, but he would be more diligent the next time they set out.

Mathias grumbled as he attacked the mess. But he did attack it and with alacrity.

Rhys dismounted and checked Yorath's plate-sized

hooves for ice. He scooped balls of snow from the hooves and ran his gloved hands over the fetlocks to clear them of ice that had tangled in the hair. Yorath nudged him in gratitude and Rhys rubbed his nose in return. "Tonight you shall be warm, my friend," he said. "That is, if yon squire can keep his wits about him."

Mathias grunted in response. Rhys merely shook his head and indulged himself with a stretch to relieve stiffness of long hours in the saddle. The journey had taken twice as long as expected, but it was better than the alternative of staying at court and wedding either Marcella or Jane.

Marriage. Peter assured him there were joys to be found in that holy estate. Rhys had no firsthand knowledge of such joy. His grandmother had been forced into marriage; so had his mother. Both seemed desperate to avoid it, his mother so much that she killed herself. Yet from the whisperings of the servants, it seemed as if his father had loved his mother desperately. Eventually, he'd chosen death over life without her.

A sign of weakness, his grandmother had told him. One that sent his father to hell for all eternity. Now she was in her nunnery praying for his immortal soul and for Rhys's also, praying that he be spared the same weakness.

Was it weakness? Or a sign of something so deep that he could not comprehend it? Was there something lacking in him that he could not imagine loving, or hating something so deeply that death would be preferable?

Rhys shook his head at his meanderings. He should be thinking about which woman to take as a wife, not the meaning of life, love, and marriage.

So, would it be Marcella or Jane? He weighed both of them in his mind, their strengths, their weaknesses, their beauty, their riches, and finally their intelligence. Both came up lacking and he found his temper growing shorter.

With this delay, it was unlikely they would reach Aubregate by nightfall. Rhys studied the forest before him. The trees, larger and older than any he had seen before, stretched away endlessly into the distance. The snowy ground was crisscrossed with the fresh tracks of both birds and small creatures such as rabbits and squirrels.

Rabbit would make a nice dinner if they were forced to spend another night on the road. Fortunately he had a small bow that would serve his purpose. He retrieved it from his saddle and checked on Mathias. The squire had their belongings sorted neatly beside the road and was now examining the saddle. The packhorse stood next to his mount, and both wore feed bags and munched in contentment.

"I'm going to hunt," he called out, and Mathias waved impatiently in acknowledgment. "I really should beat him," Rhys said as he stepped into the forest. There was no reply.

After a few steps he felt a strange solitude, as if he were completely cut off from everyone and everything. He turned and saw Yorath browsing along the road and Mathias working industriously. It was as if they did not even know he was gone.

The way led downward and Rhys followed, tracking

the meandering trail of a rabbit through the undergrowth. There was no direct route, but Rhys plowed doggedly through the snow with his mantle dragging behind him.

Once more he checked behind and realized he could no longer see the road, nor Yorath and Mathias. All he saw in any direction was dense forest. There was nothing to indicate north, south, east, or west. If not for his tracks, he would think he'd fallen into some sort of enchantment.

Rhys shook his head at the foolish direction of his thoughts. This north land was full of legends and stories of magical happenings. When he was a tiny boy his nurse would fill his head with wonderful tales of the fey and fairies and dragons of yore. Every night she'd tell him a story until his grandmother discovered his head was being filled with unholy thoughts and sent the nurse away to a nunnery to repent of her sins.

Rhys knew the difference between stories and reality, but in a place such as this he could see how the lines could be crossed and such legends came into existence. His skin fairly crawled with anticipation. If he were on a battlefield he might be concerned, but here it just felt . . . strange. He felt as if he'd intruded upon something magical and private. He felt as if he should retrace his steps and leave this place.

The branch of a low-lying shrub moved in front of him and he caught a flash of fur. It was the rabbit, running for all it was worth toward a small ravine. Birds and squirrels took flight as he set off after it. He notched his bow as he ran in hopes that he could get a shot at it. Rhys stopped at the top of the ravine and his eyes darted back and forth. He spotted his quarry, just as it scrambled up the opposite side and disappeared into a deadfall.

The ravine was about as deep as he was tall and was nearly the same across. The bottom held an ice-covered stream. He could see the water running beneath the surface. Rocks broke through the ice and he realized he could use them as stepping-stones to get to the opposite bank if need be.

Or he could jump. Rhys grinned at the prospect, backed up ten steps, and took a running leap. He landed solidly upon the opposite bank, or so he thought. Then the ground beneath him began giving way and he toppled backward. He landed with a thud at the bottom of the ravine. His backside crashed through the ice and was immersed in the frigid water.

He felt dazed. He saw stars and then a swirl of color swam before his face. He blinked and realized someone was staring down at him.

It was a woman. Or was it? She was dressed as a man, but there was no mistaking the delicateness of her features or the curves of her body. Indeed, the very state of her dress enhanced them, more than any courtly dress ever could. In her hands she held a bow with an arrow notched and ready.

Rhys quickly backed away. When he reached the side of the ravine, he placed his hand upon the hilt of the short sword he always wore and gazed up at her.

A long braid of bronze mixed with copper fell over her shoulder and dangled past her waist. A belt hung low on her hip, holding a sword a bit shorter than his. She was clad in a brown tunic and chausses, along with leather boots that came to her knees. Her legs were long and lithe, and her body thin and willowy, yet generous in places where it should be.

More than generous. A rich cloak of deep green lined with fox hung from her shoulders, along with a quiver full of arrows. Her arms wore leather gauntlets and her hands were covered in gloves that fit like a second skin. In her fingers she held the bow ready, yet aimed at the ground.

She looked down at him with vivid green eyes. *Her eyes look like emeralds.* . . . Her skin was as white as the snow except for the tip of her nose which was red from cold. At her side stood an immense dog.

She was extraordinarily beautiful, and he felt the impact of her gaze like a punch in his gut, and lower. Not even the icy cold water drenching his chausses could keep his response at bay. Her choice of clothing left little to the imagination. Indeed, it revealed much, even though she was warmly dressed and completely covered except for the top of her head.

Yet there was something peculiar about her, something strange that he could not quite identify. Was she part of the enchantment he'd felt earlier?

"You trespass, sir," she said in a voice that sounded as melodious as the water trickling over the rocks.

"I was waylaid upon my journey," he replied cautiously. "I merely seek a rabbit for my dinner."

She relaxed her hold on the arrow and reached behind her hip. She pulled forth a rabbit, which hung from a thong upon her belt. "This rabbit?" she asked.

"If you found yon rabbit coming from this direction, then yes, 'tis the one I seek."

"The rabbit is mine as you can clearly see," she said. "I suggest you hunt for your dinner in yon fields instead of these woods lest you meet the same fate as other trespassers in these woods."

"And what fate is that?" Rhys asked. He wanted to laugh at her bold threats but was fairly certain she would not take such a response well. Considering the fact that she was holding a bow and seemed quite capable of using it, he held his humor in check.

Mayhap she sensed his amusement. She looked at him intently, her emerald eyes moving over his body from the top of his head to the tip of his snow-covered boots. He waited for her to speak, but instead of answering his question, she placed the arrow back into her quiver, slung the bow over her shoulder, and turned away from him.

"It will be dark soon," she called out as she walked away. "I wish you luck in finding your way out."

The beast of a dog looked down at him. Its mouth hung open in the semblance of a friendly grin. Rhys did not wish to test its friendliness. Finally the animal turned and bounded after its mistress.

Rhys jumped across the stream and pulled himself up far enough to see into the forest. She was gone, vanished as quickly as she'd appeared.

He looked once again, his eyes searching back and forth until he could no longer make out anything in the dim light of the forest. Night was coming, and quickly. He was nearly frozen after his partial dunking in the stream. He clambered back up the bank on the side he'd come from and was relieved to find his tracks still there.

Had he really thought they would be gone? Her warning made it seem as if they would. He hurried back at a slow run, keeping his gaze fixed on his footprints as if they would disappear before him. A sense of relief washed over him when he saw the way lighten, and the dark form of Yorath came into his sight. He quickened his pace and burst forth from the forest as if he were being pursued.

"Milord?" Mathias asked questioningly. He turned from the packhorse, where it appeared he had just secured the last bundle. "Do you think we will make Aubregate before nightfall?"

"Let us give it a sincere try," Rhys answered as he went to Yorath. "I have had my fill of this journey and am anxious to see its end."

"I regret my part in our delay," Mathias said contritely.

"You have set it aright as best you can," Rhys replied. "And hopefully learned a lesson."

"Yes, lord," Mathias said. "I have."

Rhys set off without another word. The sun still hung in the western sky, and the lack of clouds above promised a moon to guide them. They would press on. If they were lucky, they would arrive in time for a hearty meal with Edward. If he was able.

Peter had said that Edward's health was failing. Was that the reason for his summons? He would have his answer soon enough. Preferably after a warm meal and an even warmer bed.

The thought of warm beds brought to mind warm and willing women to fill them. Would he find such at Aubregate? He usually had no trouble finding an eager maid, no matter where he visited.

If the women of Aubregate were anything like the woman who'd come upon him in the woods, then it would be a most delightful warming indeed. In all his experience, he had never seen one such as her. Or mayhap it was just her unusual form of dress that made her seem so different. *Nay, 'twas the woman. . . .*

The entire incident seemed unreal in his mind. Could he have struck his head and imagined the entire thing? A warrior woman of the forest, complete with bow and sword? If he were going to dream, then why not conjure up a willing mistress instead of an Amazon or a fey, or even an elf? The stories his nurse had told him were often of the elves who'd supposedly inhabited the land centuries ago, before the legends of Arthur, Merlin, and Avalon even existed.

Whoever she was, she was extraordinary. She was beauty and strength in one delightful package. Her skin glowed with good health and her teeth were white and straight. She was perfection from the tip of her toes to the top of her head. Except for her ears.

Rhys pulled Yorath to a stop. Her ears. They were pointed. The tops of them slanted up into tips. That was what was so strange about her. Between his fall and the fact that she'd held an arrow notched and ready to fly into his chest, he had not taken time to think about it.

"Milord?" Mathias asked.

Rhys shook his head. "Nothing," he said. "I thought I saw something, but I was mistaken." He urged Yorath onward with a quick squeeze of his thighs. He'd been too long in the snow, and the cold was affecting him. He'd imagined the entire episode. Or had he?

Chapter Five

"I should have killed him."

Llyr had no reply. He just kept on walking while Eliane led Aletha up the trail that led to Madwyn's home in the forest. It was not the first time she'd said it. Anyone who trespassed into the woods was fair game. Usually those who went in that deep never came out again. All those who lived in the area knew it. The townspeople never ventured into the forest unless they were in the company of a woodsman. The inhabitants of other estates only entered it hunting game or the treasure that was rumored to be hidden there. The fools did not know that the treasure was not something that could be taken.

So, who was the knight who had ventured into the forest? She recognized his knighthood at once. Who else but a knight would wear a mantle of wolf pelt lined with velvet of the deepest blue? Who else but a knight would wear silver spurs or carry a sword with a ruby set into the pommel? Who else but a knight would have the audacity to say that he was merely hunting rabbit for his dinner when he so brazenly trespassed? Who else but a knight would have the impudence to look at her with eyes as dark as the blackest sin and make her insides go weak at the thought of putting an arrow through his heart?

He'd seen her ears. Why, oh why, had she taken off

her cap? Because it itched. Because she hated it. Because she should not have to hide who and what she was, especially when she was in the forest.

What tales would he tell when he returned to the outside world? Why was he here? What was it about him that had stayed her arrow and shaken her confidence when he gazed upon her?

"I should have killed him."

Llyr loped on ahead as Madwyn's cottage came into view. It was set atop a small hillock that backed up to a stone cliff. Next to the cottage a spring bubbled forth from the forest floor. Steam rose from the spring in the frigid air and Eliane longed to soak in its warmth. Mayhap that would relieve the tension that gathered in her neck and shoulders as if she carried a heavy weight upon her back. Mayhap it would make her forget about the things that troubled her, for a moment or two. Then again, mayhap it would not. She let out a long sigh.

The cottage itself looked as if it were part of the hillock. Made of daub and stone, it was of the same shape with a perfectly round window in the front. The sides seemed to grow out of the stone face of the cliff. Ivy, strangely thriving in the cold, grew up the side and over the thatched roof. A well of stacked stones had been dug by the arched door, and a path of stone set into the earth and swept free of snow. Smoke rose merrily from the stone chimney, and the smell of baking bread greeted Eliane as she strode up the path. To the side of the cottage was a three-sided shed where Madwyn's palfrey stood. The mare turned at their appearance and neighed a greeting to Aletha.

Eliane loosened Aletha's bit and dropped the reins, sure in the knowledge that the mare would stay put.

Her stomach rumbled in anticipation as she ducked beneath the arch of the door and greeted Madwyn. Llyr already lay in front of the fire and held a huge bone between his paws. His tail thumped as Eliane removed her cloak and hung it on a peg by the door. Overhead, dried herbs hung from the rafters and a loom in the corner held the beginnings of a thick rug. Pelts of several small animals were stacked in a corner, just waiting to be sewn into the lining of a cloak or a pair of boots, and bread sat rising on the hearth. In the back was a huge bed, draped with curtains of deep velvet and piled high with blankets and furs. It sat against a wall covered with a huge tapestry that was so old, Eliane could not even guess whence it came. In the corner next to the window, a snowy white owl perched upon a branch that had been inserted into the daub of the wall. It stirred when Eliane came in and looked at her intently with its great golden eyes.

"I've brought a rabbit," she said by way of greeting.

Madwyn smiled as she took the rabbit and placed it in a basket for cleaning. "That is not all you bring," she said as she looked carefully into Eliane's face. "What troubles you this day?"

"Is it that apparent?" Eliane asked. "Will I ever have any secrets from you?"

Madwyn shook her head and took Eliane's hand in hers. "'Tis only because I know you so well," she said. "Indeed, you are quite adept at hiding your feelings. It is only here that you reveal them."

Eliane looked into Madwyn's beautiful face and saw no judgment, only earnest caring.

"Come and sit," Madwyn said. "Tell me of your troubles."

Eliane sat at the well-worn table while Madwyn mixed herbs and steaming water together in thick mugs and set one down before her. "The list is long," Eliane said. "I am not sure where to begin."

"Begin at the beginning," Madwyn said as she sat down across from Eliane.

Eliane took a sip of her tea and looked at the woman across from her. She was ageless. She looked the same as she had when Eliane was a child crying in her arms for her mother. Thick blonde hair streaked with silver tumbled down her back to her hips. Vivid blue eyes beneath upward-slanted brows looked at her with concern. Her face was remarkably smooth, with only a few creases around her eyes from laughter, and her hands were as fine and spotless as Eliane's.

"I saw Gryffth's son," Eliane said.

Madwyn's laugh tinkled merrily. "Is it your intent to find out the details of my midwifery?" she said in reference to one of the many roles she played at Aubregate. "Is that the first priority on your list of troubles?"

"Nay," Eliane admitted. "It only reminded me that Gryffth wished to bring the babe for Father's blessing. I bade him wait."

Madwyn touched her arm to stop her. "This is one thing you do not have to hide from the people, Eliane," she said. "They know of Edward's decline. They will mourn his passing with great sorrow."

Eliane nodded. "I fear they will miss him even more when they see that I am all that is left to protect them."

"Is that what troubles you so? The responsibility?"

Eliane nodded. "I fear I am not worthy."

"You have always known what lies ahead for you. Why does it suddenly weigh upon you so much?"

"Because of something my father said this morning."

"What did he say?"

"He said the time has come for me to marry." The words tumbled forth now. "Yet I do not know whom he expects me to choose. I have given him leave to choose for me, but there is no time left. There is no one handy, except for Renauld, and I would rather die than marry him. Yet the alternative is to become a ward of the king, a pawn in his political maneuvering. How will that serve Aubregate and its people?" She looked at Madwyn with hope. Hope that the other woman would have answers for her.

Madwyn gently patted her hand and sipped her tea. "Your father is a wise man," she said. "He will make sure all is taken care of before he passes." Her answer was not what Eliane had hoped to hear.

"Do you know something I do not?" Eliane asked impatiently. "Do you know where Han is?" She narrowed her eyes. "Papa has bade me to dress as a lady on the morrow," she added. "Does someone come? Someone I do not know about?"

"Han is here," Madwyn replied. "You just missed him. I am surprised you did not see him on the trail. He is on his way to the keep as we speak."

"Because I stopped to hunt," Eliane said. "Which led to something else. Something I must tell Han."

"What is that?"

"I found a stranger in the forest. A very richly garbed stranger. A knight for certain, possibly even a lord."

"A lord? Here?" Madwyn's blue eyes widened with interest. "What happened? What did you do?"

Eliane told the tale, concluding, "I released him. I

bade him find his way out if he could. Yet I feel that I should not have done so."

"He did not discover anything. He could have been merely hunting, as he claimed. He would not know of any reason not to enter the forest if he was not of these parts."

What Madwyn said made sense except for one thing. "I was not wearing my cap when I came upon him," Eliane admitted.

"Oh," Madwyn said. Eliane watched as Madwyn's hands went to her ears. She pushed the silver and blonde locks behind the fragile peaks so similar to her own. Han possessed them too. Most inhabitants of the forest had the same ears and did what they could to make sure they were not seen by any outsiders. The townspeople and the castle folk were all used to the anomaly; occasionally the strangely formed ears would show up on the new babes born to the townspeople or crofters. None seemed to care. Everyone knew the trait was a throwback to the days of yore when all were of the forest.

Eliane's mother, Arden, had had ears that were rounded and normal. She remembered as a child touching the curve of her mother's ears, then her own pointed tips in wonder. When she realized that her ears were different from nearly everyone she knew, she wondered why. Why her?

The only thing that kept the gossips from questioning Eliane's parentage was the fact that she had the same bright hair as her father, along with his temperament. It was also not prudent to bandy about rumors concerning one's lord and benefactor.

Madwyn had reassured Eliane many times that it

was not strange she had the ears. Her mother's people had been forest folk going back more generations than she could count. Still it was difficult for Eliane to accept her difference when she realized at an early age that she was the only child in the keep with misshapen ears.

"I thought I would be safe." Eliane shrugged as Madwyn considered her tale. "I was not thinking clearly," she added. "It is hard for me to recall the last time I did think clearly about anything."

Madwyn took her hand and gave her a reassuring squeeze. "It has been many years since any of us have run across a stranger in the forest," she said. "You could not have foreseen it happening this day."

"It is my responsibility to protect the forest and all within," Eliane said. "What will happen when this strange knight returns home and tells the tale of my ears? Will others come to discover the truth of it?"

"They will more than likely think him drunk or under a spell," Madwyn replied with a smile.

"That does not reassure me," Eliane said. "If a spell was cast, they might come looking for the pointy-eared witch who cast it."

"Eliane," Madwyn exclaimed. "There are no witches about. And no need for you to worry. No one would think such a thing."

"People condemn what they do not understand. There are those in the Church who would call us demon possessed. If they knew what lay within these borders, they would condemn it." A tremor of fear ran down her spine. "They would kill us all and burn the forest to the ground."

"Hush, child," Madwyn said. "You are trying to

weave a blanket with nothing more than a thread."
She pushed the mug of tea into Eliane's hand. "Drink.
It will calm you. I will send a message to the huntsmen
to look out for a strange man in the forest. If they find
him still wandering about, then they can take care
that he does not live to tell the tale. And if he is gone,
then we will watch to see if anyone takes note of his
ramblings. If he has any wit, he will keep his tales to
himself so as not to damage his own reputation."

Eliane let out a sigh of relief. She seemed to be doing that quite a bit lately. It was easy to let Madwyn
solve her problems for her. She'd been doing so for
most of her life. Could it all be so simple? The stranger,
if found in the forest, would be killed.

A vision filled her mind. The strange knight lying
facedown in the forest with his body full of arrows.
The thought disturbed her for some strange reason.

"Nay," she said. "Let him be." She looked at Madwyn, who had already gone to the owl's perch to send a
message. "He is wise enough to find his way out and he
should not have to pay with his life for my mistake."

Madwyn smiled. "Your father has taught you well,"
she said. "To recognize wisdom in others and mistakes in yourself. 'Tis the mark of a wise ruler."

Eliane shook her head and then lowered it to the
table with a thunk. "What you call wisdom others
may call foolishness. You see me as a mother sees her
child."

"I see you as you are, Eliane," Madwyn said firmly.
"Do not think me so foolish as to be carried away by
feelings. I have lived many years and seen many things."
She crossed over to the fireplace and peered at the
bread in the oven before she turned and addressed

Eliane with her hands on her hips. "The problem lies in the way you see yourself. If you see yourself as weak and ineffective, then those you are trying to lead will see the same thing. You must learn to trust your instincts just as you did this day. Something stayed your bow. Something told you not to kill this knight. You must trust that it was the right thing to do and await the day when the reason is revealed to you."

"What if the reason is nothing more than a lustful heart?" Eliane cried out. She thunked her head upon the table once more as if she could drive the thoughts from her head. "I was weak when I gazed upon him. His face had the look of both angel and devil. He was beautiful, yet frightening, and I felt as if my body was not my own when he looked up at me."

Madwyn's lips lifted at the corners and Eliane waited in fear that she would laugh at her confession.

"I am sorry I missed him," Madwyn said finally. "He sounds . . . interesting."

"I feel as if a spell has been cast upon me." Eliane hit the table again with her forehead. "See how worthless I am? How easily swayed by a handsome face?"

"Pish!" Madwyn exclaimed. "Enough of this wallowing." She turned back to the oven and, with a cloth, reached in and pulled out two loaves. She placed them on the table before Eliane and slid the rising loaves inside. Madwyn added two short logs to the fire and turned back while wiping her hands upon her apron. "I will send word to the keep," she said. "You will stay here with me tonight. We will soak in the spring and I will wash your hair and rub scented potions into your skin. Then we will talk of happy things."

Eliane looked up at Madwyn, who peered down at

her expectantly. Her suggestion sounded wonderful. A momentary escape from what awaited her come morning. Her father had commanded her to put away her chausses and tunic and dress as befitting a lady. He must have a reason for his instructions.

"So be it," Eliane sighed. It was a much better prospect than continuing to beat her head upon the table. "Let us be merry tonight, for who knows what tomorrow may bring?"

Chapter Six

Finally. Renauld Vannoy waited impatiently in the audience chamber for his chance to speak to the king. For weeks he had cooled his heels, hoping to speak to King Henry about his concerns, and now that he'd been invited in, he still had to wait. Renauld knew the delay was intended to remind him that his problems were minor when compared to those of a king.

All this nonsense about Church and state . . . He had no patience for politics, especially when the Church stuck its long nose into the fray. As far as he was concerned, might meant right. Whoever was strongest was meant to survive. And Renauld was not above using the strength of others when his own was insufficient to his needs.

For his current task he needed the strength of a king. A king who would grant his request because of a small indiscretion Renauld had witnessed as a squire.

Renauld had learned early that it was best to walk carefully and stealthily in castle corridors. As a boy, he'd come upon his father tupping one of the serving wenches with a knife held at her throat.

When the wench slipped away, his father took out his anger upon his son, knocking him into a wall. The wench paid for her escape later that day with the loss of her tongue. She learned to stand his father's perverted desires and Renauld learned to tread lightly when walking about the halls. He was six at the time. The lesson had served him well.

When Henry was newly crowned and drunk with the power of being king, Renauld had witnessed the king's transgression. Henry did not want to remember, thus his reluctance to grant Renauld an audience. But Renauld had also learned the value of persistence as a small boy. He was not too proud to take a beating or two if it eventually led to what he wanted.

And Renauld wanted Aubregate. He wanted its fields, he wanted its town, and he wanted the natural harbor that lay at the base of the cliffs. He wanted the keep, the buildings, the livestock, and the vassals that inhabited the land and worked industriously for their lord instead of cheating and stealing and hiding their crops. He wanted the forest and the bountiful game that hid within its borders. He wanted the treasure that was rumored to lie at the heart of the woods.

But most of all, he wanted Eliane. He wanted her for the same reason that Henry would allow him to have her. He wanted her because he remembered. He remembered the look of disgust on her face that day he saw her watching him from the woods. What business was it of hers what he did? She was just a girl, nothing more than a child. She had no right to condemn him. Yet condemn him she did. She even came out of the forest and killed the dog with her bow. Then she threatened to kill him if she ever saw him torture another helpless animal. He was a squire, about to be knighted, and she was a child. What did she know about the ways of the world? What business was it of hers what he did on his property, with his property?

He would show her what he could do. He would wipe that look of contempt off her face as he should have done ten years ago.

When he was master of Aubregate, he would be master of Eliane. He would do what his father could not do, nor his father before him, or *his* father before *him*. All had desired Aubregate and died trying to get it. Renauld would succeed because he would have the help of the king.

"Lord Renauld Vannoy of Chasmore," a page intoned. Renauld stepped forward and bowed.

"Milord," he said casually. He dared much, as always. The look Henry gave him told him so.

"Come closer, Renauld," Henry said. "It has been a while since you've come before me."

"A long while," Renauld replied. "Since you knighted me."

Henry nodded. "It seems the years have been kind to both of us," he said. "And you have been content . . . until now. . . ."

"I live only to serve," Renauld reminded him. "And Your Majesty has not had need of me these past years, except for the levies he requires for rebuilding. I have embraced the task of acquiring the funds that you require," he added, omitting the fact that he'd had to threaten each one of his vassals with death to do so.

"Yes, it has been a time of peace," Henry said.

Which to Renauld's ears meant that if England had been at war he would have been long dead and Henry's secret with him. He graced his king with his best smile.

"Tell me, Renauld, what brings you from your lands in the dead of winter to speak to your king?"

"My concern for my closest neighbor, Edward Chandler of Aubregate," Renauld replied. "He has fallen quite ill."

"I am glad to see you bear no animosity toward Edward," Henry said graciously. "He is, after all, the man who killed your father."

"My father's sins are not my own," Renauld reminded him. "Nor his enemies or his battles."

"A wise sentiment," Henry said coolly.

Renauld inclined his head at the compliment. "I am concerned for Edward's daughter, the Lady Eliane."

"You know her?" Henry asked, interest written plainly on his face.

Renauld allowed himself a self-satisfied smile. After all, he was the one who'd started the rumors about Eliane's deformity after he'd seen her ears. It served his purpose for others to think her deformed so they would not seek her out for the riches she would surely possess someday. Someday soon. As he recalled, she was an unattractive wench even without the ears. All skinny arms and legs with bright red hair and spots on her nose and cheeks. He was sure the woman she had become would be much the same.

"We are neighbors, sire," Renauld said. "We have been at peace all these years. I am concerned about what will become of her when her father is no longer with us."

"You wish to offer for her?" Henry asked directly.

"I doubt her father would allow it," Renauld said honestly. "While I bear no animosity toward him, I am afraid he still carries some for me, owing to the nature of my father's crimes against him."

"He truly loved his wife," Henry said. "And he has kept his daughter close at hand."

"Indeed, sire," Renauld said. "To protect her. As I would protect her." His eyes stayed on Henry, to remind him of the secret he knew, while his words were for the courtiers who listened with interest to his request. "It is my greatest desire to keep the peace of the kingdom," he said. "And what better way to maintain it than by an alliance between two neighbors? We share a border. The Lady Eliane will soon have need of a protector and I have need of a wife. The alliance would benefit both the house of Chandler and of Vannoy, and together we would serve your kingdom well. That is, if *you* allow us to merge." He concluded his plea with a bow, yet still kept his eyes upon the king, willing him to see once more the secret he'd carried for so many years.

Renauld heard the expectant inhale of breath of all those who awaited the king's ruling. Would Henry simply hand over the Lady Eliane into his keeping? Renauld could not help holding his breath too as he awaited the king's word. He felt as if he were playing chess and had just put his queen at risk to corner the king. He'd put it all on the line, because he was determined to succeed where his father had failed.

The king looked at Renauld with eyes that seemed full of disappointment. Then suddenly he brightened. With a crook of his finger, he called, "Peter."

Damn . . . Peter Salisbury. Renauld had been relieved when he'd noticed the other man's absence. He had hated Peter Salisbury with a passion ever since the day at Anjou when Edward's squire had had the audacity to lay his fists upon him. Especially since he'd done so in front of young Rhys de Remy, who should have died in the mud that day. Both had been a thorn in his side ever since. And now here was Salisbury walking toward the king.

"Refresh my memory, Peter," the king said. "Did we not hear a similar plea from Lord de Remy just a few days ago concerning our *dear friend* Edward's health?"

Renauld felt his stomach sink when Henry referred to Edward as his friend. That was not something he had counted on. Since Edward was never at court, Renauld had hoped he would be nothing more than a name to the king. Was there something he'd overlooked? Something he did not know?

"Lord de Remy was summoned to Edward's side, milord," Peter explained loud enough for all to hear. "As you recall, Rhys owes Edward his life." Peter looked directly at Renauld, who resisted the urge to allow his hands to curl into fists.

De Remy had been summoned to Chandler's side? When? The last and only time he could recall seeing Rhys was three days ago.

"He departed immediately with your blessing, milord," Peter continued. "He was beginning to find court life a bit . . . suffocating."

The crowd laughed quietly at Peter's remark and Henry smiled broadly.

"I'm sure he was," Henry agreed quite jovially. His gaze fell upon Renauld. "It seems as if Lord Edward has reached out to someone in his time of need," Henry said. "But I am sure he appreciates your sentiments," he added graciously.

Renauld took a step forward before he could stop

himself. Henry's eyes flared and Peter's hand went to his side, poised above the hilt of his short dress sword. Henry raised his hand.

"Still," he said. "I am curious about Lady Eliane. If Edward's situation is as dire as I've been led to believe"—he looked pointedly at Renauld—"then it is my sincerest desire to give her aid, comfort, and *my* protection. So I bid you, Renauld, and you, Peter, to ride to Aubregate and bring her back to me . . . but only after she has buried her father."

"Milord," Renauld spoke up. "Bringing the lady here might not be the best thing for her. She is . . . different." He wanted to say deformed, but he had to be careful. After all, Salisbury had served as Chandler's squire. Chances were he'd seen Eliane's strange ears and would know that they could be easily hidden at court. However, if there was a chance that he could keep her away from Henry's protection, then he would take it.

Once more those assembled waited with bated breath for their monarch's reply. "Nonsense," Henry said. "She will find us accepting and full of love and respect for her no matter how different she may be," he said, and then he turned to Peter. "And bring back Lord de Remy also. I am sure there are many who are quite anxious to hear his decision."

Once more the crowd laughed, but Renauld did not hear it. He was concentrating on trying to hold back the red tide of rage that swelled within him. De Remy was at Aubregate or would be soon. If Renauld realized that, he could have followed him, killed him, and made it look as if it were the fault of the woodsmen.

If only he had known. It occurred to him that if

he'd had friends, he probably would have known. But friends meant trust, and trust was not something he could afford. Renauld trusted no man. He preferred to use his coin to get what he wanted. However, without the riches of Aubregate, his coin would soon come to an end.

Renauld found Henry looking at him expectantly. He bowed and without another word turned and walked away.

"Vannoy!" It was Salisbury, of course. Who else? Renauld stopped and gathered himself before he turned to greet the man who followed him out of the king's chamber.

"Salisbury," Renauld said. He had to admit the years had been kind to his foe. The last time he'd seen Peter had been at their knighting, which unfortunately had been done jointly. Salisbury had filled out nicely and now had the weight to go with his height. Though Renauld was not as tall as Salisbury, he was as stout and possessed great strength. Still, he'd always been envious of those who were graced with height, such as de Remy.

Could I take him? It occurred to Renauld that he could eliminate all of his enemies in one trip and have Eliane. They would be passing by his lands. His men-at-arms would be traveling with him. But what if Salisbury brought his troops also? Surely he would leave some behind to care for his wife. Still, it would be hard to do anything with so many witnesses. Witnesses who could not be bought, for he had no doubt that Salisbury's men would be loyal to him. Men such as Salisbury demanded such loyalty, as if it were their birthright.

Still, he would think on it.

"Will the morning be soon enough for you to leave?" Salisbury asked. Renauld could tell by his tone that he was not looking forward to the company either.

He thought for a moment. He needed time . . . time to prepare.

"First light?" he said finally.

"Agreed," Salisbury replied, and took his leave without another word.

Renauld watched him go. Salisbury possessed an air of confidence that irked him to the core. It always had, from the time Peter showed up with that whelp de Remy beside him and then challenged Renauld to a fight. Unfortunately, the challenge was issued in front of witnesses and, even more unfortunately, the fight had been with fists instead of weapons.

It had been difficult to determine a winner; both were giving as good as they got. They kept it up until Lord Allan pulled them apart and sent Salisbury on his way. After that, de Remy was not nearly as malleable as before, although Renauld did his best to make the youger squire pay for his insolence. Especially after he realized Rhys wasn't going to say a word about his *accidental fall* that day on the bridge.

Perhaps *he didn't know* Renauld had pushed him into the muddy torrent. But there were times when he caught the whelp staring at him . . . watching him . . . with those dark eyes of his that never showed fear or weakness. De Remy made sure he was never alone with Renauld after that day. Until Renauld was sent back to his own estates to learn their management from his father's steward before he was knighted.

That was when Eliane came upon him. The bitch.
She would pay, de Remy would pay, and Salisbury
would pay.

He smiled. He would have all his enemies together
in one place. The king had thought to outsmart him,
but instead he'd left him with one more move. One
more brilliant move. One that required he send a message to Chasmore at once.

*Be prepared, Your Majesty . . . I am about to declare
checkmate.*

Chapter Seven

*R*hys stretched mightily in the luxurious bed he'd been shown to the night before. He sighed in contentment and tossed a pillow at Mathias, who still slept heavily on a pallet before the fireplace. The lazy twit should have been up already and heated the water for his bath. They both should have been up hours ago, but the weariness of their journey had caught up with them.

There had been no lady of the castle to greet them upon their arrival the night before. Neither Lord Edward nor his daughter was about. Whether they were asleep or missing, he was not told by the man-at-arms who allowed them entry. Rhys assumed that Lord Edward's absence was due to his illness; still, the daughter should have appeared to welcome them.

Granted, they'd come late, guided by the crescent moon and the innumerable stars that reflected off the ice-encrusted snow. As they'd entered, Han had waved lazily at them from a comfortable pallet in the main chamber. That their guide was warm and well fed was of some annoyance to Rhys, especially since they'd been in Han's company early this morning. Why could they not have taken the same route as Han? Did the woman who'd threatened him with her bow in the forest have anything to do with Han's warning of yester morn? And did the man ever take off that blasted cap? He even wore it as he slept.

Mathias stirred and blinked heavily as he rubbed the sleep from his eyes.

"Be up, lazabout," Rhys said. "I require a bath, clean clothes, and food, preferably all served by someone more attractive than you."

Edward's daughter mayhap? Rhys had to admit that his curiosity was piqued. Especially since she had not greeted them last night. It was part of the lady's duties to greet guests, offer to bathe them and clothe them. Unless her deformity was such that she was unable to perform such duties? It was all very puzzling, as was the reason for Edward's summons.

Mathias stumbled up from his pallet. He stretched, yawned, scratched, and hitched up his chausses over his bony backside. He then knelt before the fire and added a few sticks of wood to bring it roaring back to life. The addition of a log made the flames pop and crackle, and a warm glow soon filled the room. The squire leaned back on his heels and briskly rubbed his bare arms to warm them.

Rhys looked at the pale white skin of Mathias's thin back as the boy flexed his shoulders to relieve the stiffness that came from sleeping on the floor. How long would it be before a scar marred that youthful skin? Rhys had been thirteen when he'd received his first wound in battle. An arrow had grazed his left arm—he was lucky the shaft had not pierced the muscle and left the arm useless.

He'd been lucky many more times in the innumerable small skirmishes he'd been involved with. None could really be called a war, although he'd been victorious in all. He had scars, across his back, on his side, and a particularly nasty one on his thigh where he'd been run through with a sword. Lucky he'd not been crippled or lost a limb. Lucky he'd survived his many battles.

He considered himself extremely lucky that he had not died the day just past. There'd been no mistaking the threat in the woman's emerald eyes just as there'd been no mistaking the fact that her ears were strangely pointed. The encounter seemed much more real to him now in the safety of the castle of Aubregate than it had when he'd come out of the forest. Very strange indeed. Should he mention it? Say that a woman with pointed ears had drawn a bow on him and threatened his very life while he lay with his arse freezing in a stream?

Mathias pulled on his chainse, tunic, and boots and left to do Rhys's bidding. Rhys lay back beneath the furs and lazily contemplated a ray of sunlight that filtered through the curtains of his bed. Curtains that kept our the cold that penetrated the stone walls of the castle.

Aubregate's riches were evident, but not ostentatious. The hangings on the bed frame were velvet and the rugs were thick and plush. The headboard was intricately carved, along with the posts that held the drapes around it. His mattress was well stuffed and without lumps, and his pillows smelled fresh and clean.

Hanging on the wall across from him was a tapestry unlike anything he'd ever seen before. It featured a woman of incredible beauty with long golden hair standing next to a pure white unicorn in a forest glade. The sunlight that pierced his bed hangings danced upon the tapestry, and golden threads woven throughout the maiden's and the unicorn's mane and tail glittered in the morning air along with a few careless dust motes.

He turned on his side and propped up his head with his arm to study it better.

It was evident the tapestry was very old, yet it seemed well cared for. Something about it made him sad, almost melancholy, as if he should have known the woman. As if he had missed something truly wonderful. Rhys shook his head at his thoughts. Another flight of fancy, just like the strange woman in the forest.

"Let us hope that I am indeed warm and dry in a bed and not freezing to death in some ditch," he said as he threw back the blankets and furs and rose to meet the day. His shaft pointed ahead of him, aiming at the tapestry as if the woman there would relieve its need. He hoped there would be a solution to that problem with the arrival of his bath. After the lazy days at court and the abundance of willing partners, he was unaccustomed to going without.

And you still have to decide between Jane and Marcella. . . . That thought did nothing to banish his sudden bout of melancholy at all.

He had no more than wrapped a fur about his naked hips than the door burst open and a line of servants came in with a tray of food, steaming buckets of water, and a tub made of hammered copper.

Mathias brought up the rear with a wide grin on his face. "Just as you requested, milord," he said.

Rhys cocked a questioning eyebrow at the servants. There was one somewhat dusky wench who carried the tray of food, but the rest were men. Unfortunately, the wench placed the tray upon a table, dipped a quick curtsey, and left while the men arranged the tub in front of the fireplace and poured the steaming buckets of water into it.

"Is this not as you requested, milord?" Mathias asked innocently. He stuck his tongue sideways in his cheek to keep from laughing out loud. "Did you not ask for someone other than me to bathe you?"

"I will beat you eventually," Rhys said.

"Do you make a habit of beating your squire, milord?" a voice called out. Rhys turned to find a tall woman standing in the doorway holding a basket with soap, oils, and towels. She seemed older than he, yet her face was remarkably smooth except for a few lines around her mouth and her strikingly blue eyes. Her head was completely covered with a thick veil and a long blonde braid shot with silver hung down her back. Her clothing was simple, yet rich, a dark blue bliaut of velvet with intricate silver embroidery on the sleeves that flared at her elbows to reveal a lighter blue sheath beneath. The sleeves of the sheath tightly hugged her arms, ending past her wrists in points between her thumbs and fingers. A wide silver chain belt with a small dagger rode low on her hips. The artistry of both was exquisite. The dagger held a large blue sapphire much like the ruby in the hilt of his short sword.

The woman carried the basket past him, across to the tub, and set it on a small stool. Placing her hands on her hips, she turned to look at Rhys. The look she gave him was appraising, as her eyes swept from the top of his head, down his chest, over his hips, to slide down his legs, where his toes curled into the thick pile of the rug beneath his feet.

"Which do you require first?" she asked as the serving men left the room. "To break your fast or bathe?"

Rhys dropped the fur. "A bath," he said, and strode casually to the tub.

She lifted an eyebrow as her sharp eyes took in everything about him and Rhys graced her with a smile, stepped into the tub, and sat down in the warm water. He could not help flinching as the heat seared his skin, especially the tender region between his thighs, but he kept his gaze upon the face above him. She might be older than he, but she was beautiful and he had found in the past that older women were most generous and ingenious in the art of lovemaking.

"Are you the lady of the castle?" he asked. He knew that Edward's wife had died many years ago but had not heard whether he had ever remarried.

"No," she said. "I am but a simple servant." She held out a bar of soap for his approval. He sniffed it. Sandalwood, of course, with a hint of something else . . . pine possibly? He nodded his approval and she dipped it into the water along with a cloth and lathered them together. "My name is Madwyn," she continued as she picked up his arm and began the process of scrubbing the days of travel from his body. "Milord and lady both bade me to apologize for their lack of hospitality this past eve. Milord is not well and milady and I were not present when you arrived."

"Is your lady at home now?" His curiosity was once more piqued about Edward's mysterious daughter. Mayhap she was hidden away in a convent where no one would see her.

"Yes," Madwyn replied as she moved around the tub and started on his other side. "Milady Eliane and I returned early this morning. She is attending to the needs of Aubregate and her father. She will send word when he is ready to meet with you."

Rhys reclined against the back of the tub with his

eyes closed while Madwyn went about the business of washing his body. The heat of the water spread into his muscles and relieved much of the tension he'd carried with him during the journey. The feel of the cloth sliding across the planes of his chest was pleasurable and Madwyn's touch was firm, yet gentle. All in all, it was quite an enjoyable bath and he had high hopes of it leading to more pleasure before he met Lord Edward. Still, he was curious about the missing daughter. "Will the Lady Eliane be present when I meet with Lord Edward?" he asked.

The answer he got was a hot towel draped across the lower half of his face. He opened one eye to find Madwyn standing over him with a blade in her hand. "Shall I shave you?" she asked. The glint in her eye gave him pause and he heard Mathias smother a snort across the room.

Rhys was not one to back down from a challenge. He nodded his agreement and laid his head back against the rim of the tub to allow her blade access to his throat. Her hands were deft and sure and he could not help admiring the closeness of the shave when she finished.

"Mathias," he said after she wiped the remnants of the soap from his face. "Did you lay out my best clothes?"

"Yes, milord," he replied.

"Then go attend to Yorath," he instructed. "Make sure he is content."

"Milord?" Mathias questioned. The squire knew full well that his master's horse was well cared for in the Aubregate stables.

"Go," Rhys barked. The boy needed to learn

prudence, especially when his master wanted to be alone with a woman. "Now." He heard the door close somewhat loudly behind the squire as he left the room. "I shall surely beat him before the day is out." Rhys sighed as he closed his eyes once more. Madwyn had given him a thorough cleaning from the waist up. He was now ready for her to proceed with the rest. More than ready. So ready that the tip of his shaft poked up through the water. His entire body tingled in anticipation as he imagined her hand, slick with soap, moving around it, grasping, squeezing, and pulling. Maybe she would even take him in her mouth.

His fantasy was quickly doused when she poured a bucket of icy water over his head.

"I beg your pardon, milord," she said in a breathless voice. "I fear I used the wrong bucket."

Rhys shivered, coughed, and sat up.

"Did you not wish for me to wash your hair, milord?" she asked. "Or should I take my leave now?"

"I can finish up on my own," he said. "You may go now." He watched her warily as she dried her hands and left the room without a backward glance. He heard the tinkle of her laughter as she closed the door behind her.

"Wench," he said as he leaned forward and finished lathering his hair. He slid beneath the surface of the water to rinse it. Luckily for him, his most pressing problem disappeared with the blast of icy water.

"What amuses you so?" Eliane inquired.

Madwyn stood in the upper hallway outside her room with her hand over her mouth. Her shoulders shook with the effort it took to suppress her laughter.

Eliane eyed her in suspicion. There was something afoot in the castle and she seemed to be the only one who did not know what was going on. Llyr stood patiently by her side as Madwyn wiped tears of laughter from her eyes.

After a most peaceful eve, followed by a restful sleep and an early awakening, Eliane and Madwyn had made their way through the gloaming of the forest and arrived at Aubregate with the first light of morning. Eliane felt heartened by the beautiful sunrise, which made everything look as it if were covered in beautiful jewels.

Her cheerful mood quickly turned to dismay, however, when Ammon told her of a lord and his squire who had arrived at the castle in the deep of night. According to Matilde, the pair were now ensconced in the guest chambers across from her own on the uppermost floor of the keep. Who was the mysterious visitor? No one seemed to know, except Han, and he was as closemouthed as ever.

"You have seen the visitors," Eliane said accusingly as she narrowed her eyes at Madwyn. She saw that Madwyn had changed into the clothing that she kept at Aubregate, clothing that was usually reserved for special occasions or visitors. "Who is he? What is his business here?"

Madwyn held up a hand as she composed herself. Still, her eyes danced merrily while she led Eliane from the hallway into her chamber. "Hush, child," she whispered, "lest he hear your shrewish questions."

"Shrewish?" Eliane gasped before Madwyn placed her hand over her mouth to quiet her. "This is my home and I am entitled to ask questions of strangers who enter," she said when Madwyn released her and the door was safely closed behind them.

"It is your father's business and he will let you know all in good time," Madwyn assured her. "But first we must make sure you are suitably dressed to meet this visitor." The older woman went to the chest that held Eliane's gowns.

"Tell me what you know, Madwyn," Eliane said. She crossed her arms and plopped down on her bed. "I will not move until you do." Llyr, seeing her position, jumped up on the bed and stretched out in his usual place.

"Then we are agreed," Madwyn replied tartly. "Since it is your father's desire that you stay in place until he calls for you." She rummaged through the chest, holding different gowns up to examine their worthiness.

Eliane bounced off the bed. "Am I to be kept prisoner?"

Madwyn grabbed Eliane's hands and led her back to the bed. "You are to obey your father," she said. "As you promised you would." She stroked her hand down the side of Eliane's head. Her hair was once more neatly braided after the thorough washing and brushing Madwyn had given it the night before. "We will dress you in your finest," she said, "and loosen your hair as befitting a maiden."

Eliane bit her lip as she looked into Madwyn's eyes. "Because I am about to meet the man my father has chosen for me to marry?" A shiver of fear trembled down her spine.

"Yes," Madwyn said.

"Who is he? Where does he come from?" The

questions formed quicker than she could ask them. "What does he look like? Is he old? Young? Can he hold a sword? Is he clean? Does he have all his teeth or is his mouth filled with rot?" The thought of giving the kiss of peace to someone with rotten teeth made her stomach roll in protest.

Madwyn put a finger to her mouth to quiet Eliane. "I am glad to hear the questions of a normal maiden," she said. "The normal fears—"

"There is nothing normal about this," Eliane said. She looked about her chamber as if it would offer some means of escape.

"Yes, there is," Madwyn assured her. "How many maidens do you suppose have asked these same questions before meeting the men they are to marry?"

"How many maidens have the legacy that I have?" Eliane cried out. "How many maidens carry the secrets that I must carry? How many maidens have to protect what I am presworn to protect?"

"The situation may be different, but the feelings are the same," Madwyn soothed. "Do you not trust your father?" she asked. "Because that is what it comes down to."

"Tell me, Madwyn," Eliane said. "What did you see in yon chamber?"

"I saw a man eager to have a wife," Madwyn said with a quick smile. "One who is most handsome, and strong, and young . . . and with all his teeth."

"In truth?" Eliane asked anxiously.

"In truth," Madwyn replied.

Footsteps sounded in the hall. They both looked toward the closed portal. Llyr jumped from the bed and went to the door. He lay down and sniffed at the

crack as a hard rap sounded on another door. A deep
voice responded and the door across the hall opened
and closed.

"Come," Madwyn said with a smile. "Let us prepare
you to meet your husband."

As Madwyn led her to choose her gown, Eliane realized she did not even know her intended husband's
name.

Chapter Eight

He was to marry Lord Edward's daughter. That was the reason for the summons. He did not even know her name. "What is your daughter called?" Rhys asked.

"Eliane," Edward replied. "You are not foresworn?" he asked again.

Eliane . . . the sound of it was lyrical. "No." His lips lifted into a grin. "I even have the king's blessing to choose a wife where I will, as long as I make my choice by the first day of February." This would certainly resolve his earlier dilemma.

"Why must you marry by then? Was there some problem?" Edward asked. He sat against his pillows. They were everywhere, behind his back, beneath his arms and knees, all in place to give his weakened body the support it needed. The room was dark, even though the day shone bright beyond the heavy curtains that covered the windows. There were curtains about the bed too. Edward was well protected from the cold and the light.

Rhys wanted nothing more than to fling back the curtains and allow the sunshine to come in and warm the room and the body that lay dying within the huge bed. Instead he raised his hand in assurance. "The problem was mine—too many brides to choose from. This makes my path easier."

"Be honest with me, sir," Edward said. "Is your heart given where your bond may take hold?"

Rhys smiled ruefully as he ran his hand through his still damp hair. "No one has ever held my heart. Not even my mother," he added. "There are no bonds to tie me other than that which I owe you."

Edward sank back into his pillows and sighed in relief. "Then let it be done." He raised a finger and the priest came forth. "The banns are ready?" Edward asked.

"They require only the signatures," Father Timothy replied. He held a roll of parchment in his hand. "I will post them today. Three days hence the marriage may take place."

By the looks of Edward, Rhys was not sure he would last three days. He'd been shocked when he first came into the lord's chambers. The wasted invalid who lay in the bed was not the robust man he recalled from his youth. Yet the eyes were the same, vividly blue and piercing, along with the sharp nose and pronounced brow. The hair, once red, was now shockingly white and the skin, once bronzed from the sun, seemed pasty and as fragile as the parchment Father Timothy now placed before Edward.

Edward's hand trembled, his manservant Cedric grasped it within his own and guided the quill to the place where Edward must sign. Rhys heard the scratch of the nib and then three pairs of eyes looked up at him expectantly. He nodded and Father Timothy carried the parchment to a table, where he handed Rhys the quill.

Rhys looked at the words carefully written upon the page. Once he placed his name below Lord Edward's, he was pledging to care for Edward's daughter, her lands, and all that lay within the borders of Aubregate. All that was his would become hers and all that was hers would become his. His name, his sword, and his honor would be given into her keeping and he had yet to look upon her face.

He blinked as another face came to mind. A face with emerald green eyes, a proud chin, a straight nose, and delicately arched brows. All framed with hair the color of flames and strangely pointed ears. An enchantment. Nothing more. Nothing there to keep him from his duty except a strange desire to run. Something he would not do. He could not do. His honor would not allow it.

He dipped the quill into the ink, yet he could not bring his hand to the parchment. What of the rumors? The deformity? What if Edward's daughter was so hideous that she could not show her face? Mathias moved to his side, his young face full of questions at the sudden turn both their lives had taken.

Rhys gave him a reassuring smile, even though he had questions himself. The nib touched the parchment and he formed the letters of his name. Rhys Christian Roger de Remy, Lord of Myrddin.

It mattered not about the daughter who was to be his wife. All that mattered was that he owed Edward his life and he was presworn. He would honor his agreement with this man.

Father Timothy snatched the parchment up and quickly sanded the ink to dry it. Was he afraid Rhys would go back on his word? The man had much to learn and would bear watching. The priest moved to bless Edward and left the room with the parchment in his hands. The banns must be posted on the door of the church, informing everyone of the coming marriage three days hence.

"When will I have the privilege of meeting the Lady Eliane?"

"First there are some things you should know," Edward said.

So the time had come to learn her secret. To know the extent of her deformity . . .

"Aubregate goes to the female of the line," Edward began. "It has always been so and will remain so. Any daughters you have will inherit the estate and all within."

"I have my own estates for any sons born of this union," Rhys said. He was puzzled at the turn of the conversation but not concerned.

"There has not been a son born to a woman of Aubregate in several generations," Edward said. "If ever," he added.

Rhys raised an eyebrow at that statement. Was Edward challenging his manhood?

"There are many secrets here," Edward said. "Secrets that only Eliane can give into your keeping. Do not attempt to uncover them on your own lest you meet your end."

"I will not be safe on my own lands?" Rhys questioned. "Is this a trick, sir? A test of my honor?" His voice rose and his hand went to his side, where his short sword rested.

"The lands are Eliane's, Rhys," Edward reminded him. "And I only tell you this to keep you safe. Do not go into the forest unless you are accompanied by Eliane, Han, or a guide."

The woman in the forest . . . "Han gave me a similar warning yestermorn," Rhys replied. "What dangers lie within the forest?"

"That will be Eliane's task to share with you, as it was her mother's to share the secret with me," Edward said weakly. Cedric moved to his side and placed a hand against his master's cheek.

"It is time for you to rest, milord," he said.

"I need to see Eliane," Edward protested weakly. "It is time she knew her fate."

Her fate? Edward made it sound as if she were soon to climb the gallows. It was strange that she was not betrothed until now. The estate was rich enough to receive many offers, unless the fact that the females of the line inherited scared some suitors away. Surely a landless knight would have offered for her, deformity and all. Unless the deformity was such . . .

Was that why Edward had chosen him? Because no one else would have her? Because he knew that Rhys's honor would not allow him to walk away from repaying his debt, no matter what the price? It would not bother him to be shackled with such a wife. He would live his life as before. No one at court would need to know anything about her beyond that she was his wife.

Cedric left to fetch the bride-to-be.

Rhys moved to the side of the bed and looked down upon the only person who had ever shown concern for him. Edward's eyes were closed and his breathing was labored. It was easy to see that his disease had attacked the warrior from the inside, eating him up until there was nothing left but this dry shell of skin and bones, kept alive by determination alone.

"God spare me from such," Rhys murmured quietly, his hand instinctively going to the small silver crucifix he wore about his neck.

Edward's hand lay upon the coverlet. The fingers were long and thin and Rhys could not help recalling the strength they once held, enough to pull a boy from the mud and hold him up by the tunic. That hand at one time could wield a broadsword and cleave a man in two. Rhys took the hand in his and noticed the difference in color. His was bronzed from the sun, with veins that pulsed with blood and fingers that were sure and strong. Edward's was pale white, mottled with spots; his fingers felt as if they would crush beneath his grip.

"I want you to know—" Rhys began. His voice broke and he cleared his throat. He heard Mathias shuffle his feet across the room and wished he'd had the presence of mind to send the squire off. But dying was part of living. And showing gratitude to someone who saved your life was not anything to be ashamed of.

"I want you to know—" he began again, and was heartened when Edward opened his eyes. "That I will give your daughter the same gentle care you gave me," he said. "I will protect her and this land. You gave me my life and in return I will give her mine."

Edward smiled. But it was not a smile of gratitude. It was humor that crinkled his eyes and faintly turned his lips upward.

"My boy," he said. "You do not know of what you speak. Be careful what promises you make at this time, lest you find them impossible to keep."

"Milord?" Rhys asked. He bent lower as Edward's voice grew weak. Yet the words he spoke were sure and certain.

"You will find that Eliane will determine what you will give and what she will take from you. And God grant you the patience to find out exactly what it is she wants."

Rhys wore a puzzled smile as he straightened up. These were not exactly the words of gratitude he'd expected to hear.

"Your daughter comes," Cedric announced as he returned to the room. Rhys stepped away, into the shadows beyond the bed. He kept the bed curtains between himself and Edward. A bit of privacy for the coming conversation, he told himself, but he knew his hidden position would give him a chance to observe. A chance to prepare himself. He noticed Mathias also faded into a dark corner on his own. The boy was quick to notice what went on around him.

Two women entered the room. One he quickly recognized as Madwyn, the woman who'd attended him at his bath. The other was just as tall and slim. Her hair was dark and unbound and fell past her waist. He could not tell the hue in the dim light of the room. He supposed it could be red, as Edward's had once been. Most of it was covered with a veil that was held in place by a gold circlet. The veil and her hair hid her face as she bent to her father. She sat down and took his hand in hers with fingers that showed no sign of deformity. Indeed, her arms were straight beneath her sleeves and beneath the dark blue velvet of her bliaut, her spine showed no strange curves or humps. Her steps as she entered had been sure and strong also.

It must be her face. . . . Rhys prepared himself to see her. He would not show emotion, he would not show horror. He would not shame his bride in front of her father, nor would he shame himself. He glanced over at Mathias, who seemed to have sunk deeper into the shadows. If the squire shamed either one of them, he would beat the boy soundly. This time he meant it.

"Papa," she said in a clear, low voice. There was no lisping, no stumbling. Indeed her voice was musical, like water flowing over the rocks in a stream.

"Daughter," Edward said. "The time has come for you to meet your husband." She started to rise from her place on the bed, but Edward's grip held her there. It would have been a simple task to move away, even for a woman. Rhys was glad to see she respected her father. "You have said time and time again that you trust my judgment. That whosoever I choose for you . . ." His voice was weak. ". . . you will honor."

"As I will, Papa," she reassured him. "I give you my word."

Edward placed his other hand atop his daughter's and weakly squeezed them together. "Then arise, Eliane, and meet your betrothed."

Rhys willed his face to remain impassive as she rose and turned. Once again he was struck by her height. She and Madwyn both were as tall as most men he knew. He stepped forward, toward the bed, which stood between them as a giant barrier. Would it be so in their marriage? he wondered. Would it be difficult to bed her? When the candles were out, would her deformity even matter? She kept her head down, her face lost in the shadows of her hair and veil.

"Lord Rhys de Remy of Myddrin," Edward said, "has agreed to be your husband."

Her hands were folded demurely in front of her and she kept her face down as she spoke. "We thank you,

Lord de Remy," she said. "For helping us in our time of need."

Once more he was struck by that lyrical voice. It was magical, as if it could capture him in a snare.

Magical . . . Rhys stepped around the bed. The drapes blocked his view as he passed the foot, the posts, the corner, until he came to the side she stood on. She wore a blue velvet gown, deeper and darker than the color of Madwyn's, with gold trim at the sleeves. The color was rich and luxurious, especially against the blandness of Edward's coverings.

Her veil was white and she wore a belt of gold that matched the circlet upon her head. He saw that her hair was indeed red, but that one word could hardly do the color justice. The candle on the bedside table and the fire flaming brightly in the hearth behind her brought out many more hues. She kept her face downcast so that her hair hid all except the tip of her nose from his sight.

"Mathias," he said. "Open the drapes so that I may see my bride's face."

She let out a tiny gasp, almost imperceptible except for the sudden rise of her shoulders. Behind her, Madwyn put her hand to her face to cover a smile. Rhys saw her blue eyes dancing in merriment and it gave him courage. He took the clasped hands in his and pulled her closer to the foot of the bed and the window.

"The air," Cedric protested. "It is cold. Too cold for milord."

"Leave it, Cedric," Edward said. Rhys spared him a glance and saw a wide smile of approval on his face.

She kept her face down as she allowed him to lead

her. When they both stood at the foot of the bed, before the window, Mathias pulled back the drape and sunlight streamed through the thick glass. Her hair turned the color of flame, with tendrils of red, gold, bronze, and copper all mixed together. Rhys could not help smiling as he placed his finger beneath her chin and raised her face. If dreams could come true, then he would be the first to say they had. Either that or he was still struck deep in some enchantment. Either way, he would enjoy this magic to its fullest.

A finely arched brow rose in challenge as emerald eyes looked upon him in bemusement. "I see you found your way out of the forest, milord," she said tartly.

"Forsooth," he replied, jumping into the game. "It was only the thought of the reward awaiting me here in Aubregate that guided my steps and kept me on the true path."

"Oh," she replied. "Did you have knowledge of your reward before you came?"

"Nay, milady," he said. "Only the rumors I heard at court. And they were not kind."

That remark seemed to puzzle her for a moment. "What are these rumors of which you speak?"

"Lies," he said. "Lies spoken by bitter hearts." He arched his own eyebrow in challenge, and then slowly raised his hands to lift the circlet from her head. Her eyes followed his hands, even when he tossed the circlet upon Edward's bed. Then he saw the fear in those great green depths as he slowly slid the veil from her hair.

"I would see for myself," he said softly. He touched a hand to the flaming thick mass of her hair and then pushed it back behind her ear. She raised her arm as if to stop him, but the quick and stern look he gave her halted her hand. He heard Edward stir upon his bed and looked at the man. He should speak but could not, not until he knew whether his eyes had been playing tricks on him in the forest.

Any deformity would be grounds to deny her. Everyone within the chamber knew it. Better to know it now, than later, on the wedding night, when there would be even more witnesses.

Her hair felt like silk in his hand. The scent of it filled his head and brought visions of deep glades and cool water. Wisps of it snagged on the fragile tip of her ear and he carefully smoothed them away before placing a finger on her cheek to turn her head toward the window. She tilted away from him, as if she were shamed by what he saw.

There was a distinct peak to her ear that made it once again the size of what was usual. The delicacy of it amazed him. The light made it translucent, as if it were a piece of abalone shell washed up on the beach. He had never seen anything like it. "I thought I imagined it," he whispered. "I thought it some enchantment."

"I assure you it is most real," Eliane said. She turned her head back to look him in the eye and carefully smoothed her hair back into place. "As was my warning."

"Eliane," Edward chided from his bed.

"She has your spirit, I see," Rhys said. "But whence did this come?" He waved his hand in the general area of her ear. Something about the way she stared at him made him reluctant to touch her, although it was now his right.

"From her mother's family," Madwyn said. "The trait does not always show in offspring of the bloodline," she added, "but any child you sire does carry the risk."

"A consideration, then," he said. "Although if all babes born are female, the ears are easily hidden."

"If you have regrets, speak now," Edward said warily from his bed. "Before the banns are hung."

"Yes," Eliane added. "Speak your regrets now." Her eyes sparked green fire and he was reminded of the previous day when she held a bowstring taut with an arrow aimed at his heart.

"I am sure that in his haste Father Timothy has already nailed the banns to the church door," Rhys said, daring her to respond. For some strange reason, he felt compelled to challenge her. Just as he had challenged her when she held the bow. Her eyes sparked again and he could not help wondering how they would look filled with passion. "Nay," he said. "I see no need to break the agreement."

" 'Tis a good thing," Eliane said as she turned from him. "I would hate to have to kill my father's friend."

Edward laughed. "You have kept your word," he told Rhys. "It is a bargain well struck."

Chapter Nine

*T*here were rumors at court about her? What rumors? Who even knew of her existence? "Renauld . . ." She spat out the name as if it were a curse. "Vannoy."

Madwyn looked at her as if she had lost her mind. "Why do you speak of him?"

"*He* said there were rumors about me. Unkind rumors."

Madwyn laughed. She laughed long and hard, so hard that she had to sit down upon a bench. They had retreated to the solar on the topmost floor of the castle so Eliane could think and plan. There was so much to do before the wedding in three days' time. The keep would have to be cleaned from top to bottom for all the guests. She had to take inventory of the stores and make sure there were enough mead and wine on hand. She must have a dress made, if there was appropriate fabric in the coffers. Messengers had to be sent out to summon the vassals for the wedding and the fealty oath.

Fealty oath . . . The vassals would have to swear to her new husband . . . that was something she had not counted on when considering her marriage. Her mind was spinning like the wheels used for twisting yarn from wool. Wheels that now stood idle, since Madwyn had chased the maids from the solar.

"Why do you laugh?" Eliane asked her. "I see no humor in any of this day's happenings."

Madwyn's eyes danced as she looked at Eliane. "Nay," she said. "You would not. I, however, find it very funny that you have just met your husband, who was the same man you nearly killed in the forest, and all you can worry about is the rumors he may have heard about you at court?"

Eliane bit her lip at Madwyn's logic. "It seemed as if they were unflattering," she said in her defense.

"Indeed," Madwyn agreed. "Why do you think Renauld would say such things about you?"

"Because he has always wanted Aubregate, just as his father did before him."

"Spreading unflattering rumors about the heiress of Aubregate would keep the competition of unwanted suitors away, would it not?" Madwyn explained.

"Yet *he* came," Eliane said. "Milord de Remy came." She went to the window. The solar was in the southwest tower of the keep, which sat atop a small hillock close to the forest. From the window she could see all of the lands of Aubregate to the west. In the distance the gray sea faded into the pale blue of the sky. Everything was covered with snow, then a crust of ice, which was blindingly white in the noonday sun. The landscape appeared to be encrusted with jewels. The ice gave the illusion of richness, an illusion that many had pursued through the generations. The fools did not know that the treasure was the land itself. The land that was hidden beneath the blanket of snow, sleeping, waiting to come back to life with the spring thaw. "He came because of my father."

"You told your father to choose," Madwyn said. "And you would accept."

"Yes," Eliane agreed. "Yet I do not know what I have accepted."

"'Tis the way with most brides," Madwyn said. "And you are luckier than most."

"How is that?" Eliane asked.

Madwyn laughed again and shook her head in disbelief at Eliane's question. "Do you not find Lord de Remy fair of face and strong of arm?"

Eliane closed her eyes against the brightness of the day and imagined the close, dim light of the forest on a wintry afternoon and a pair of eyes, dark as night, looking up at her in challenge. His face had bristled that day with beard, but this day it was clean shaven, revealing a strong jaw and chin and smooth, unmarked skin. He was as tall as she, nay, taller, which was an oddity since the only men she'd ever met who were taller than she were of the forest. "He is both," Eliane said. "To say otherwise would be a lie, and you know it."

"Then what is the problem?" Madwyn asked. "It is more than most heiresses can claim when a husband is chosen for them. Did you not admit to having a lustful heart just this day past?"

Eliane felt her cheeks flame and she resisted the urge to lean against the glass to cool them. "I cannot stand about discussing what is done," she said. "When there is much to be accomplished."

"At least you may congratulate yourself for not killing him," Madwyn said as they left the solar to begin the preparations.

"I have yet to decide whether that was a good thing."

* * *

"What did he mean that you kept your word?" Mathias had been strangely silent since they'd left Lord Edward's chambers. It was a good thing, since Rhys had much on his mind. He placed the brush he was using on the ledge in the stall and looked at his squire over Yorath's wide back. Mathias perched on a barrel outside the stall with a piece of straw dangling from his lips. A black and white cat circled around the barrel and arched its back against it in hopes of a rub.

"Lord Edward saved my life when I was younger than you. I told him then that I would repay him whenever he asked."

"You will pay your debt by marrying the Lady Eliane?"

"It is one way to look at it," Rhys agreed.

"I think Lady Jane and Lady Marcella will find another way to see it." His blue eyes danced with humor and Rhys knew he was considering their reactions to Rhys's surprising choice of bride.

"Let us hope that word reaches them while we are a great distance away."

"I am sure we will hear their shrieks no matter where we hide," Mathias said.

Rhys turned so Mathias would not see his grin. The boy was entirely too irreverent. But at the present Rhys needed to see the humor in his situation.

He'd come to the stable because he was not sure if he could continue to hide the sense of great relief he'd felt upon finally seeing Eliane. Where had the tales of her deformity come from? He considered her ears more of a curiosity than a deformity. Someone had greatly maligned the Lady Eliane. As her husband, he would protect her reputation.

Her husband . . . the benefits of becoming Eliane's husband were suddenly at the forefront of his mind, as well as other parts of his body. He picked up a comb and went to work on Yorath's tail. "Does not your horse need attending?" he asked. "And the packhorse as well?"

"They are taken care of." Mathias looked comfortable. Too comfortable as he played with the piece of straw and teased the cat with the toe of his boot.

"Go now," Rhys barked. Mathias jumped up from his perch as the cat arched its back in his direction and let out a hiss. "Never presume that another will care for your mount as well as you. He is your partner, not your servant, and you will do well to remember it."

"Yes, milord." Mathias bowed and went to his duties, leaving Rhys alone to consider his bride-to-be.

To his surprise he found the prospect of marrying Edward's daughter exciting. The fact that she was the woman from the forest enchanted him. When he'd awakened this morning he had seriously questioned his sanity, but now there was much to look forward to. He had never been with a woman who seemed as capable as Lady Eliane. She was not a shrinking flower like Jane, nor did she seem to be a fan of trickery like Marcella. What she *was* he had yet to determine.

The next few days should be interesting, and he found himself wishing that it was three days hence and the vows spoken. Would she come willingly to the marriage bed? Or would she be shy and need encouragement? He envisioned her standing over him as she had in the forest. Except this time her long legs were bare but for the barest wisp of a gown. Her breasts, which had been covered in leather, now peeked seductively from behind her hair, which fell in a glorious mass of copper and bronze past her hips.

Rhys combed out Yorath's tail until the silky black strands hung straight and swished against the straw covering the floor of the stall. With a hand on the stallion's flank to steady him, Rhys moved up to the side of the great beast to work on his mane. His thoughts turned to how Eliane would feel beneath his touch, and his shaft rose in excitement at the prospect. Yorath tossed his head and Rhys looked up to find the object of his fantasy standing outside the stall.

"Have a care, milady. He does not take kindly to strangers." Rhys leaned against Yorath's side and placed his arms casually over the stallion's back while willing his more rebellious parts into place. It would not help his cause some three nights hence if he frightened his lady with his lust. "As a matter of fact, he does not take kindly to anyone . . . except me."

She smiled at him. A smile that did not reach her eyes. A smile that was more challenging than sweet. The dog that had accompanied her in the forest was with her again. It stood at her hip, just as it had the day before. "Llyr feels the same way," she said as she touched the dog on the top of his head. A growl rumbled deep in his throat. "Llyr, enough!" Her words seemed to chastise the beast, but Rhys realized she commanded the dog to growl as easily as she spoke to him.

To his amazement, she extended her hand, palm down, toward Yorath and spoke in a language he'd never heard before. The words were musical and lilting, and Yorath stretched his nose out and snuffled the air around her hand. Then the stallion gently nibbled her fingers. If Rhys had not seen the horse's reaction, he would not have believed it. Especially when she laughed and stroked the long path of Yorath's nose. Her emerald eyes flashed her victory as her lips settled into a smile of mischievous satisfaction. How would it feel to have that look turned upon him instead of his horse? In his mind's eye he could see her, settling over him, taking him inside her, smiling that very same smile and dazzling him with her emerald eyes.

"I have need of your squire." She continued to look at Yorath rather than him. "So that my women may consider your wardrobe."

He kept the horse between them. It was that or throw her down in the straw and have his way with her. "My wardrobe is fine."

"Did you bring garments appropriate for our wedding?" Her emerald eyes pierced him.

"I am certain I have something that will not shame you," he replied. She raised a shoulder as if she were doubtful. How smooth was the skin of that same shoulder? How would it look when she did that and her shift slid low, down her arm, to expose her breast? Yorath shifted and bumped him. He grunted in pain and gritted his teeth.

"Are you injured, milord?" A finely arched brow rose questioningly.

"You may find Mathias over there," he said, pointing in the direction Mathias had gone. She turned to go. Rhys made some adjustments to his chausses before he stepped to the rope across the stall and watched the gentle sway of her hips as she moved away with the dog by her side. She stopped to talk to a tall and painfully thin young man with a mop of brown hair. She

placed a hand on his arm and the two laughed as if
they shared a private joke.

*She should not be so easy with a stable boy. She should not
be so easy with anyone but me.* Rhys stepped back into
the stall and placed a hand on Yorath's neck. Was that
jealously he felt? She was just giving the boy instructions as was her right. "See to milord's needs. Care for
his horse as you would care for mine." What else could
it be? He chastised himself for being foolish; still, he
looked once more in her direction and found the stable
boy grinning at him. The lad yanked on his forelock
and walked away, whistling, with a shovel placed over
his shoulder.

I should beat him . . . along with Mathias. . . . Rhys realized his will had not yet mastered his body. He'd
better find someone to attend to his needs, and soon.
Or the next three days were going to be painful.

Renauld Vannoy spared a glance at his traveling companion as they rode north toward his lands. Peter
Salisbury had to be delaying on purpose. There could
be no other reason for the constant stream of bad luck
that had occurred on their trip. The first instance was
on the morning they were to leave, when the man's
wife suffered a spell that demanded Salisbury's immediate attention, delaying their departure until the noon
hour. Renauld would have gone on without Salisbury
except the king had commanded that they go together.

There was also the fact that he needed to give his
messenger time to get to Chasmore. It would do no
good if he arrived before the deed was done. Renauld
gritted his teeth and put up with the delay.

The second morning on the road, Salisbury realized

that he'd forgotten some very important business, so he took time to write a letter and dispatched his squire, along with two men at arms to deliver it. Then he discovered that his horse had a loose shoe and insisted that they detour to the closest blacksmith. Since Salisbury was well acquainted with the lord who owned the keep where the blacksmith lived, they were invited to dinner. Salisbury enjoyed the meal so much that their host insisted they spend the night. Though Renauld was grateful for the bed to sleep in, he chafed at the delay.

On the morning of the third day he realized that they still had two days of travel to arrive at Aubregate. And that was if the weather cooperated. Fortunately for him, it seemed as if it would. Still, he was as impatient as Salisbury seemed reluctant.

Does he know something? Something about de Remy's trip to Aubregate? Renauld watched from the back of his horse as Salisbury walked back to their host as if he'd forgotten to tell him something. If that were remotely possible. The two men had talked about everything under the sun the night before. Finally, Salisbury mounted his horse and greeted Renauld with a smile.

"Are you ready?"

Renauld resisted the urge to lop off Salisbury's head with his sword. "I've been ready," he ground out between his clenched teeth, "since daybreak."

Salisbury looked around as if he just now realized the sun was shining. "Well, then. Let us be off."

He knew something. Renauld could only hope that his men had taken care of their task. If they failed, they would suffer for it. But they knew better than to fail.

Chapter Ten

"What language was that you spoke?" Rhys asked. They had ridden most of the morning in an uncomfortable silence, except for the tidbits of information she'd given him as they toured her lands. *My lands now . . . but only with her approval.*

Eliane looked at him in confusion. She rode by his side on a leggy mare that seemed more spirited than the usual lady's palfrey. It suited his betrothed much more than the stout and sturdy mounts most women rode. She had no difficulty handling the mare, even with Yorath snorting at her side. He commiserated with his stallion, which tossed its head and chafed at the bit. It seemed Rhys's only thought since coming across Eliane in the wood was to bed her.

"In the stables," Rhys added when she did not answer.

She shrugged. "I know not its name, only that it is the ancient language of my mother's people. I learned it as a child just as I learned our common tongue."

Common . . . there was nothing common about her. She rode astride while wearing a sensible brown skirt over her leggings. The leather tunic he'd first seen her in was beneath her fox-lined cloak of deep green. The hood was thrown back so she could enjoy the warmth of the day. She wore her fiery hair braided and wrapped about her head like a crown, which left her ears exposed. He studied them again and felt the strangest desire to trace the edges of them. He should have done it the day before when she was more compliant. Now her bow and quiver hung from her saddle along with a bag full of cakes, which she passed out to the children they'd seen along the way. He had no doubt in his mind that beneath the cloak she also wore the blade he'd seen upon her hip in the forest.

The people know who she is and what she is . . . whatever that may be. The news of the coming marriage had spread quickly. As they toured the lands, he was greeted with deference and curiosity by the families that poured out of the fields and thatched cottages to greet them. *She feels safe here. . . .* He'd noticed ears like hers on some of the people they'd met. They were a part of the land, or perhaps the forest. The forest seemed to be the source of all the mystery. A forbidden place with warrior women who had pointy ears. Who would have thought such a place existed?

They were accompanied by Lord Edward's steward, a man named Hubert, who formally invited all to the wedding celebration the day after tomorrow. Mathias and four men-at-arms from Aubregate also rode with them. His own men-at-arms should be at Myrddin by now. He'd seen no need to pay for their upkeep at court when he would not be there.

The day was sunny and unseasonably warm compared to the ones just past. The dog that was her constant companion loped beside them as they rode. The fields, while fallow beneath the snow, seemed well tended. There was no sign of disease or starvation among the vassals they had seen this morn. It was apparent that Eliane was well liked, and she called each one by name and thanked them when they asked after her father.

Could he call each one of his vassals by name? He knew he could not. He relied on his steward to tell him whom he was dealing with when he rode his lands. Could he say that his vassals received him as the people of Aubregate received Eliane? That he could not answer. He knew they respected him, because he had never treated them unfairly, but the subjects of Aubregate seemed to love their lady.

Rhys frowned. Love was not real, but respect was. The people here would learn to respect him and trust him, just as the people of Myrddin did. They would find him a just and fair lord. He would not fail Edward in that promise.

"If it pleases milord, we will have our repast at the mill," she said as they continued on. "Matilde is to have it awaiting us. From there we can go down to the village by the sea and come back by way of the town." Her tone was as formal as it had been the day before when she'd found him in the stable and inquired about his wardrobe.

"The prospect of a meal pleases me," Rhys said. "As does your showing me the land, for you know the way far better than I." He was sincere in his compliment. He'd recognized her intelligence during the course of the morning. And she seemed without guile or malice. He found her company most refreshing after the machinations of Marcella and the pretended innocence of Jane. He found Eliane different from any other woman he'd ever known.

She looked sideways at him from beneath veiled lashes, her eyes glittering like emeralds in the sunlight. It suddenly occurred to him that he had no bridal gift for her. There were emeralds among the jewels at

Mryddin. Emeralds would suit her. Emeralds and nothing else. He would gladly see her naked upon his bed wearing nothing but emeralds.

"What does Yorath mean?" Once again he was taken by the music in her voice.

"'Tis Welsh." He stroked Yorath's proudly arched neck as the stallion pranced beneath him. "The translation would be 'handsome lord.'"

She smiled slightly and nodded. "It fits him." Perfect teeth caught her lower lip as she once more quickly glanced his way. "How is it you know the language?"

"It is the ancient language of my mother's people." He found that he enjoyed turning her words upon her as if it were a game. Could it be that she had not heard the tale of his parents? He watched her as she rode, deep in thought. Then she turned to him, the knowledge of his history apparent in the widening of her eyes.

"It seems that not even isolated Aubregate has escaped the tales of my family's woes." He shrugged as if it were nothing.

"Our halls are often visited by troubadours," she admitted. "Aubregate's larder and appetite for entertainment on a cold winter's night are equally large."

"A good story for a hot meal and a dry bed. The troubadours get the best of that exchange."

"It must have been hard for you." Her emerald eyes were upon him now, searching his face for a weakness he dared not show.

"No harder than for any other child who is orphaned," he said. "The country is full of them. Some fare better than others. There was nothing lacking in my upbringing." Nothing that he would admit.

She had no response and finally turned away from her perusal of his face to watch the road. The dog bounded ahead and took off through a field, churning through the snow toward the woods in the distance.

"Llyr!" she called out. "Come."

"Did you not know that his name is Welsh also?" he asked when he heard her call the beast's name.

"Nay, I did not." The dog came back to the road and rejoined them. "It just seemed to fit him."

"It means the sea," Rhys said.

She laughed. The sound was joyous and bubbling. "We found him in the sea," she explained. "My father pulled him forth when he saw him trying to swim to shore. He was just a pup then, small enough for me to carry in my arms. We never knew whence he came."

The sky was as blue as he'd ever seen. The fresh air was welcome against his face after weeks of being cooped up at court. The men at arms and Edward's steward seemed in high spirits from the sound of their voices. Mathias occasionally joined into their conversation as he soaked up whatever bits and pieces of knowledge that came his way. The boy was intelligent enough to ask about something he did not understand.

Rhys felt an easing in his shoulders as if a great weight had been lifted. The woman at his side was comely and agreeable, intelligent and strong. Mayhap this marriage would have the benefits that Peter spoke of. Beyond the obvious ones. He'd awakened this morning in the same state as the morning before and knew that it would be two more days before he could expect any relief. He found himself most anxious for the days to pass.

The road curved toward a stand of trees and a small

stream. The terrain was sloped here, the start of its downward journey to the sea. A flock of sheep filled the road before them, their woolly fleeces dingy against the white of the snow. Llyr pricked his ears as they heard a dog barking.

"Go," she said as the dog looked at her expectantly. He took off with a bound. "He is quite enamored with the shepherd's dog," she explained, then suddenly turned away as her cheeks turned a fiery red.

Rhys grinned at her embarrassment. It was obvious she knew what was expected of her two nights hence. Madwyn must have instructed her on what was to come. There was no doubt in his mind that she was a virgin. He had never lain with one and found the prospect added to his anticipation. So much so that he had to shift himself in the saddle, which set Yorath off again. The mare tossed her head and nipped at the stud. The stallion rose on his hind legs and Rhys settled him with a sharp command. Yorath snorted his impatience but settled back into a walk with a shake of his head.

"It seems that Llyr is not the only one enamored," he said.

Eliane turned away again. He saw the flush creep up the graceful curve of her neck and over her ears. Rhys grinned wolfishly at the thought of kissing those ears. Of the enjoyment to be had by running his tongue over the exquisite peaks . . . and other peaks that were hidden beneath her clothes. A sudden realization made him laugh out loud as he shook his head.

"Something amuses you, milord?" Her look this time was more direct, as if she were surprised at his sudden outburst.

"Now I know why I have never seen Han without his cap. Even in the heat of summer." He was pleased to see that she immediately understood what he spoke of. Eliane smiled mischievously and he felt the pull of her attraction deep in his groin. He would be a lusting beast by the wedding night. If he could last that long without cornering her in some dark corner of the keep.

"People are often suspicious of what they do not understand," she said. "Han has served my father well for many years."

"And he has not aged a bit in the time I've known him," Rhys replied, suddenly curious. He'd been so caught up in the surprise of his coming marriage and the prospect of his bride that he'd forgotten another part of the bargain. What was the secret of the forest? "You have shown me the fields and the flocks. You have spoken of the mill, the fisherfolk, and the town. When will we see the forest?"

Gone was his compliant companion. The warrior woman from the forest was once more before him. "When I deem you ready," she said. With an imperceptible touch of her heels, her mare sprang forward and she galloped ahead, leaving him wondering at the sudden change and wanting her all the more for it.

"I hope there are some willing women in the town," he ground out from between clenched teeth as he shifted uncomfortably in the saddle.

"Milord?" Mathias had ridden up beside him as her men-at-arms rushed to join their lady.

"See to milady," Rhys barked. The last thing he needed was for Mathias to recognize his condition. The boy heeled his horse and took off to join the men-at-arms. Rhys heard the steward chuckling behind him. The man missed nothing. He would have a good story to report to Edward when they returned.

Edward will rest content, knowing I am most anxious to take his daughter as a bride. He could put up with a moment's discomfort if it would give the man some peace. He would have his own peace soon enough, along with another chance to discover her secrets when they had their repast. He saw the mill in the distance, its wheel turning as the stream made its way down the hill.

The sound of a yelp, then a shout, brought Rhys to attention. The sound of steel brought his sword out and he pressed his knees into Yorath's sides. The horse took off at a run, his mighty hooves churning up the mud from the melting snow. Rhys did not see the snow, or the mud. All he saw was the red haze of anger. His bride was under attack.

Who would dare? Since her mother's death, there had not been an attack this far inside Aubregate. There had been skirmishes on its borders, raiders after sheep and cows, or those who thought to find the rumored treasure in the forest, most of them from Renauld's lands. In all Eliane's memory, there had never been such a brazen attack. Thoughts of her own safety were lost in the anger that bubbled up inside Eliane. *Who would dare raise an attack against us?* She pulled out her short sword as the man-at-arms who rode beside her fell with an arrow sticking from his chest. She heard the clash of steel and heard Llyr's growl as he leapt from the ground and knocked an attacker off his horse.

"Llyr!" He went for the man's throat, but his victim was able to deflect him by dropping his sword and wrapping his hands around Llyr's neck. Eliane tried to urge Aletha forward but suddenly found Mathias blocking her way.

"I must get to Llyr!"

"Milady, we must be away!" Mathias cried out as he ducked beneath an arrow. The remaining three men-at-arms fought valiantly but were outnumbered three to one. Did the attackers seek to rob them? The steward, with his bag of Aubregate gold, was well behind, with Rhys. She suddenly realized that she should not have left his company.

The battle was vicious. Horses screamed and lashed out as the fighters hacked at each other with their swords. They bumped into each other and a sudden kick knocked Llyr away from his victim. He yelped and the man he'd taken down grabbed his sword from the ground as he rolled from beneath the horse's dangerous hooves.

His intent was to kill Llyr. Eliane knew it as surely as she knew these men did not belong here. If only Mathias would get out of her way.

"Llyr! Come!" Eliane twisted in the saddle, trying to spot him, then saw another man wearing the green and gold of Aubregate go down. There was more at risk here than Llyr. As dear as he was to her, he wasn't a man, and men were dying. Who was attacking and why?

"Do not harm her!" someone shouted. She did not recognize the voice. Four men broke off from the battle with the remaining men-at-arms and moved on her and Mathias.

"Go!" Mathias drew his sword. He was just a boy. What did he expect to do? He wore no armor. He had no shield. She would not leave him here to fight four men on his own. She reached out and grabbed his bridle, then kicked her heels into Aletha's sides. The mare took off, eager to leave the noise and confusion. Eliane heard the sound of pursuit behind. They intended to capture her, but they had orders not to harm her. Mathias, however, was another story. She swung the flat of her sword down on Mathias's horse's hindquarters and raised her arm to defend them both.

She saw the dark form of a man and horse crash into the four riders who were breathing down their necks. Rhys! She heard his deep-throated war cry and heard the clash of steel. She felt the stream of blood that splattered across her back and Aletha's hindquarters.

"Away, Mathias!" Rhys shouted. "Take milady away!"

"To the mill!" Eliane said. There would be men there. Crofters and laborers, townsfolk. All would come to their aid with whatever weapons they had. She was relieved to see Llyr running at her side as she bent over Aletha's neck. She looked over her shoulder at Mathias. His face was as pale as death and splattered with blood. Was he wounded?

He has no shield . . . no armor. . . . Rhys at least wore his sword and leather hauberk, but he was not prepared for battle. They were on Aubregate lands. They were supposed to be safe. This was to have been a day of celebration, not desperation.

The flock of sheep scattered before them as they pounded through. Eliane caught a glimpse of the shepherd, who seemed as shocked as she was that anyone would dare to venture an attack on Aubregate lands. *Who? Why?*

Eliane slowed Aletha. "We need to capture one of them."

"Milady?" Mathias gasped beside her.

Eliane did not answer. She looked beyond Mathias. What she saw chilled her.

Rhys de Remy fought like a madman. He stood in the midst of three men, fighting them all at once. Bodies lay around the group, her men, the attackers, a horse; all were silent except for the grunts of the men and the clash of steel. Yorath stood off to the side, steady and waiting for his master's command.

"I must stop him." She turned Aletha to ride back to the battle.

Mathias merely looked at her. His blue eyes were wide in his pale face. He placed his hand on his cheek and looked at it in horror when it came back streaked with blood.

Eliane grabbed his arm. "It's not yours." She tilted her head toward the battle. "We must help him."

Mathias swallowed hard. "Yes, milady."

"We must save one for questioning." What that questioning would entail she did not want to know. Was Rhys capable of torture? One look at him fighting assured her that he was.

Mathias swung his sword and they rode back to the battle with Llyr once more bounding by her side.

One of Rhys's combatants had fallen. Two were left. Rhys swung viciously with his sword at the back of a leg, and the man fell to one knee. He dropped his sword and raised his arms in surrender. Rhys turned to face the last one. The attacker thrust violently with his weapon. Rhys stumbled back and tripped over the man who had surrendered. He fell on his back with his sword extended up.

The man with the wounded leg once more grabbed

his sword. He fought without honor. Rhys was down with two men swinging at him. He used his sword with both hands, quickly parrying their thrusts as he tried to get his legs beneath him.

Eliane did not hesitate. With a cry she raised her arm and slashed her sword at the unwounded man as Aletha charged through. He toppled sideways. Rhys rolled to his feet and jabbed his own blade through the remaining man. He fell just as she turned Aletha.

Rhys looked at her with dark and frightening eyes. The eyes of a demon. He did not say a word but stalked to her with the intensity of a wolf after its prey. The look on his face was desperate, yet terrifying. He snatched her from the saddle before she could take a breath. His face was streaked with blood and his black eyes glowed like coals. He buried his hand in her hair and her braid came loose and tumbled down her shoulder. He said one word before he lowered his mouth to hers.

"Mine."

His lips claimed her. They branded her. His hand was splayed across the back of her skull so she could not move. She felt the steel of his blade and the heft of the hilt at her back as he wrapped his sword arm around her. Her arms were trapped between them. The leather of his hauberk pressed through her clothes and she knew there would be bruises where the buckles touched. She felt the ridge of his erection as it pressed against her stomach, and her body lurched at the brazenness of his claim.

No man had ever kissed her. No man had dared to touch her, yet this man laid claim to her with the blood of his victims smearing his face as if he were a

Viking chieftain of old. Ancient Viking blood ran in her veins, and she felt the stir of it deep inside her, like a wolf calling to its mate. Indeed she heard Llyr's rumbling growl beside her as Rhys made his claim. She could not breathe; she could not move; but she did not want to protest. It was his right to claim her.

He finally stopped, his lips pulling at hers as he moved away and she gasped, clinging to his leather-clad shoulders as she drew in air. He studied her, intently, his dark eyes studying her face as if he were seeing her for the first time.

"Milord?" she was finally able to say. "Are you hurt?"

Her braid had come undone. It fell across one shoulder and he picked up the end of it. He rubbed the loose strands between his fingers, and then stopped, suddenly, when he realized they were covered with blood.

He looked down at Llyr, who looked up at him with his hackles raised. The two of them took each other's measure with their dark eyes until finally Rhys turned away. "Mathias?" He released her and she staggered at the loss of his strength.

I have killed a man. . . . She looked at the body and placed her hand to her mouth to keep the contents of her stomach from fouling her lips, from diminishing his kiss. *I would do it again. There was no other way.*

"Here . . . sir." The boy's voice was weak. He sat on his horse, looking, it seemed, everywhere at once. He swiped at his mouth with his hand and Eliane knew that he had lost his breakfast sometime during the kiss.

"See if any are alive," Rhys said. "Before the sun sets, I want to know who ordered this and why."

Chapter Eleven

"I've never seen anyone fight as he did," Eliane confessed. Madwyn ran the brush down the length of Eliane's freshly washed hair. She had hoped to wait until the day of her wedding to wash it but the blood must be rinsed out.

"Did he frighten you?"

Did he? He fought like a man possessed. He fought as if he were one of God's avenging angels, or mayhap Satan incarnate. Did he frighten her? Not in the way Madwyn meant. She was not afraid he would run her through with his sword or strike her down with his fists.

"He does not."

There was another fear. One that she dared not mention, even to Madwyn, who knew everything there was to know about her. In truth she did not know if she could put into words exactly what it was that frightened her, only that she was truly frightened. But not by Rhys de Remy. He was presworn to protect her and keep her safe. Her father would not give her into the man's keeping if he felt there was danger there. It was her own foolishness that terrified her.

What had happened when he'd kissed her, nay, branded her? That was no simple kiss of peace they'd exchanged. That was a turbulent whirlwind of . . . something. Eliane touched her fingers to her lips. She had not told Madwyn of the kiss, only the attack and the resulting deaths of all involved, save one who galloped off to the east, according to the steward, who had stayed safely back during the episode.

"It should please your father to know Lord de Remy is more than capable of defending Aubregate."

"He needed neither armor nor shield to slay nine men."

"Your father said he was trained by a great warrior," Madwyn reminded her. "Your father met him at Anjou. He was blooded at a young age." Madwyn placed the brush on the table and dipped her hands into a crock. She smoothed the ointment into Eliane's hair to tame the ends and enhance the shine. "Some men thrive upon battle," she continued. "They embrace fighting as they embrace their wives." Madwyn pulled back a side section of Eliane's hair and worked it into a small braid. "Indeed, for some, battle is all they desire. Some go so far as to seek their death in battle."

Eliane still felt the heat of Rhys's embrace, despite the time that had passed since he jerked her from the saddle and took her into his arms. The thought of his embrace warmed her to her very core, in places that Father Timothy had often warned her against thinking about because it would lead to sin. But it was not sin with a husband. Desiring one's husband was a good thing. If only she knew exactly what it was that she did desire. She knew about the act. One did not grow up around animals of every kind without observing it. But the wanting she'd experienced, the warming, the feelings tumbling about inside her were things she had never known, until Rhys de Remy branded her with his kiss.

Eliane knew her color would give her thoughts away to Madwyn, who could read her face as well as any words put to parchment. She concentrated instead on the soothing feel of Madwyn's hands in her hair.

"His gifts of the bandit's horses to the families of those who fell were most generous," she said.

Rhys had given instructions to the steward for the possessions of the attackers to be divided among those who'd suffered the most. Unfortunately those possessions held no clue as to where the attackers had come from. Nor did it explain the why. Men from both the keep and the forest searched for the escaped rider, but Eliane held no hope for his capture.

"Do you think it was Renauld?" Eliane asked.

"Word is he is still at court," Madwyn protested. "How could it be possible? And why now?"

"Why not now when my father is nearly . . . dead?" She did not want to say it, but she forced the word from her lips. "What better time than now?"

"If he were close at hand, I would say yea, but from court . . ." Madwyn shook her head.

"He is devious enough and greedy enough to send men to take me. He would think nothing of getting me with child, so he could claim me as wife." The thought made her bile rise, even though it was a threat she had lived with her entire life. "Then he would kill me so Aubregate would be his." Eliane rose from her stool and paced to the window in her tower. It looked over the forest, now nothing more than a black mass in the distance. The forest was her refuge and her sanctuary. It was where she went to worship, to think, and sometimes to hide as she had done just a few days past, before she learned that she was to be married. If only she could run to the deepest part of it and hide. If only she did not have the weight of all Aubregate resting upon her shoulders.

Rhys de Remy had showed himself to be a mighty warrior today. Was he strong enough to protect the secrets of Aubregate?

Madwyn joined her at the window. "Let me finish your hair so you may dress. You must go down and play the gracious bride and hostess. You must put on a brave face for your father and smile and tell him that he leaves you in good hands."

His hands upon my body . . . She could still feel them, one in her hair and the other fisted against her back. So different from the first day when he barely touched her cheek, just enough so that he could turn it and look at her ears. He could be gentle, or he could be strong. Which Rhys would come to the marriage bed? Which one did she want to come? Which one did she fear the most?

"Are you certain there will not be a backlash?" Rhys asked. Father Timothy took the parchment from him and bent to sand his signature. The contracts were finalized, noting all the details of his alliance with Edward's daughter.

"The church cannot grant a dying man the peace of seeing his daughter well wed?" Father Timothy's voice held a hint of hostility in it. "There are special dispensations that allow a hastening of the banns. Certainly this situation warrants one."

Edward's face on the pillow was anxious and desperate. Cedric hovered beside him.

"I was thinking about the bride," Rhys said in hopes

of relieving some of Edward's anxiety. While he hoped to coax a smile from Edward, he did not speak in jest. Eliane *was* all he'd thought about since the attack. He would never forget the sight of her charging toward him with her sword in her hand and that fierce look on her face when she swung the blade.

Having the wedding within the next hour was not soon enough for him. After hearing of the attack, Edward and Father Timothy were of the same mind. The marriage must be consummated at once so that Eliane and Aubregate would be safe.

"She will do as she is told." Edward's voice was weak, but it rang with conviction. She would do as her father bade her. Rhys had doubts that she would be as obedient a wife as she was a daughter. The Eliane he knew was hardly compliant.

"She knows it is for the best." Edward must have seen Rhys's doubt. His words cost him dearly and he collapsed into a fit of coughing that racked his ailing body. Cedric supported his frail frame and held a piece of linen to his mouth. It came away bloody. The hand of death was upon Edward. Eliane must consent to the marriage now, or Edward would not live to see it.

"Bring me my daughter," Edward gasped.

Father Timothy followed Rhys from the room. "We need witnesses," he said. "It would help if it was someone of title."

"It seems that noblemen are in short supply in these parts or you would have had a groom long ago," Rhys said.

"Your squire?"

"Nay, he will be just a knight, and only if he survives my training." They arrived in the main hall, where Ammon, the stable boy, sat on a bench at the table with a young maid. "Tell him to call forth those of importance from the town." Father Timothy nodded at Rhys's instructions. "They will have to suffice."

"You," Rhys said to the maid, who looked at him with brown eyes full of fear. He did not recall seeing her before. "Fetch the cook." She dashed off, nearly tripping over her skirts as she left the bench.

"Milord?" Ammon asked when Father Timothy was finished speaking. "How is Lord Edward?"

Rhys saw the concern in his eyes. Would any of his vassals ask after him with the same worry were he on his deathbed? He thought not. Would any of them dare to address him directly? Never. But these were not his vassals. They were Edward's. Tomorrow they would be his and Eliane's. Would they be more afraid then?

"He still lives for now." He tilted his head toward the door. "Go, and make haste." Ammon was gone, passing the cook on her way in. Rhys looked around and wondered where Mathias had gotten off to. There had not been time to counsel the boy after the battle. There was too much to be done, and now he was even more preoccupied. He was to be wed within the hour.

The cook bustled up and bowed her head as she wiped her hands upon her apron. "How goes the wedding feast?" he asked.

The woman's wide face stretched into a smile. "Well, milord. Tomorrow the kitchens will be busy, but all should be ready."

"The wedding will be this eve," Rhys said. The woman's eyes grew wide, and she spared a look upward to the lord's chamber. " 'Tis his last wish." Rhys placed a comforting hand on her shoulder. "To see us wed."

Tears welled in her eyes but she nodded. "All will be ready, milord." She hurried off.

Was he this kind with his servants at Myrddin? His grandmother had taught him fine manners and he was never harsh or abrasive in his speech. But he never really cared what they were feeling. He knew they laughed and cried and sickened and died, but it never seemed to involve him. There was always someone else available to step in and take a missing servant's place. Meals were served, horses were fed and groomed and saddled for him when he desired to ride. Crops were planted and levies paid. But at Aubregate Eliane was not the only one who would grieve for her father. The servants and vassals would mourn him as well.

"Matilde? Have you seen Mathias?"

"I saw him earlier," she said. "He passed through the kitchen and has not come back."

Rhys let out an exasperated sigh. He did not have time to hunt for his squire. His thoughts were jumbled, wondering what was happening in Edward's chambers with Eliane. Would she object to this hastening of their vows? She seemed practical. Surely after the events of the day, she would see the need, but still . . .

If only he knew who was behind the attack. That they'd been after Eliane was evident, but for what reason? Did they hope to ransom her? Why now? There had not been an attack on Aubregate since Edward's return from war. Did it have something to do with Rhys's arrival or the announcement of Eliane's marriage?

"First things first." The wedding was the first order of business. Everything else could be dealt with afterward. Before the ceremony he needed to bathe the blood and dirt from his body. To do that he needed his squire. He followed Matilde to the kitchen, where she pointed out the direction Mathias had gone.

Rhys found the boy in the kitchen garden, sitting beneath an arbor on a long flat stone. Mathias sat with his legs pulled up before him, his arms wrapped about his limbs and his chin resting upon his knees. His cloak spilled about him and blood smeared his cheek. His eyes were tightly shut, as if he wanted to blot out his visions from the battle.

Rhys well recalled his first blooding. He was nine and newly squired to Lord Allan. The battle of Anjou was not a pleasant one. Most of it he'd put from his mind, but sometimes at night the horrific images still haunted him.

Mathias saw him and jumped to his feet. "Milord?"

Rhys tilted his head toward the castle. "'Tis a wise man who knows when to escape the madness of preparations for a marriage."

"Sir?"

"It seems that I am to be wed before the sun sets," Rhys said. "I would prefer not to be covered in blood when it happens." He added an encouraging smile.

"I will go prepare your bath at once," Mathias said.

"Mathias." Rhys stopped him with a hand on his shoulder. "Thank you for what you did today."

"Milord?" Mathias's blue eyes darted to Rhys, and then away as his face turned pale once more.

"You pulled milady away from the battle. It was your first thought, was it not? To protect the Lady Eliane?"

Mathias nodded. "I had my sword—" he began.

"But no armor or training. You made the correct decision under the circumstances. Protecting milady was your first duty."

"I had fear of the beating you would give me were I to do otherwise, milord," Mathias said. His eyes darted again to Rhys's face, but this time there was relief in them, instead of fear.

Am I too kind to him? Mayhap he was. But Edward's kind words, and Peter's helpful instructions, had had more impact on him than any sharp cuff or curse he had received at Allan's hand.

"I still may beat you," Rhys said. "If the bath is not to my liking. Now go. And see to yourself as well. Do not humiliate me in front of my bride."

Mathias gave him a quick bow and was off.

Rhys did not follow, knowing that it would take a few moments for Mathias to prepare. Instead he ducked through a narrow passage in one of the bailey walls.

He turned to enter the castle but was stopped by a call from Han. He stood in the passageway between the inner and outer bailey with a boy leaning heavily against him.

"Another attack?" Rhys rushed to his side. Several huntsmen stood behind the pair with an injured man carried between them on a long plank. They moved through with their burden while Han stayed with the injured boy.

"Nay, not against us," Han said. "We found these two in the forest. Escaping from those who sought to kill them."

The boy who leaned on Han straightened when he saw Rhys. "I am William, squire to Peter Salisbury," he said.

"Peter?" Rhys questioned.

The boy's head was bloody and a bruise marred his cheek, but his eyes lit upon Rhys with relief. "Milord bade me say if it is your purpose to marry the Lady Eliane, then please do so in all haste. The king's attention has been directed this way by Renauld Vannoy, who desires to make her his own."

The earth beneath Rhys's feet suddenly tilted. *Renauld Vannoy desires Eliane.* "Is there more?" he asked as his mind whirled around the one statement. *Renauld Vannoy desires Eliane.*

"Yes, sir. He bade me memorize the message."

"Do you know who attacked you?" Rhys asked. He knew. But he needed proof. He needed this squire to tell him.

"No," the boy said. "We were attacked when we came to your border. One was killed, and we escaped into the forest. Milord's purpose was to cause delays to give you time to complete your task."

"Cause delays." The realization came to him. "Is Peter on his way here?"

"Yes. He rides by the king's command with Vannoy. The king bade them return both you and the Lady Eliane to court as soon as possible after the death of her father."

Renauld Vannoy . . . It was he who was behind the attacks. *He wants her.* "Take him inside and see that his wounds are tended," he commanded. Han nodded and they moved on, leaving Rhys alone in the opening between the inner and outer bailey.

Rhys looked toward the outer bailey. The walls were stout and would withstand assault. Torches had been placed at both gates. Men walked the walls, their eyes turned outward. They had lost comrades this day. They would not be surprised again.

Vannoy wants her. . . . Did she want him in return?

Surely they knew each other. After all, their lands adjoined. There was a long-standing feud between the families, but feuds between parents were often reasons for rebellious sons and daughters to come together.

Did Eliane want Renauld as her husband even though her father would never permit it? Had she led her men into the ambush, hoping the attackers would take her away from an unwanted marriage?

Nay . . . she'd killed one of them. Killed one to save his life. Or was it to keep him from speaking the truth? Would she sacrifice her own men and an innocent boy to go with Renauld?

Surely not.

She is mine . . . mine. . . .

That was why Renauld was at court. He was seeking to force the king's hand. He must have made promises to the king. Promises regarding the rumored treasure of Aubregate and its deformed daughter.

Mine.

Her ears . . . Renauld knew of Eliane's strangely shaped ears and spread rumors of her deformity to scare off other suitors. And now he was coming for her.

Mine.

Thunder, strange for this time of year, rumbled to the west. Lightning followed it, slashing across the sky and revealing the high swell of dangerous clouds. Rain would soon be upon them.

"Mine," Rhys said as he went into the castle to prepare for his wedding. But he could not help thinking, *Does she want Renauld?*

Chapter Twelve

*T*he wind blew the witnesses into the castle, rattling the windows and causing the fire in the great hall to flutter wildly in the hearth. Those who'd just entered did not pause to talk. Instead they made their way through the crowd directly to the roaring fire to dry off. As they stood before the hearth they discussed in low tones the attack and the sudden urgency for the vows about to be spoken.

In the solar above, Madwyn was attempting to keep Eliane's mind from running off in several different directions at once.

"My father?" Eliane asked.

"Cedric is to bring him down," Madwyn said. "They have put pillows in his chair."

"He should not leave his bed," Eliane said. "He is too weak."

"He desires it," Madwyn said. "That is all that matters."

"Rhys?" She stumbled over his name. She should not stumble over it. What if she stumbled during the vows?

"He is still in his chambers," Madwyn assured her. "He has bathed. I believe he is as eager as you," Madwyn added with a wry smile.

She was more anxious than eager. Too much had

happened in too short a time. First the attack, and her father's decision to move up the ceremony, then the appearance of Han with Peter's squire and the message he carried. *I am to go to the king? Why?* The most unsettling thing was the way Rhys looked at her when it was revealed that Renauld was on his way to Aubregate with orders from the king to return her to court. There was something in his eyes that frightened her, almost as much as the prospect of leaving her home did. Something that had not been there before. Not even when he kissed her. Llyr must have sensed her disquiet, because he came from his place on the rug and placed his head in her lap.

"Eliane," Madwyn scolded. "He will soil your dress." Eliane looked at the dark head lying on the pale blue velvet and rubbed behind his ears. Llyr's brown eyes conveyed the sadness she felt. How could she leave Aubregate?

"I will not leave this place while Papa is alive."

"You should eat something," Madwyn scolded as if she had not heard her. Eliane looked at her untouched food. Her stomach rebelled at the thought.

"He cannot last much longer," Eliane continued. She put a hand to her lips to stop the sudden burst of emotion that sought to escape from her heart.

"Hush, child," Madwyn said. She placed her hand beneath Eliane's chin and lifted her face. "Think happy thoughts. Think of your marriage. Think of your wedding night."

Eliane jumped from her stool. That was the one thing she did not want to think about. She did not know what to think, how to act, or what to do. She had thought herself prepared—she knew what was to happen, what he would do, what she must allow him to do, but still she worried.

What if he found her . . . lacking? What if he refused her at the bedding ceremony because of her ears or because he found her undesirable? The entire thought of being stripped and put on display made her stomach heave into her throat, and she was suddenly grateful that she had not found time to eat this day.

The sound of a door opening and closing across the hallway turned her head. She listened to footsteps, two sets, Rhys and Mathias, until they faded away onto the steps that led down to the great hall. Madwyn took her hands and gripped them tight. She looked Eliane over, adjusted the gold circlet that held her veil, and said, "It is time for you to be married. But we must not rush to it. Let the groom wonder where you are. It will do him good to wait."

Edward sat in his chair beside the hearth. He seemed lost in it, as he was lost in his fine velvet tunic and cloak. Pillows were placed around his body to keep him upright, and his fingers were curled into a fist on his left hand so that his ring would not slide off.

Cedric stood as always by his side, ready to see to his lord's slightest whim. Han stood on the opposite side, his icy blue eyes watching the room before he bent to whisper in Edward's ear as each of those who'd been summoned moved to greet him. Rhys had to look again to make sure it was Han, but there was no mistaking those pale blue eyes, the smooth face, and the upward-slashing brow.

Han's clothing was as fine as Edward's. His tunic

was deep blue velvet, embroidered with silver thread, and his boots were soft gray leather that came over his knees. His pale hair was unbound and fell down his back to his waist. As he had when he came upon Eliane in the forest, Rhys had a vision of the forbidden stories his nurse had told him as a child about the hidden world of the elves and the fey. Mayhap the tales were true after all.

Edward watched him as he stood beside the stairs, waiting for his bride. He did not want to appear too anxious, so Rhys made his way through the crowd of well-wishers to Edward. A maid offered him wine and he took it, downing it all in one gulp.

"Nerves, milord?" the steward asked, and the crowd laughed merrily at the sight of him with his empty chalice.

"Nay," Rhys said. "I am only anxious to have the wedding behind me so that I may engage in more pleasant pursuits."

It was what they wanted to hear. Edward smiled weakly from his chair and Rhys wondered where he found the strength to remain upright. His skin was gray, and it seemed as thin as parchment over his bones.

Comments were made about the desirability of the bride, and the prowess of the groom. It seemed all were anxious for the bedding ceremony to come. But first, there must be a wedding. Father Timothy cleared his throat loudly and all heads turned to where the staircase entered the main hall.

Her bliaut was of palest blue velvet with a kirtle of white silk beneath and trimmed with thread of silver and gold around the hem and the ends of her sleeves. Blue, to signify her purity. Was she pure? Had she already given her body to Renauld and then sent him to petition the king for their marriage? *You will drive yourself mad with these thoughts.*

Her garments hugged the long lines of her body as faithfully as the chausses he'd seen her wear. Her form was long and lithe, but well curved, with a nipped-in waist and high breasts that moved slightly with every breath she took. A girdle of golden mesh encircled her hips, and a jeweled dagger hung at her side. A long white veil covered her hair, and a gold circlet with a sapphire was set upon it. Her hair hung heavy to her hips with just the ends curling up. A few slight wisps of copper framed her face, which was as pale as her gown. Her left hand twisted in the fur of her dog's neck as her emerald eyes landed upon her father. *She should always wear emeralds. Emeralds and nothing else.* Eliane stepped forward to go to her father but had to stop when Rhys moved into her path and took her hand.

"I've waited long enough," he said into her ear. Her brow arched in surprise as he guided her, none too gently, toward Father Timothy. Rhys placed a hand in the small of her back to urge her forward and was surprised to find her trembling. Llyr, on her opposite side, growled at him and Madwyn quickly grabbed him by the scruff of the neck. The dog yelped and Eliane looked around as if seeing the room for the first time.

"Your hand is cold," Rhys said. He placed his other atop it as they took their place before Father Timothy.

She only nodded, and he noticed her teeth were chattering. The dog growled in protest as Ammon took him away.

"Llyr?" Eliane protested.

"I will keep you warm," he whispered against her veil. His breath moved it slightly, and he saw the peak of her ear hiding in the mass of copper hair. Eliane looked at him, her emerald eyes wide, her lips trembling, and then she looked beyond him, to her father, who nodded and smiled.

"Proceed," Edward commanded, and waved a frail hand in the priest's direction.

"Is this the same wench who slew a man this day?" Rhys smiled at the gathering while he whispered in her ear. "The same one who threatened to kill me in the forest?"

"Telling her of your plans for later this eve, milord?" A voice rose above the crowd, which laughed in response.

He kept his eyes on Eliane and watched the play of emotions over her face, watched her gather herself, watched as her eyes narrowed.

"Do you think me afraid, milord?" Only he could hear her. She gazed at him as if she were trying to see inside him, trying to discern his intent. As if she wanted to see his soul.

"We all fear the unknown," he whispered once more against her ear, a wry smile upon his lips at her sudden bravery. Once more she was the huntress from the wood. All that was missing was her bow.

"Is marriage a state you are familiar with?" She turned away, not giving him the satisfaction of watching the play of emotions on her face.

His heart leapt at her challenge. Back was the Eliane whose company he much enjoyed. "Nay, wife, only what comes after. I am most anxious to show you that."

She looked at him, her eyes glittering in the fire-light, her nose tilted haughtily in the air, as if she found him lacking. She would soon see that he was not. "I am not your wife yet."

"A condition that I would like to change with haste," Rhys said loudly. "If yon buffoons would stop laughing at their own jests long enough for the priest to say the necessary words over us."

Father Timothy puffed up his barrel chest while the assemblage quieted down. He opened his mouth to speak, but Eliane interrupted. "Wait."

Was she about to cry off? Fear gripped him, and he squeezed her hand without thinking. She placed her other against the velvet covering his chest, and her eyes implored him. "I want Llyr by my side," she said. "He has been there so long that I feel his absence dearly."

It was as if she touched his heart with her hand. *Anything* . . . She could ask for the moon and he'd fly to the heavens to pluck it from the sky. Once more he had to gather himself. He seemed to lose himself whenever she was near. He could not act the besotted fool for this group. What was wrong with him?

You will be fine once you have her. Once you rid yourself of this lust for her.

"Bring forth the beast," Rhys snapped over his shoulder. "So we may be done with this."

"The marriage bed will be crowded, milady, with two beasts in it," someone ventured. The jest was in poor taste and nervous laughter covered it.

Eliane cast her eyes downward, demurely, as the dog, released by Ammon, bounded to her side. Her skin turned as bright as her hair. She flattened her hand, pushed the palm downward, and the dog sat still as a statue by her side. "I did not mean to anger you, milord," she said quietly.

Father Timothy cleared his throat before Rhys or anyone else could respond. When the room quieted, they knelt before him in the rushes. His thigh touched hers and he was amazed to see they were near the same length. It thrilled him to imagine those thighs wrapped around his waist. He should be listening; he would need to speak soon, but he could not concentrate.

Her lower arm rested upon his thigh as he held her hand clasped in his, and the long muscle beneath his skin clenched with her touch. He wanted nothing more than to raise her hand to his lips and kiss it, to take each finger into his mouth and suck, but Father Timothy was looking at him as if he expected Rhys to say something. Her hand flexed within his.

"Repeat after me," Father Timothy said once more. Rhys forced himself to focus on the priest's round face as his voice rang strong and clear through the hall. Eliane's soon did the same. Father Timothy called for the rings. Rhys had not even realized there would be rings. Luckily he wore one, as he always did on formal occasions. It was the ring his Welsh grandfather had sent back with him when he rejected him. For some strange reason he'd taken a liking to the ring and kept it with him wherever he traveled. The craftsmanship of it had always intrigued him. Two continuous vines of silver and gold made a perfect circle. He slid it off his smallest finger and onto hers, once more repeating the vows.

Confusion crossed Eliane's face when Father Timothy

looked at her expectantly. Han moved to her side and placed something in her hand. Her father's ring. An emerald set in gold. The colors of Aubregate. The color of her eyes. Her teeth caught her lip as she tried with some difficulty to slide it over his knuckle, but she smiled when it finally slid into place.

Father Timothy added the Lord's blessing and then bade them stand. "You may seal the vows with a kiss."

Her lips parted with a gasp as he placed his hands on either side of her face. Her emerald eyes searched his, questioning him, but he cared not. He wanted nothing more than to drag her from this room to the chamber above and throw her upon the bed. But he could not. Not until the feasting and the toasting and the boasting was done. He lowered his face and brushed his lips over hers.

"Hail, Lady Eliane! Hail, Lord Rhys!" Tankards of ale were thumped upon the long wooden table and a cheer went up around the hall. Llyr's deep bark joined the cheers and Eliane was whirled from his side as congratulations abounded. A tankard was shoved into his hand.

Servants poured into the hall with trays of food. Musicians followed, and a merry tune soon filled the room. Rain pounded against the stone of the castle and turned to ice, sheathing it in glittering crystal.

Mathias grinned sheepishly at Rhys from the corner. One of the maids kissed the boy and pushed a tankard into his hand. Tomorrow his head would be splitting and he would be sorry, but tonight he could be young and foolish.

Rhys's eyes found his bride, by her father's side. Edward's hand gripped hers and he looked up at her with tear-filled eyes. She bent and kissed his forehead. Her father pulled her hand to his cheek and looked beyond her to Rhys, his face shadowed with coming death.

Renauld grabbed the front of the messenger's shirt and pulled him close enough that the stench of the man's rotted teeth gave him pause. The smell was so offensive that he flung him back so that his head snapped against the tree beneath which he sheltered. He should be warm and he should be dry. He should have Eliane and Aubregate under his thumb. All should be as he desired, but instead he stood beneath a tree in the freezing rain hearing things he did not wish to hear.

"Tell me again." It took great effort not to rip the man's head off.

"The Lady Eliane is to marry Rhys de Remy. The banns were posted two days ago." The man stuttered and spittle jumped from his mouth as he spoke. He was frightened, as well he should be. The men in Renauld's employ knew the penalty for failing him. Yet they were desperate enough for his coin not to care. That was why he used them. They'd known starvation and they knew about torture and would do anything to avoid either.

"There was an attack on the lady this day," the messenger continued, his tongue tripping over his rotting teeth. "She is now safe inside her keep."

"Damn," Renauld muttered. He did not dare say more since Salisbury was watching him. De Remy had gone in and taken the prize. If only he had drowned in the mud all those years ago. How many nights since then had Renauld considered it? If only the boy had died, if only Edward had minded his own business. If only his father had succeeded where his forefathers had failed.

At least he had the satisfaction of knowing de Remy was saddled with a hideous wife. The last time Renauld had seen Eliane, she'd been nothing but skinny arms and legs, wild red hair, and a face covered with hideous spots from the sun. And her ears . . . he'd only seen them the one time, the time she drew her bow upon him. They were an abomination. They should be cut from her head, or at the least shaped to look normal.

That had been his plan. Take his knife and trim her ears. He'd ached to do so since the first time he'd seen them. And now Rhys de Remy had taken his prize.

Renauld pounded a gloved fist into his hand. He needed an outlet for his frustration. He would love to hit the messenger and knock the rutted stumps of his teeth from his head, but he could not. Because Salisbury watched him.

I will have Aubregate. De Remy did not deserve it. It should be his. His father had died because of it. He'd waited years for it. With Edward dying, the time was now right. But if de Remy took Eliane as his wife before he got there . . .

"When were the banns posted?"

"Two days ago."

"Then the wedding is to be in the morning." Renauld looked at Salisbury, who stood with his men beneath a thick stand of firs. It was too wet to travel, too wet for a fire, too wet to bed down, and it would be dark soon. If they pressed on, they could make Aubregate before midnight. The roads might be close to impassable, but he did not care. They had dallied long enough thanks to Salisbury.

"Tell the men to make ready for my coming," he told the messenger. He grabbed the reins of his horse and swung into the saddle.

"Where are you going?" Salisbury strode forth from beneath his shelter.

"To Aubregate," Renauld said. "I have no desire to spend another night freezing cold and soaking wet." His men quickly followed suit. "You can do what you like." He sneered at Salisbury. "You know how to find the place." Renauld pulled his cloak over his head and rode into the rain.

Chapter Thirteen

*E*liane shivered. It was not from cold, even though the rain that had begun at eventide had now turned to ice. Indeed, it was most warm in her chambers with the press of bodies and the fire popping in the hearth. Her shivering was due to fear. She could not seem to control the tremors that racked her body. Never in her life had she felt so vulnerable. She might be able to slay a man with her sword, or take down a deer with her bow, but nothing in her training had prepared her for this moment.

She stood naked in the midst of her father's vassals while Madwyn held her hair up so that all could examine each and every part of her body. She would not think of them as her vassals. Not when their eyes were all upon her, searching her from head to toe for any flaw while smiling and laughing and making jokes about what was to come.

Eliane knew she was not as *soft* as most women. She knew her height was such that most men found her too tall. The man she had married . . . *my husband* . . . was used to the delicate creatures of court who were sheltered and pampered, not a redheaded hoyden who rode astride and climbed trees and hunted in the forest. Would he deny her because he found her undesirable? Her hands moved self-consciously to cover that

most private part of her body and her skin flushed as
red as her hair. She said a prayer of gratitude that Ammon and Han had chosen to stay below. *Thank you,
God, for their discretion.* She would come completely
undone if Ammon saw her thus.

"There is no doubt you will be warm," someone
said in jest. "With all that fire in your bed."

"Yea, milord, watch that she does not burn you,"
Madwyn rejoined loudly over the laughter that filled
the room. Llyr's confused barks joined in.

Rhys seemed to have no fear of being burned. If his
erect state was any indication, he was most anxious to
see the deed done. She could not help staring at the
part of him that seemed most eager and realized with
some relief that he did not find her hideous. Even
Mathias and Peter's squire, William, stared at her with
their eyes wide and their jaws hanging open.

"My poor and much abused lady will freeze if we do
not cover her," Madwyn said, her eyes on Rhys, who
nodded his assent. "The rest of you out," she commanded. "You've had your fun. I am sure there is ale
left below. Go see if you can finish it so that the only
sound I hear is your drunken snores instead of your
sorry attempts at humor."

Madwyn guided her to the bed and pulled back the
sheets to show that they were white and unstained.
They would be checked again come morning for the
telltale signs of her lost virginity. Eliane slid beneath
the sheets and pulled them over her naked breasts as the
room emptied. A maid quickly picked up the clothes
that had been scattered during the ceremony while
Madwyn handed Rhys a robe.

"Have mercy on the girl, please," Madwyn said. Rhys cast a mischievous grin in her direction as he belted the robe around his waist. Madwyn ignored his look and went about the room, straightening things, stoking the fire, and blowing out candles. Llyr jumped into his place on the bed, as was his nightly custom, and turned three times before lying down.

Rhys cleared his throat. Loudly. Eliane, who had decided that the best course at the present was pretending she was someplace else, blinked innocently. When she saw the direction of his gaze, she surprised herself with a nervous giggle. She quickly covered her mouth with her hand to keep from laughing out loud at the sight of Llyr sprawled across the foot of the bed so that there was barely room for Rhys to sit, much less take his place by her side.

Madwyn turned at the sound and saw Llyr. "Oh," she said. "That will not do at all." She patted her thigh. "Llyr! Come!" The dog grunted his disdain as he ignored her command. He rolled over on his side and raked a long leg over the sheets to arrange them to his satisfaction.

"Though I did not mind his presence during the ceremony and afterward," Rhys said, "I *am* certain that I will mind it *tonight*."

"Come, Llyr," Madwyn repeated with more authority. A maid knocked, then brought a tray of food and a bottle of wine.

"Llyr," Eliane said. "You must go." Her heart was not in the command, and Llyr realized it. "Mayhap he could be persuaded to sleep on the rug instead?" she asked hopefully.

"And take a bite out of my arse when I am most

vulnerable?" Rhys quipped. "I think not." He leaned over the bed so that he stood over Llyr, who quickly moved to a sitting position. Rhys adjusted his stance so that he was once more over Llyr and stared him in the eye.

I imagine he was stubborn as a child. . . . Eliane could see him as a small boy with his jaw thrust out and his arms folded across his chest.

"Down," Rhys said firmly, and pointed to the floor. Llyr growled. Rhys did not back down. He commanded the dog again. Llyr looked at Eliane, who merely shrugged, trying hard to keep from laughing out loud at the test of wills.

"I said *down!*" Llyr dipped his head and moved slowly and sullenly from the bed. Madwyn grabbed his neck and with the maid on the opposite side, they herded him from the room. Rhys shut the door firmly behind them as they left.

Eliane's desire to laugh was suddenly gone. The look Rhys turned on her drove all thought from her head save one. *He means to have me.* The time had come to conquer her fear. Nay, the time had come for him to conquer her.

Rhys strode to her with quiet determination, his dark eyes glowing beneath the slash of his brows. There was one thing on his mind, and one thing only. He wanted her. His desire thrilled her, but it also frightened her. She must not let him know that it did.

He shrugged the robe from his shoulders and let it drop to the floor. The fire behind him cast his body in sharp relief but left his face in shadow, his eyes hidden beneath his dark brows as he walked to the bed.

Warrior . . . His body seemed to be hewn from

stone. From the tendons in his neck and shoulders, to the long length of his thighs, each muscle stood out as if chiseled with a sculptor's tool. His left arm was scarred, right where the biceps dipped into the shoulder and she recognized it as an arrow track. Smaller scars were scattered about, including a sword wound on his thigh. They, along with his build, revealed an active life.

He had not a mark upon him from the earlier battle. She knew, after seeing him fight, this was due to his great skill. Her father had chosen wisely when seeking a protector for Aubregate. Time would only tell if she could say the same for Rhys as husband.

He was most willing to prove that part. His shaft stood straight out, as if leading him to where she lay, waiting . . . *Just let it be over with.* He wore a crucifix around his neck on a narrow silver chain. She let her eyes settle on it, focused on it, as if the Lord himself would step down and save her from what was to come. She knew she was not destined for the Church, but she suddenly wondered if mayhap it would be a more desirable choice than experiencing this fear that twisted around inside her.

The mattress dipped as he knelt on it. She scooted to the opposite side to give him room, yet she kept the sheet safely knotted in her hand and over her breasts as she leaned against the pillows. His hand reached out, took the sheet, and pulled it away, his fingers grazing her breastbone and the softer skin beneath as he revealed what she hid.

"Did I not promise to keep you warm?" He knelt over her, with one arm on either side of her waist and his knees beside her hips. His dark hair fell forward, brushing his neck, curling about his ears, dipping over his brow.

She did not know what to do with her hands, which she held clutched against her breasts. She chewed on her lip as she looked up at his face. His lips brushed her forehead, moved down her cheek. With his nose and cheek he pushed her hair back over her ear and traced the outline of it with his tongue. A tremor ran down her neck, into her spine, and settled into a warm pool between her legs.

"Oh." It was just a small gasp, but it stopped him. He moved his head back and looked at her with a bemused expression on his face.

"Does that please you?" he asked.

She looked down at her hands, which now rested on the sheet that covered her from the waist down. "Should it?"

He smiled. "I hope so. It was my intent." He bent to her ear again and whispered, "Should I try harder?" His tongue traced her ear, and she could not hide the shiver of delight that overcame her.

"I honestly did not know what to expect," she admitted.

"You will know all soon enough," he said, and nuzzled her neck. His mouth settled in the curve of her shoulder, and her head moved back upon the pillow of its own accord. She felt his mouth move, as if he smiled, and she closed her eyes with a sigh. His hair was soft and brushed against her cheek. The crucifix pressed into her skin, making her wonder exactly how much of this night she would have to confess to Father Timothy. Her hands still felt awkward, so she moved them, her knuckles brushing against the heavy ridges of his abdomen. She felt them contract, heard his sharp intake of breath.

I did that. . . . So strange that an accidental touch would have so strong an impact upon him. How much more would an intentional touch, a stroke, a caress? Still she did not know what to do, so she placed her hands upon his waist and marveled that there was no loose skin, only solid strength beneath her grasp.

Suddenly he was above her, his body stretched over hers. With his hands about her waist, he gently slid her down until she was flat on her back.

His lips seared hers with a kiss and his hand cupped her breast. His thumb flicked over her nipple and without thinking about what she was doing, she flexed her legs and felt her toes curl. She reached an arm back and grasped the edge of the headboard. She was afraid she would fly off the bed, even though he was above her, trapping her with his body. Her other hand moved up his back and carefully, cautiously, traced the line of his spine with her fingertips. Her hips flexed and he settled onto her. The sheet still lay between them from the waist down, yet she held no doubt as to what was going to happen. Her only questions were when and would it feel as wonderful and magical as this felt right now? His shaft settled into place between her thighs and burned through the sheet, igniting her. *Did I not promise to keep you warm?* There was a difference between being warm and burning with desire.

He swallowed her sudden gasp as his tongue plundered her mouth, twisting around hers and guiding her into the kiss. His hand continued its play with her breasts and to her amazement she realized that she moved against him as if it were the most natural thing in the world. He broke the kiss and moved his mouth once more over her cheek and down the line of her jaw. His tongue made a trail over her breastbone and down until it swirled over the tight peak of one nipple. His hand teased the other until she thought she would scream.

He raised his head and looked at her. He moved his body up, sliding his skin over hers, pressing his chest against her breasts, his stomach against hers. His hands grasped her head, and twined into her hair. His gaze was dark and intent, fathomless. *It's as if he is seeing me for the first time.* He studied her as if he searched for something within her, and her heart quickened a beat at the intense emotion that flashed between them.

"Milord?" she asked with trembling breath.

"Say my name."

"Rh . . . Rhys."

" 'Tis lovely, the way you say it." She closed her eyes in happiness at his compliment. "Eliane," he whispered, and she opened her eyes once more. "It suits you. Eliane. Like music. Like a song. Eliane with eyes like emeralds. That's what the troubadours will sing about when we go to court."

A sudden fear flashed through her. "I will try not to hurt you." He misunderstood her fear. "I will not lie." It was not the act she feared, nay, she wanted it. Desperately. He had woven a spell over her and she was helpless against it. "It will hurt, but only at first." He did not realize that it was the mention of court that frightened her so. She would not tell him now. She might not tell him ever.

Rhys shifted on his side and drew back the sheet. He

flung it over his hip and moved his hand up her thigh. Her eyes widened as it trailed upward. "Eliane," he said again, and bent to kiss her just as his hand found the moistness between her legs. Her heart raced. She felt it pounding in her chest as he once more nuzzled her breast. It wasn't until he raised his head and let out a violent curse that she realized the pounding was on the door to her room.

"Milady! Milord! Lord de Remy!" The knocks became more insistent. "Eliane!"

"'Tis Han." She looked at the door in trepidation. Rhys leapt from the bed and crossed to the door, still naked and most obviously still wanting. He snatched the door open wide, nearly ripping it from its hinges, and stared at Han, who brushed by him without any regard to Rhys's condition or either of their state of undress. Eliane covered herself with the sheet and pushed back her hair with a trembling hand.

"Your father calls for you." Han held out her robe, which had been conveniently left on a low stool. "The time has come."

"He's dying?" Eliane asked. Her heart jumped into her throat as she looked between Han and Rhys. *Now?*

Han turned to Rhys. Her husband jerked his robe on and tied the sash as if he wielded his sword. His face and every line of his body showed his frustration.

"He must see his daughter now." Han turned once more to Eliane. "Before it is too late." He turned his back so he would not see her nakedness. Once more she was grateful for his discretion.

Eliane looked at Rhys. He rubbed his forehead and ran his hand through his dark hair. She saw a tic in his jaw and realized that he was angry. Extremely so.

"Go." His voice snapped, but the dark eyes he turned upon her were full of pain. He took a deep breath and his mien suddenly became calmer. "Go see to your father. Our time will wait."

Without a word, she grabbed up her robe and followed Han from the room.

Chapter Fourteen

He did not know what was expected of him. Rhys sat in the chair by the fire and stared at the flames as he sipped the wine left by the maid. The food was untouched. He had no appetite for food. He hungered for something else. It was his wedding night and he was painfully alone, except for his throbbing cock, a constant reminder of his unsatisfied state

His thoughts were jumbled. Should he go to Eliane? Comfort her as her father died? Wasn't that his duty as her husband? Or should he leave them in peace? After all, he was practically a stranger to them. If Edward had wanted him there, would he not have asked for him also? Or was he so far gone that the only name he could speak was his daughter's?

What of Eliane? Should he wait until she sent for him? Would she send for him? How long did it take for a man to die? A man who had already been dying for years?

The keep was quiet. Unnaturally so. He knew the revelers from the wedding most likely slept where they'd fallen in the great hall below, snoring amongst the rushes and the hounds. The two squires, Mathias and William, were asleep in his former chamber across the hall. The servants had to be exhausted from their labors and deep in slumber. The only people who could possibly be awake at this late hour were those who watched for Edward's last breath. Eliane, Cedric, and certainly Father Timothy. Were Madwyn and Han there also?

What was their relationship to Eliane? Were they related by blood as their ears suggested? They were people of the forest as Eliane's ancestors were. They spoke a common language that was unlike anything he had ever heard before. What did it have to do with the secrets of Aubregate and the rumored treasure? What exactly had he gotten himself into with this hastily conceived marriage?

Rhys's frustration became unbearable. He needed to do something, anything, to relieve it, yet he felt trapped, by the walls, by the weather and the circumstances. *By the marriage?*

She was so beautiful. So innocent, yet knowing. The way she'd responded, the way she'd moved, betrayed a great passion waiting to be revealed. He'd been so close to claiming her. So close to losing himself inside her.

How long had she been gone? How long until she returned?

He could sit no longer, so he got up and moved about the chamber. Everywhere he looked, he saw Eliane, especially when his eyes fell upon the bed. The posts were carved to look like tree trunks and the canopy and the drapes were shades of green, as if one were looking upward at the leaves. It called to mind the first time he'd seen her, standing over him in the forest, with her bow notched and ready.

On the wall between the window and fireplace hung a tapestry of exquisite craftsmanship. It showed a glade with a stream running through it and a stone portal beyond. There was a snowy white unicorn with a foal at her side. Both drank from a stream that was shot with silver thread as if to indicate the purity of the water. The portal caught his attention and he could not help wondering where it led. The dim light of the fire did nothing to show what lay beyond.

Tiring of questions that had no answers, Rhys moved to the window. The rain that had come with their wedding was now sleet. It covered everything with a sheen of ice. Only the torches beneath the overhangs still burned and they gave but a weak light. Anyone who went out in this weather would have to be mad. Or desperate. Renauld was out there, traveling this way, in hopes of getting his hands on Eliane. But he could not travel in this mess. Or would he? Was he desperate enough? Surely he'd taken shelter at his own estate. Was the ice enough to keep him away? There were no answers to be had by staring into the darkness, so he turned away from the window and once more saw the bed.

Rhys closed his eyes and saw her as she'd been, beneath him, staring up at him with those emerald eyes full of wonder and surprise. He'd been determined to show her, to seduce her, to make her want him with the same longing he'd felt since the first time he saw her. If Edward could have waited a few more moments, it would be done. But would a few moments have been enough to get his fill of her?

He took another drink of the wine and cursed himself for a fool. *You are crying like a lovesick troubadour.*

Mine. She will be mine. With a snarl, he flung the wine away and watched it crash against the stone of the wall. He was tired of waiting. Tired of wanting.

A sound broke the silence as what was left of the wine trickled down the wall into a puddle. It was a mournful, deep tone that seemed to shake the stones around him. It sounded as if a large and powerful creature was in deep pain. Rhys had never heard anything like it. The sound faded away into the distance, but its echo remained. He turned to the window again and looked upward. Fat snowflakes now mingled with the sleet. The sound came again, and he realized it must be some type of horn, but he could not imagine what it was. If he had been in the forest, he would have said it was mystical, but here in the keep it was haunting. Whoever was making the noise was in the tower above him.

Edward is gone. Rhys found his chausses and pulled them on, yanking the cross garters into place with frustration. Had he become so lazy that he needed Mathias to tie them for him? He grabbed up his linen chainse and threw it on, leaving the ties undone. He jerked on his boots and left the chamber. The noise sounded again as he stepped into the hall. Voices sounded from below, sleepy, disgruntled, confused, and then a keening wail from a woman. *Edward.*

William opened the door, clad only in his chausses, his hair on end, and his eyes red and swollen. "Where is Mathias?" Rhys asked.

"Here." William moved so Rhys could see Mathias, flat on his back in the bed, still fully dressed and snoring to high heaven. "He is drunk," William added.

I will surely beat him later. "Leave him," Rhys command. "He would be worthless anyway. You can serve in his stead."

"What has happened?" William moved to get his chainse and boots.

"Edward is gone." He took the winding staircase down, two steps at a time. The door to Edward's chambers was open. A sheet covered the frail form on the bed. Cedric sat in a chair, his head in his hands, and Eliane . . .

She stood before the window, looking out at the driving snow. Her hair tumbled down her back in a mass of tangles to her hips. Tangles he had made in his passion. Tangles she had not taken the time to comb out in her haste to be by her father's side. Her arms were folded about her and he could see the ring he'd given her on her finger as she clutched her upper arms as if she were chilled. The dog was by her side and leaned into her, butting her arm with his nose as if he could offer comfort. She dropped her hand to touch him and twined her fingers into the hair of his neck.

Rhys came up behind her and the dog rumbled deep in its throat without turning its head to look at him. *So we are to be at war, you and me.* He stared at the dog until the beast dipped its head, acknowledging that *this* time, Rhys had won the battle. Both knew they were still at war.

Eliane turned. Her cheeks were stained with tears, her eyes swollen, and the tip of her nose quite red. He did not know what to do. He'd made it a habit to avoid women when tears were involved. It usually meant they wanted him to stay when he wanted to go. He always walked away, not letting the tears trap him into foolish words that would later haunt him. Words and tears were ready weapons in a woman's arsenal. Weapons that a wise man avoided at all costs.

"He's gone." Her words were simple, yet spoke volumes.

Rhys flexed his hands, placed them on her upper arms. Stepped closer to her. "I'm sorry." Was that enough? Should he say more? Should he say that he too would mourn for the only man who ever gave a damn about him? How could he compare his grief to hers? Edward was everything to her. Rhys had no knowledge of what it was to feel something so strong for anyone.

Her teeth worried her lower lip as she looked at him, her eyes moist and as deep as the sea. She nodded her head, up, down, agreeing with whatever it was he said; he could not remember after looking into her eyes. Very slowly, she lowered her head and tentatively placed it upon his shoulder. She stepped to him and put her hands upon the skin of his chest where his chainse was open. His arms seemed to fold around her of their own accord and he rested his chin on top of her head as she found what peace there was to be had in his embrace. Were there words he should speak? Words of comfort that would be meaningless against the tide of grief she felt. She seemed content without the words, so he held her and hoped that his still throbbing cock would not chase her away.

Whatever passed between them in that moment was short-lived. Han rushed into the chamber. He was once more dressed in his usual garb, and his woolen cap was covered with ice. Had it been he who blew the mournful horn? Madwyn came behind him. She too had changed out of her wedding finery.

"Visitors approach," Han said. "Vannoy." He spat out the name.

"How can you be sure?" Rhys asked. Eliane moved away from him, her face pale with worry. She once more twisted her fingers into the hair of the dog's neck. The dog stood at attention, watching the faces around him, as if he could read their intent.

"He knows, believe me," Madwyn said. "Han can see things. Further and deeper than most."

"He hopes to stop the wedding," Han said. "He has no way of knowing it has already occurred."

"He cannot stop it! We are wed. The papers are signed." Eliane's voice was panicked and she looked between the three of them for some sign of agreement.

"Not all is complete," Madwyn said. "You must be bedded before it is binding."

"Wha . . . what?"

"The wedding is not complete until I bed you." Rhys saw her fear. Was it of him? Before, she had seemed willing. Most willing. "Our marriage can be put aside without it." He looked at Han. It was the first time he'd seen him other than calm. "How long before they arrive"

"Not long. I had the gates closed. He is on *your* king's mission. We will have to open them eventually."

Rhys grabbed Eliane's hand. "We must hurry." He pulled her from the room with Madwyn on their heels. The dog followed. The dog would be a problem.

"Where do we go?" Eliane asked. "What is happening?"

"You must trust your husband," Madwyn said. "You must do as he says."

They passed William on the stairs and Mathias behind him. He looked ill.

"Your master will soon be at the gate," Rhys said to William as he pulled Eliane up the curving stone steps. "Do what you can to delay their entrance to the chambers above."

"Renauld would not dare," Eliane said. "A Vannoy has never set foot within these halls."

"One will tonight," Rhys said. "By order of the king." They burst through the door of her chamber. Madwyn was still with them and he turned on her as she crossed the room. "Do you intend to watch?"

"Don't be a fool," she said. She handed him a crock with a carved lid. "This will ease the way," she said. She grabbed the dog by the neck once more and hurried him out. "Bar the door," she added. "I will do what I can without calling the king's vengeance down upon us."

Rhys pulled the chain that hung beside the frame over the door. He wondered if it had ever been used. Its only purpose was to protect the occupants in case of an attack. He went to the trunk where Eliane's weapons lay and picked up the short sword. He should have sent Mathias for his weapons, but there was no time. No time at all.

Eliane stood where he'd left her. Did she not know what she had to do? What he had to do? "Take off your robe and get into bed," he said gently. He tossed the sword and the crock on the mattress. He pulled off his chainse and loosened his chausses. He dared not strip further. If he had to face Renauld, he would not be vulnerable. There were shouts outside. They drifted through the icy air and rang against the window. Renauld had arrived.

Eliane raised her eyes to him. Her expression was grief-stricken, her eyes wide: confusion, desperation, sadness, despair, and fear all mingled on her face. She was stricken. He felt as if he were going to betray her. He had no choice. "We must hurry." He yanked the robe from her body. She did not help him, nor did she fight him. He picked her up and carried her to the bed. She said not a word. He pulled the top sheet away with one hand and dropped her upon it.

He heard another thump, the sound of horses, more shouts, and then a scrambling on the stairs. There was a scratching sound and he reached for the sword. A bark, then a howl.

"Llyr," she gasped.

Her hair was wild and her eyes, her beautiful emerald eyes turned up to him. A tear coursed down her cheek. Understanding dawned on her face and she lay back and slowly spread her legs. His cock strained forward. He needed no encouragement. He was ready to burst.

God . . . He had to do it. Even though she was not ready. Rhys stuck his hand in the crock and brought out his fingers covered with a smooth unguent. He placed one hand on her stomach to steady her and found her opening, pushed his covered fingers through her barrier hard enough to break through. A few drops of blood fell to the sheet as he pulled his fingers free. He grabbed her hips, pulled her body close, and plunged inside her in one mighty shove.

She did not say a word, although her face twisted in pain. She kept her eyes upon him, even when the tears came and ran into her hair.

"I am sorry to cause you pain," he managed to say. She was so tight, but the unguent eased his passage and he was able to move inside her. As soon as he did, he was lost. Somehow he placed her legs around his waist and fell forward, propping himself on his elbows, his legs still on the floor. He wrapped his hands in her hair. He needed something to hold on to . . . someone . . . Eliane closed her eyes and he hated himself. Still, he moved because he could not stop moving, pumping inside her, grinding against her hips, with the pressure building and the dog howling and scratching at the door as if to tear it down. The howling was so loud, Rhys could not hear anything else. The keep could be falling down around their ears and they would not hear it. He could only hope that Han and Madwyn and perhaps Peter were keeping them safe. Then he could not think at all.

Still, he said it over and over again. "I am sorry." Until all he could say was her name. Then the world spun around him and the stars came, dazzling, into his mind and he shut his eyes in release. But through it all, he could still see the betrayal on her face.

Chapter Fifteen

$\mathcal{S}$he was weak and she hated herself because of it. Why else would she cover her face and turn away from her husband when all he'd done was save her and thus save Aubregate? While she lay on her side with her legs tucked up close to her, Llyr howled and scratched at the door. She felt Rhys move from the mattress where he had collapsed when he was finished. She heard the heavy sigh he let out as he stood and moved about the room. She could do nothing to stop Llyr's howling, just as she'd been able to do nothing to stop what had just happened. It was her duty as a wife to submit to her husband.

"Eliane," he said. "Look at me."

Submit to you, husband. . . . She recalled the words of the wedding vows she'd spoken, and she opened her eyes. His gaze was upon her, his eyes fathomless black pits in his haggard and weary face. Did he feel the pain of her father's passing also?

He is gone. . . .

Rhys grasped her shoulders and pulled her up to sit. She was grateful to see he was covered once more, but only from the waist down. She did not think she could stand to look upon him otherwise. The pain between her legs was still fresh, and inside she felt raw. Was this what submission meant? To accept her husband's possession, even though there was pain? What about before, when he'd kissed her and held her and touched her? There was no pain then, only a longing for something she could not explain. Was this all there was to being married? Was this what her father mourned all those years after her mother was gone? Her name was the last that he spoke. He died with it upon his lips, as if he saw her.

"Drink this." Rhys handed her a goblet half-filled with wine. She obeyed, drinking it all down when he placed an encouraging finger beneath the cup to hold it up. When she finished, he took it from her. As he moved away to replace the cup on the table, Eliane saw the blood of her lost virginity splattered upon the sheet. She once more closed her eyes. She felt her robe come over her shoulders and then Rhys gently guided her arms within and pulled her hair from beneath it. How could he be gentle with her now, when before there had been nothing but pain? Yet he'd seemed to enjoy the mating. The sounds he made bespoke great pleasure. Was it thus for men? Was that why they sought the act so desperately? Was that why women were encouraged to submit to their husbands?

"I would speak with you if only yon dog would stop howling." He looked over his shoulder. "And if we did not have visitors bearing down upon us."

As if Llyr heard Rhys's request, he stopped howling and they both turned their eyes upon the door. There was the sound of growling, and then Llyr yelped. Eliane stared at the door, unable to move.

Someone pounded on the door. "Open in the name of the king!" The pounding continued.

"Vannoy." Rhys spat out the word and picked up his sword.

It had been years since Eliane had heard Renauld's voice, but Rhys seemed certain. He turned grim eyes upon her before he turned to the door. The pounding increased. Renauld had to be putting his shoulder to the door. The portal seemed to bow inward with each heavy thump. There were more shouts and Madwyn's could be heard among them.

"Rhys."

He turned and looked at her, his eyes betraying no emotion. She did not know him well enough to guess what he was feeling.

"I will not shame you . . . husband."

Something flashed in the dark depths of his eyes, and a smile flitted across his features before he turned once more to the chain. He removed it and then moved back to the bed. He sat down before her on the edge of the mattress with the sword in his hand and the blood clearly visible on the sheet beside him. She took shelter behind him, exceedingly grateful for his presence. If not for him and her father's forethought, her situation would be dire. This was what she had always dreaded, but never had she imagined having the stalwart presence of a husband such as Rhys de Remy protecting her. Renauld would have to look over or through him to see her.

The door gave way and slammed against the table behind it. It seemed as if the entire population of the keep stood in her doorway, with Renauld Vannoy foremost in the room. Llyr bounded through and jumped upon the bed, taking up a position at the foot of it.

Renauld's hawkish eyes took in everything. The disarray of the sheets and her hair, Rhys sitting casually upon the bed, with his chest bare to the world, as if he'd just risen from a lengthy night of lust. Eliane tightened the belt on her robe and placed a hand on Rhys's shoulder to steady herself. She felt the warmth of his skin and the tension of his muscle beneath. He was ready to strike if need be. The thought gave her comfort.

"It appears that you have rushed your vows." Renauld swaggered into the room, his eyes roaming about as if taking inventory of her belongings. Her skin crawled at the thought of him in her room, in the keep, with her father's body not yet cold and still lying below. She did not realize that she had tightened her hand upon Rhys's shoulder until she saw the skin beneath her fingers turn white. She relaxed her hand.

Rhys's eyes followed Renauld as he stalked about and finally came to a stop before them. Behind him, in the doorway, she saw Peter, Mathias, William, Han, and Madwyn. She was sure there were more in the hall beyond. Were there servants and townsfolk lined up on the staircase, waiting to parade past and see for themselves that she was now wedded and bedded? Surely Renauld had to know that the deed was done and could not be undone in the eyes of the Church or the state. *Can it?*

He saw. His eyes lit upon the blood, which was glaringly obvious against the white of the sheet. Rhys even pointed her sword tip toward the mattress in case anyone missed it. He did it casually, as if he were doing nothing more than playing with a toy. A very deadly toy.

"The banns called for the ceremony to be tomorrow. I am certain the king will wonder why there was a need for such haste when he has just now called Eliane to court to be his ward."

"It was her father's dying wish to see her properly wed," Rhys said.

"Edward is dead?" Peter asked. Dear, sweet Peter. His face seemed stricken while Renauld did nothing to suppress the satisfied look on his countenance.

"He is," Han said evenly. "As I tried to tell you when yon fool pounded down the doors to the keep." His contempt for Renauld was obvious even though his words were as calm and stoic as ever. It was miraculous that he had not slain Renauld before their long-standing enemy set foot within the keep. Han was wise enough to know that it would do more harm than good to slay the man when he was on the king's business.

Peter bowed low in the direction of the bed. "I am so sorry, Lord de Remy. Lady de Remy. Your father was a great man and will always have a place in my heart."

"Thank you, Peter," Eliane said. She moved a bit from behind Rhys so Peter could see her face and the genuine gratitude she felt at his kind words. She saw Renauld's eyes upon her and felt Rhys stiffen beneath her hand. The look on Renauld's face was one of amazement, as if he'd never seen her before. She turned her head away from his stare and wondered at it. She knew her ears were well hidden beneath her hair.

Llyr's growl rumbled and the dog rose to stand awkwardly on the bed. She steadied him with a down motion of her hand. Llyr kept his eyes upon her, waiting for any sign to attack. He sensed the tension in the room as clearly as everyone else present. The air about them fairly crackled and popped like a fire.

Had she changed that much in the years since Renauld had last seen her? She'd been nothing more than a child at the time, but her hair was much the same hue and her frame already taller and leaner than most. She cast a quick glance in his direction and saw he looked much the same, except now he carried a man's weight instead of a boy's. She still could not stand the sight of him, and the memory of what he had done to that puppy still sickened her as it did Han. She could tell by the look on his face that he wanted to throw their uninvited guest from the nearest tower.

Rhys stood, her sword held lightly in his hand as Renauld continued to stare. "Have you business with *my wife*?" He twisted the blade in his hand casually. "If so, then you may speak to her *through* me."

"Tell your *wife* that the king has bade me return both of you into his care as soon as possible," Renauld spat out. "He gave Salisbury the same task. Since her father is dead, we need only wait to put him in the ground to be on our way." He turned on his heel and left.

Elaine could not believe the cruelty of his words. Tears came once more. Surely the king was not so cruel as to demand her presence so soon after her father's death.

"Vannoy!"

Renauld stopped at Rhys's shout. He had no choice since his way was barred by those who stood at the door. He turned and stood with his hand placed upon his hip, close to the hilt of his sword.

"*You* will show Lord Edward the respect due him," Rhys said. "*We* will observe the proper time for mourning and then *my wife and I* will journey to present

ourselves to the king. You may return to him with the
knowledge that you have delivered his message, and
give him my wife's gratitude for his concern. As we
are now in a state of mourning and there is scant place
for your comfort, we will not be offended if you return to your own lands until you see fit to deliver *my*
message to the king."

Eliane watched Han's eyes flicker in acknowledgment
of the words Rhys left unspoken. Renauld would be
delivered to the borders of Chasmore at once. Either
upright on his horse or stuffed in a sack and dragged
behind. Either way, it would be done.

"Leave us for a moment," Rhys commanded those
watching as Renauld stormed off, quickly followed by
Han. Madwyn stood in the door for a moment, her
eyes questioning.

Eliane had no answers for her. Too much had happened in too short a time. She could not think. She
merely nodded in what she hoped was a reassuring way.

"I will be waiting to attend you," Madwyn said as
she shut the door. Llyr whined and came to her, his
nose bumping her arm. He placed his head in her lap
and settled with a huff of air.

Rhys stood before the fireplace, his hand on the
mantel and his head bent as if he studied the embers.
The fire was dying. It needed to be stoked. He rolled his
shoulders, and the muscles rippled beneath his smooth
skin. She watched in fascination as they moved, and
marveled at the power she had felt, seething beneath
her hand. Had it taken greater strength on his part to
hold back? Surely he'd wanted to kill Renauld for his
impudence and disrespect. Did fear of the king's reper-
cussions stay his hand or fear of Renauld? She knew

nothing of Renauld's fighting skills, only of his black heart and evil ways. Was there some history between the two men that she did not know of?

What did she know of her husband beyond the tales told of his birth and the fact that her father had saved his life when he was just a lad? She did not even know in what manner her father had saved him, only that Rhys owed him his life. That was why he'd married her. To honor his debt to her father. Did he find the bargain ill met now that he had Renauld Vannoy as an enemy?

Rhys turned, finally, from his contemplation of the fire. He gathered his clothes and put them on with great care. When finally he was dressed once more, he came to the bed. He gazed down at her for a long moment and then picked up a tendril of her hair that curled over her arm. Llyr growled and Rhys silenced him with a look. He rubbed his fingers over the locks, as he had before, when her braid came undone during the battle. " 'Twoud be a shame to hide such a thing of beauty."

"Milord?" Why would she hide her hair?

"At court. The fashions of women escape me at times."

Of what does he speak?

His face changed, his moment of whimsy gone. He dropped her hair as if it burned him and straightened. "I am sorry for the pain I caused you this eve. Rest assured that I will not do so again."

She shook her head in confusion. He was so formal, so stiff. Where was the man who teased her? Who fought for her? Who nearly drove her mad with his kiss? "I do not understand."

Rhys looked down, beyond, above, and then finally at her, with dark eyes full of desperate pain.

"I will not touch you again, Eliane. Unless you desire it."

Desire it? The door closed behind him. "I have lost something precious," she said to Llyr. But for the life of her, she could not put a name to what it was she had lost.

Renauld snatched his arm from the huntsman's grasp. *He dares much, this servant of Edward.* No longer Edward's servant. Now de Remy's through his marriage to Eliane. *Eliane . . .*

"Do you need help to find your way?" Han asked.

Renauld's hand touched the hilt of his sword. If only he could wipe that self-satisfied smirk off the huntsman's face. But he dared not. Not when he was within the walls of Aubregate. He stepped out to the bailey and turned his face upward to the snow, hoping it would cool his temper . . . for the moment.

His men-at-arms and horses were sheltered beneath an overhang by the gate. Apparently Aubregate had not extended the same hospitality to his men that they had to Salisbury's. Another slight that he would remember when he was master of this keep. Another thing that he would enjoy using against Eliane. *Elaine . . .*

"Tell your master I will see him at court," Renauld said as he swung into the saddle. He knew his men and horses were exhausted, but he had little choice. The walls were full of armed men just waiting for an excuse to bury him beneath a barrage of arrows.

Someday they will swear to me. . . . Someday soon

they would all be under his rule. De Remy would be dead and Eliane would be his. As his horse settled wearily into a slow trot through the snow, he allowed his thoughts to dwell on the most surprising revelation of this eve. Eliane.

When had she become so beautiful? She was not as he remembered. Not at all. Never in his wildest imaginings had he pictured her thus. His cock had sprung to life at the sight of her with her hair tumbled down and her face raw with emotion. The sight of her virgin's blood on the sheets had nearly driven him mad with want. To have been the first to touch her as de Remy had been . . . It should have been he. She had been under his nose all these years and he had not seen it. He'd been biding his time, waiting for Edward's certain demise, waiting for the exact moment to go before the king . . .

They would both pay. De Remy with his life and Eliane with bits and pieces of her body. The first thing he would take would be the tips of her ears and after that . . . he would just take whatever part tired him first.

He summoned one of his men to his side. "Ride ahead. Make sure there is a woman available for me when I arrive." The man nodded wearily and spurred his horse onward into the snowy night. Renauld dropped his hand to the knife he wore tucked beneath his tunic as he shifted uncomfortably in the saddle. His throbbing cock would soon be sated and he would practice his plans for Eliane on whatever wench had the misfortune to find herself in his bed this night.

Chapter Sixteen

*H*e had promised not to touch her unless she wanted him to. But there was no reason why he could not watch her. So watch her he did all during the day of bitter cold as they set out to answer the king's summons.

Traveling with a wife was an eye-opening experience. It required a cart and a horse to carry a tent, bedding, household items, her wardrobe, and a maid named Khati, who was much more excited than her mistress about the summons to London.

Four men-at-arms wearing Aubregate colors and a boy from the forest named Jess, whose sole purpose was to carry messages to and from Aubregate, traveled with them. Rhys had yet to determine whether the boy had ears like Eliane's, because he was wearing one of the woolen caps that Han seemed so found of.

Edward's man Cedric traveled with them also. He'd sworn fealty to Eliane and, through her, Rhys and declared that he would continue his role as attendant to the Lord of Aubregate if it pleased Rhys for him to do so. Rhys had never had anyone beyond Mathias to look after his personal needs. The true test of Cedric's worth would come at the end of the day when their camp had to be set up.

The day was waning. That time would soon be upon them. He motioned for Cedric. "Ride ahead with Mathias and see if he can find an acceptable place for us to spend the night. I fear it has been a long day for milady and I would see to her rest."

"I will see to milady's comfort," Cedric assured him, and the two rode on ahead, their horses plowing through the snow that had finally ceased falling the night before.

The snow made traveling with a cart difficult, but there was no help for it. He would not consider allowing Eliane to sleep without shelter, even though she assured him she was quite capable of doing so. Of her capability he needed no assurance. He'd marveled at it as he'd stood by her side during her father's funeral and the swearing of fealty afterward.

Rhys found he had great doubts about his own capability. Not touching her was much more difficult than he'd imagined it to be when he made the promise. At times it was necessary to touch her. He'd taken her arm as they climbed the steps of the church for the swearing, placed his hands about her waist to help her from her horse as they came to the cemetery for Edward's burial. It was also customary for a husband to serve his wife during meals, and this he did with great care as she watched him with those emerald eyes that were full of grief for her lost father. He could see the hurt in them, caused by his own brutal attack on their wedding night. How else would she consider it? It had been tantamount to rape. She'd had no choice but to submit.

She ought to anticipate their lovemaking eagerly and with passion. But would it ever be so? Rhys shook his head at the twisted trail his thoughts followed. He could not undo what was done. He could only hope that she would understand that completing their union was the only way to ensure her safety against Renauld.

He turned in his saddle to check on the progress of his caravan. Four men-at-arms rode before him, two of Peter's and two of his own. Eliane rode behind him, speaking earnestly with Salisbury. It was good that they talked. They had shared memories of Edward, for whom Peter had squired when she was just a child.

"How fares your wife, Peter?" Eliane asked.

"Lydia fares extremely well, especially when breeding. We have another child due in late spring."

"How many does that make?"

"Four. Two sons and a daughter so far. Lydia hopes for another daughter."

There are only daughters born to the women of Aubregate. . . . What would it be like to have a daughter by Eliane? To see her grow big from his seed . . . Once more Rhys stopped his musings. There would be no child until she chose to let it happen. He would not put her through the agony again. He could not stand to see that betrayal in her eyes.

"She has sent a gift for you," Peter said.

"Indeed? That is kind, indeed, as we have never even met," Eliane exclaimed.

"I admit I have told her much about you," Peter said. He looked toward her hair. "Including the thing that makes you different from the women at court."

Her hand went self-consciously to her ears. She should not have to hide her ears. *They are beautiful as she is.*

"I do not know much about the fashions of women," Peter continued. "But the current head gear does much to hide the hair and what lies beneath." He pulled a carefully wrapped package from beneath his cloak. "It is called a wimple." He shrugged as if knowing what it was called would explain its purpose.

Eliane took the packet and dropped it into the pack attached to her saddle. She looked at Rhys with confusion plainly written on her face.

"I am certain you will know what to do with it once you look at it," he said simply. "But I will leave the choice of whether you hide your ears or reveal them up to you. It matters not one way or the other to me." Except that he would not see her hurt.

"We should camp soon," Peter commented. "I fear the wind is ever increasing and with it the cold."

"I sent Mathias ahead to find us a place. And Cedric to make sure it is practical."

"'Tis a good way for Mathias to learn," Peter agreed. "And Cedric is wise enough to let the boy think it through on his own. That is the way I learned from Edward."

"I feel I do not spend enough time giving him the instruction he needs," Rhys said.

"Is not the best way to learn by watching?" Eliane asked. "And asking questions? Mathias seems to have no fear of asking if there is something he does not understand."

"Believe me, he has no fear of talking at all," Rhys replied dryly, and once more her musical laugh brightened his day.

"A rider approaches!" one of the leading men-at-arms called out. Rhys and Peter immediately put hands to their swords, but it was only Mathias.

"I have found a place," Mathias said eagerly as he rode up. "Not more than a mile ahead."

"What thinks Cedric of your choice?" Rhys asked.

"He must approve, milord, or he would not have sent me back to tell you."

"I will surely beat you," Rhys said as Mathias grinned wickedly. "Only the fact that you are well padded at the moment and numb from cold keeps me from doing so."

"Surely you will not," Eliane exclaimed. " 'Twould serve no purpose except to warm him up, and that would be a reward on such a day as today."

"It would also take too much effort." Peter joined in the teasing. "It is hard to achieve a full swing when one's arm is hindered by a cloak." Mathias merely shook his head and made his way back to the front of the troop to lead them onward.

"My grandmother found neither her cloak nor her robes to be any hindrance at all," Rhys said. "As she usually had some sort of weapon handy such as a stout stick or a willow branch, which was especially painful when applied to bare skin."

"Rhys!" Eliane exclaimed. "Surely she did not."

"Every chance she got." Rhys shrugged. "Do not let it trouble you," he said when her look conveyed her dismay. "It was simply the way of things. She was convinced I had the devil inside me and the only way to remove it was by beatings and prayer."

" 'Tis a shame she did not have Vannoy in her grasp," Peter commented, then rode ahead.

"While Vannoy's ways are not pleasing to me, I find I owe him much," Rhys said softly with his eyes steady upon her face. Her concern for his childhood beatings heartened him. Could it mean that she cared for him somewhat, despite the horrible events of their wedding night?

"Whatever for?" Eliane's curiosity was piqued.

"If not for him, I would never have met you."

The campsite chosen by Mathias was tolerable. It sat in a hollow and was surrounded by trees, which would help break the wind. The branches were thick enough that the snow was not deep and a stand of yews had kept the snow from drifting into it. There was a stream that ran beneath a sheet of ice close by. Cedric had taken advantage of his time alone to snare several unsuspecting rabbits and had those roasting by the time the group arrived. The tents were quickly set into place, the horses cared for, and all concerned ready to seek their rest in whatever warmth they could find.

Eliane, with Llyr by her side, yawned from her seat by the fire. The dog yawned also and stretched as Khati went to Eliane's side and whispered into her ear. Eliane nodded and with a gracious smile to the men about the fire followed Khati to the tent while the dog went off to sniff at the trees before retiring with his mistress. Eliane stopped for a word with Cedric, who nodded and pointed to a small tent at the opposite side of the fire. The boy Jess was rolled up in a fur-lined cape by the fire and the men-at-arms were visiting the trees to relieve themselves before seeking their rest.

"I have told William to set the guards." Peter interrupted Rhys's perusal of his bride as she went into the tent. "I will retire now. Shall we try for an early start?"

Peter was, no doubt, most anxious to see his wife. "Yes," Rhys agreed. "I think I will check on Yorath before I sleep." He used his horse as an excuse to avoid his wife.

Peter looked toward the tent where Eliane had

disappeared, then back at Rhys with a bemused expression on his face. "It seems to me that you have found exactly what you most wanted to avoid."

Rhys well recalled their conversation on marriage, held after the king's edict. "At least I did not have to choose a bride. I had one chosen for me."

"Yet you still find yourself at the whims of another." Peter chuckled as he made his way to his tent. "But still, there are benefits to be had."

No benefits, more's the pity.

The guards were set; the rest of the men found what warmth they could in the tent provided for them. Rhys went to check Yorath but kept his mind on his wife as he ran his hands over his steed's legs and flanks.

What rituals did she have when she made ready for bed? Did Khati comb her hair? Did she apply lotions to her face and hands? Did she bundle up in woolen gowns and socks or did she prefer the cool feel of the sheets beneath heavy piles of blankets?

Rhys moved to the stallion's head and ran his hand down the long nose. Yorath's dark eyes flickered in the firelight and he tossed his head as Llyr padded silently up to them and sat down.

Rhys looked at the dog in surprise. It was the first time the beast had come to him and certainly one of the few times Llyr had not growled at him. "Have you come to the realization that we are stuck with each other?"

Llyr merely looked toward the tent.

"I hoped to delay until she was asleep. But now I find my need for warmth overtaking my need for prudence." He took a step, then looked around. "Where is Mathias?" Neither animal had an answer. Rhys ran his eyes over the campsite and realized he had not seen the boy since before dinner. Where had he gone?

Rhys ducked his head into Peter's tent. "Has William seen Mathias?"

"Not since dinner, milord," the squire replied sleepily from his pallet.

"Have you misplaced him?" Peter asked.

"Mayhap he is asleep with the men-at-arms," Rhys said. "If not, I will call you to help search."

"Here's hoping that you find him. It is too cold a night for anything but sleep."

Rhys checked with Cedric, who shared a tent with the men-at-arms and the guards. No one had seen Mathias since dinner. Rhys stopped to ask Jess, but the boy was sound asleep; the only thing visible beneath his furs was the tip of his nose and his woolen cap. Rhys went on to his own tent to ask Khati if she had seen Mathias.

The tent was cast in darkness, the only light coming from the fire beyond. The door of the brazier glowed with coals, and the floor around it seemed cluttered. He recognized the height of Elaine's mattress to the side and was certain Khati was upon a pallet on the floor. He would bid her sleep with Eliane for warmth. But would the maid think it odd that he did not join his wife in bed? Would he embarrass Eliane before her servant?

Llyr passed him, taking a roundabout route to the mattress. Rhys realized why when he tripped, then caught himself before falling flat on his face. He peered down at what had tripped him and realized it was Mathias. He was sound asleep on a pallet and covered with his cloak and a blanket. Mathias snorted and rolled over onto his side. Khati giggled from her pallet.

Eliane sat up. The light from the fire beyond the tent wall illuminated her profile. "I bade him sleep inside," she said in hushed tones. "There was no room in the other tent and it is much too cold outside for a boy."

"Jess does not seem to mind."

"Jess is accustomed to it," Eliane said. "He does not feel the cold as we do." That answered the question as to whether Jess's ears were like Han's and Madwyn's and the rest of the mysterious forest folk.

Eliane lay down again and Llyr joined her, taking his customary place at the end of the bed. Rhys stepped over Mathias. With Mathias and Khati both on pallets, there was no place for Rhys to lie except beside Eliane on the mattress. He bumped his way around, realized that the thing caught on his ankle was a small stool. He straightened it, removed his cloak, and dropped it upon the stool. His weapons came next, and then he sat down upon the stool.

"The least he could have done was attend to me before he fell asleep." His anger at Mathias was unjustified. The squire was just a boy and had done as he was bade by his lady.

"I am at fault," Eliane confessed. "I saw he was weary. He did naught but obey my command."

"Shall I attend to your needs, milord?" Khati asked sleepily.

My needs would send you screaming into the night. . . .

"Nay, Khati," Eliane said. "I will see to my husband."

"I can manage," Rhys protested, and started on his laces. Elaine rose from the bed and came to him. She wore a thick linen gown of white and her heavy braid hung over her shoulder. She knelt before him and he realized she was shivering with cold. Her hands tangled with his as she reached for the laces. She brushed his thigh, and his cock responded as it always did when she was near, coming to full attention. She was an innocent; she would not know what kneeling before him would do to his lustful body. *The devil inside me* . . . His grandmother's beatings had done nothing to remove it.

Rhys gritted his teeth and thought of disgusting things: uncovered trenches full of shite; maggoty wounds; rotten teeth, and pustules. Anything to keep him from throwing her down and having his way with her again. He would not touch her until she was ready. Until she wanted him in the same way that he wanted her.

He brushed her fingers aside and she knelt back, her emerald eyes black in the darkness. Was she watching him? Could she see his lust? He dropped his cross garters and she moved behind him. He wore a leather jerkin over his tunic and he loosened the buckles as his body waited, coiled and tense, knotted in dread and anticipation at what she would do next. She lifted the heavy leather from his shoulders, set it aside, and then placed her hands on his upper arms. She moved them down until she found the hem of his tunic and lifted. Rhys raised his arms as she gently removed the tunic and set it in place with his jerkin.

Her hands touched his shoulders again and she bent to his ear. "I am sorry that I am not versed in the proper way to disarm a husband. I will do my best to please you if you will have patience with my feeble attempts."

If only she knew how well she disarmed him. She clenched her fingers into his muscles, sensing the tension gathered across his back and neck. Her hands were strong, and he felt her touch down into his very bones. His head lolled forward and he sighed, deeply, at her ministrations. No one in his lifetime had ever given him such tender care. He felt his worries slowly fade away and thought that he might just be able to sleep, until she leaned into him and he felt the brush of her breasts against his back. He straightened.

"It is cold and I must seek my rest." His voice seemed bitter to his ears, snappish . . . but the words were spoken and he could not change the tone any more than he could alter the words themselves.

She went to the bed and slid beneath the coverings. He had no choice but to follow. He did not remove his chainse or chausses. She would think it was because of the cold; he knew it was because he needed barriers between them.

Eliane lay on her side facing the tent wall. He would have the warmth of the brazier behind him, but he would also be between her and anyone who came in during the night. Such choices a husband was required to make. Which was more important, the bit of warmth the coals would give or the amount of time he could give her to escape if there was an attack? He grabbed his sword and placed it on the floor next to the mattress.

He slid in behind her and lay on his back so he could see the shadows that crossed between the fire and the door of their tent. He was certain sleep would elude him, so he would watch. He would not put it past Renauld to attack them again before they reached the protection of the king.

As soon as he pulled the coverings up over them, her feet found their way to his calf and worked their way beneath it. She wore heavy woolen socks, but he could feel the chill in her feet.

"Your feet are like ice," he whispered. *I promised to keep you warm. . . .*

"I am sorry," she said. "I was trying to put them beneath Llyr."

Rhys looked down at the dog that stretched across the end of the mattress. Her idea had merit. He pushed his own feet beneath the heavy mass and instantly felt the warmth provided by the huge dog.

"He is proving useful," he admitted, and she released a low tinkle of laughter. Both Khati and Mathias stirred at the sound and she quieted. His body still reacted to her nearness, so he thought about all the things that would come on the morrow and the day after.

"Rhys?" she asked softly after a few moments. "May I ask you a question?" Her face was shadowed in the darkness, yet her eyes held the glow of the coals.

He turned his head her way. "Do not fear to ask anything of me."

A faint shadow of a smile flitted across her lips. "You said that if not for Renauld we never would have met. How could that be possible?"

He turned his body to face her so his voice would not carry to the two who slept on the floor. Llyr groaned at the disruption but stayed in his place. "Did your father not tell you the story?"

"No. I know only that he saved your life, not the why or the how. Was Renauld there?"

"He was," Rhys said. "We were both squires for Lord Allen. Renauld was older and stronger—he made a point of bullying me whenever he got the chance. He took my food, my blankets, did whatever he could to make my life miserable. He pushed me into the mud that day, hoping I would drown."

"He has a devil inside him," Eliane said when he was done.

"My grandmother said the same of me," he reminded her.

"Nay . . . you are not the same. Not at all." Her mouth stretched into a yawn and she shivered once more.

"Enough of Renauld, lest he haunt you in your dreams," he said. "Sleep now."

She yawned again, turned onto her back, and then with a sigh, rolled to face the other way. Her movement had closed the distance between them, and her backside nestled up against him. His arm moved of its own accord around her and she let out a contented sigh.

Open trenches . . . maggoty wounds . . .

Her breathing deepened and he realized she had fallen asleep. His left arm was trapped beneath him, so he moved it under her pillow, trying his best not to disturb her until he was able to bring it across her chest and pull her as close as possible. She nestled deeper within his arms and Rhys tucked her head beneath his chin. He let the fresh scent of her hair wash over him. How could one smell of springtime when it was the dead of winter? Yet she did. The fragile tip of her ear peeked between the strands of her hair. He resisted the urge to kiss it. He did not want to wake her.

The members of court were bound to be curious about her. There would be questions. They would want to know what her reported deformity was. There were those who would hide in corners and spy on her just so they would be the first to know.

I will protect you as best I can. . . . Thank God, Peter's wife had had the foresight to send the wimple. 'Twould be a shame to cover her glorious hair.

He would leave before she awakened, because he knew what state he'd be in come morning. For now he would just enjoy the closeness. This thing that was called marriage. Peter had told him there were benefits. Was watching one's wife sleep one of them? Having a warm body to help you fight the cold? Knowing that someone trusted you enough to let you hold her when she was most vulnerable? Mayhap he should have his own talk with Peter come tomorrow and see what advice his friend could give him about being a husband. The thought was uppermost in his mind as he drifted off, content with Eliane in his arms.

Chapter Seventeen

She woke suddenly, chasing the wisp of a dream, her mind quickly trying to identify where she was. Something struck her, grazed her arm, and she froze until the flickering light of the fire beyond the wall of the tent reminded her where she was. She had never left home before. It was a strange feeling, waking and not knowing where one was, especially when one was not used to sharing a bed.

"Can't . . . breathe . . ." Rhys tossed his head beside her. One arm was beneath her, and he jerked it. His movements were agitated. He pushed at the coverings with the other as he flopped onto his back.

Quickly she moved to face him. She placed her hand on his cheek. "Rhys. 'Tis just a dream."

His eyes opened. He blinked. He sat up so fast that he knocked her away and she fell against the pillows. He snatched up his sword from the floor beside the bed and stood, ready to defend or attack, whichever was necessary. He looked around the tent, searching for the threat, but there was nothing there except Llyr, who growled deep in his throat, and Khati and Mathias, who stirred uneasily in their sleep. Eliane raised a hand to stop Llyr. If Llyr saw Rhys as a threat and attacked, Rhys would kill him before he realized what he was doing.

Rhys looked toward Llyr, and then turned to her.

"Eliane?" His face was haunted by the specters that had visited him in his sleep. Did they come often? Did they plague him much? Her heart swelled with tenderness for the little boy who'd been left in the mud to drown and would have if not for her father's grace.

"You were dreaming."

He returned his sword to its place and rubbed a hand over his face before he sat down on the mattress.

"What was your dream?" Madwyn often told her to speak of her dreams, as if they were the keys to understanding the happenings of the day more clearly.

The coals within the brazier had died and her breath showed in the bitter cold. Eliane pulled a fur over her shoulders. Rhys leaned forward, his arms across his knees and his head lowered on them. He seemed so vulnerable. Not at all the strong warrior who had slain so many to protect her just a few days past. What further battles would come when they arrived at court?

The story he'd told her about Renauld was horrible. But he'd spoken of it as if it were nothing. To be so young, so alone, and the subject of such brutality. Drowning in mud. It seemed as if Renauld always targeted the helpless. Puppies and small lonely boys. Thank God her father had been there to save Rhys. Thank God her father had seen the honor in him, evident when he was naught but a boy. It could have been so easy for Rhys to choose not to honor his promise to her father. He might never have written to her father. He could have dallied instead of answering the summons. He could have taken the easy way and disregarded the man who'd saved his life; instead he chose to honor the man and the promise he'd made to him.

"Were you dreaming of the mud?" She placed a hand on his back and felt him flinch. Was it so painful for him to be touched by her? He worked so hard to avoid her, only touching her when it was necessary or when someone watched them. She pulled her hand away. She'd only meant to comfort him, just as she had done when she rubbed his shoulders. Still, he rejected her touch. She was a disappointment to him as a wife, and especially as a woman. What else could it be?

Yet he warmed me . . . held me when I was cold . . . He shows nothing but tenderness where I am concerned. If only Madwyn could have made this journey with her. There had been too little time for her to ask questions, for her to learn what it was to be a wife.

He sat up, his resolve once solid, unyielding. "It will be dawn soon. Peter wants an early start." Rhys left the bed, taking his warmth with him. "It seems he is most anxious to see his wife." Was that bitterness in his voice? He shivered as he picked up his things, hastily pulling on his tunic, lacing his cross garters, pulling on his boots. He kept his face hidden, looking anywhere but at the bed and at her.

To Eliane the night seemed as black as it was when they fell asleep. Dawn surely was a long way off. There was no light beyond the walls of the tent save the flickering of the campfire. Rhys placed his cloak over his shoulders and gathered his weapons. He started to leave but stopped when he noticed the coals had gone out in the brazier.

He knelt before it, placed a knot of wood and some tinder inside, and blew into the coals. The flames came to life and illuminated his profile; his strong jaw, covered with a stubble of dark beard, his full bottom lip, his straight nose, his broad forehead with its arched brows. His dark hair brushed against his shoulders and fell across his face as he leaned forward to check the heat before he closed the grate. " 'Twill keep you warm," he said with a glance in her direction. "Sleep some more. I will wake you when it is time."

He left and to her surprise, Llyr went after him. *Traitor.* . . . She felt terribly alone. She longed for the comfort of Aubregate, of her big bed in the tower, the familiar sounds of the keep, the knowledge that her father was below and all was well with the world. She missed Madwyn and Han, Matilde and Ammon. She was going to a strange place where no one knew her. Where they would look at her with disdain because of her ears. Where she would be nothing more than a pawn in a rivalry between Renauld and Rhys. *Could wedding vows be put aside by the king?*

She should have run to the forest and hidden where she would never be found. Instead she was here, freezing and terribly alone. Eliane shivered at the cold and burrowed under the blankets and furs, seeking what heat Rhys had left behind, knowing that when it came time to wake once more, he would send Khati to her. She'd failed miserably as a bride and had no one but herself to blame for it.

Eliane woke the second day of the journey as she had the day before. Alone. Once more Rhys had joined her in the bed after everyone else was asleep, as if lying with her was the last resort. Yet she felt his presence in the night, felt him gather her in his arms to warm her, felt his soft breath against her ear as he held her. But when she woke in the morning, he was gone, causing her to wonder if she had only dreamed about him.

Today she would meet the king. They would be in his presence before dinner this eve. Rhys had made use of Jess and sent him ahead with a message to assure Henry that he was indeed on his way and most anxious to appear before his liege with his new wife. Jess had returned with an answering message. Rhys and his bride were to come directly to the king as soon as they reached the city. There was no mention of congratulations, or of the king's favor. Rhys made no comment about the message, merely read it to her and bade her dress in her most formal attire for their meeting with the king.

Khati handled the thing called a wimple with some trepidation while Eliane pulled on her best pair of boots. They were dark brown leather and came to midcalf. She had green slippers embroidered with gold thread that matched her gown, but the boots would be more practical. They had not yet reached London, and even though the roads were clear of snow here, they were still messy. There would be no time for her to change beforehand. Everything must be perfect now. She also slipped one of her daggers into a sheath especially sewn into the lining of her boots and her jeweled dagger into her gold chain belt. She would not go unarmed, especially when she did not know what to expect. It mattered not that she would be in the presence of the king. Rhys expected Renauld to be there.

Eliane smoothed the skirt of her dark green velvet bliaut. Beneath it she wore pale gold in the softest wool. The hem and wide sleeves of the dark green were embroidered with gold thread in an intricate design of stags and trees. The colors and the pattern symbolized Aubregate. It reminded her of her purpose, to protect the land at all costs.

Elaine fumbled with the clasp of the heavy crucifix that had come to her from her father's family. Khati ceased her examination of the wimple and fastened the chain about her neck. Her father had been orphaned while a squire and only possessed a few items of value, the cross being one of them. It hung heavy against her breastbone and seemed to weigh her down, yet she wanted to wear it, because it had belonged to him. Rhys now wore her father's ring of emerald and gold. She twisted the one he'd given her about her finger and wondered if there was some tale behind it. The band was quite plain, as it was not embellished with a stone, yet she found that it suited her much better than a heavy ring. She forgot she wore it at times, until it caught her eye, and then she would study the intricate carving and melding of silver and gold and marvel at the artistry.

Khati smoothed her long braid. "It seems a shame to cover your hair."

Eliane shrugged. "It must be done. If my ears are discovered, it will only lead to unpleasant questions. It is a risk we cannot take."

"Milord de Remy will not care for it," Khati said.

"Why do you think so?" Eliane looked over her shoulder at Khati as the maid tied a piece of ribbon about the end of her braid.

"Do you not notice how he looks at you? How he touches your hair every chance he gets?"

No, she had not. She only noticed that he did not

touch her or kiss her as he had done at first. Yet, when thinking on it, she knew there were instances when he would pick up a lock of her hair and rub it between his fingers. There were times when she would turn and his eyes would be upon her, with a strange look in them.

"As much as I desire to please my husband, I must wear it, Khati," she said. "There are many travelers on the road who would carry tales to the king, and I would not have the secrets of Aubregate revealed."

Khati put the linen veil in place over her hair and brought the fabric strap beneath her chin before tying it in place on the side. Eliane put her hands on it. "I would much rather wear my wool cap. I feel as if a stiff wind will take me into the sky."

"Do you think that whoever decreed this a fashion suffered from an overabundance of chins and found this the best way to hide them?" Khati's voice held a hint of laughter. Unlike her mistress, she was excited about seeing the city and all it held.

"I am certain it is so," Rhys said from behind them. He'd entered the tent without Eliane's noticing. How much had he heard? He walked to where she sat upon a stool and flipped up the end of the fabric. A wry smile flitted across his lips. He was dressed in the same clothing he'd worn for their wedding. A tunic of dark burgundy over a white linen chainse and gray chausses with black boots. His hair was damp and neatly brushed back from his face, and his jaw was smooth and clear of stubble. He was very handsome and well he knew it. *Father asked me if there was anyone I would choose. I wonder if he asked the same of Rhys.* Was there a woman waiting for him to return? Would her heart be broken when she learned of his marriage? Sliding the knife into her boot had been the right decision. Knowing it was there steeled her resolve for what was to come.

"Is my dress appropriate for meeting the king?" Eliane rose from the stool so that he might see her costume better. He looked her over, from head to toe, his gaze lingering long on her face. Her hand went to the wimple, its feel strange upon her head and beneath her chin. She resisted the urge to stick her finger beneath the band.

"The king will be swept away by your beauty," he said. She studied his face and saw that he spoke what he believed to be the truth, although his eyes seemed sad.

"Are you troubled, milord?"

He nodded. "Only about the usual things that a husband must deal with. I find that I now have many to provide for, where in the past the only needs I considered were mine own and sometimes Mathias's." His tone said he was teasing her.

Still, Eliane did not want him to be burdened by their care. "I have brought funds," she began.

"Fear not, Eliane," he assured her. "That is the least of my troubles. There are things we must discuss before we arrive. Things you should know about life at court. We will talk as we ride. Cedric will follow with the cart and meet us later. It would be best if Llyr stayed with him also."

Eliane nodded her agreement. She would have to tie the dog to keep him from following her.

Rhys interrupted her thoughts. "I think it best if we find a house in London instead of staying at court."

It pleased her that he included her in his plans, but his idea gave her some concern.

"Will the king permit it?" There was much she did not know about court life. It seemed Rhys felt some trepidation about their visit. *How long will we have to stay?* Renting a house seemed to indicate a lengthy stay. She had hoped to return to Aubregate before the spring planting. Once more she realized that her will was no longer her own. *My people are depending upon me....*

"He will if I ask in the proper way and remind him of your father's devotion." He held up his left hand and her father's ring. "This should help to remind him."

Khati placed her cloak around Eliane's shoulders. Rhys looked remorsefully at her head. "I would throw that in the fire if anything else could serve the purpose so well."

"Should I?" she teased him, placing her hand against the fabric as if she would snatch it off.

"Nay." His eyes were gentle on her face. "I fear it would only make your beauty more evident and therefore a target of those who are not as blessed."

She smiled at his words. *He thinks me beautiful.* She would remember his words when she saw the women at court and hoped that he still thought them true.

Rhys led her from the tent to where their horses waited. "A sidesaddle?" Eliane asked when she saw Aletha. "For me?" Peter had the sense to turn his head, yet she saw his shoulders shake with laughter.

"Cedric said there was one in the stable, so I bade him bring it."

"Are all ladies of the court so helpless that they cannot ride astride? It is safer than sliding off," she protested. Why should she suddenly change the way she sat her horse? She understood the need to hide her ears, but riding sidesaddle?

"It's not concern for their helplessness as much as it . . . er . . ." Rhys's face turned dark red as he looked at her, then at Peter, who no longer hid his laughter.

Of what does he speak? Eliane looked from Rhys to Peter as her husband fumbled with an explanation.

"'Tis a matter of modesty and . . . er . . . virtue . . ."

"Virtue?" Eliane looked at the sidesaddle, which seemed strangely out of place on Aletha's back, at her husband, whose skin had flushed as dark as his burgundy tunic, and at Peter, who laughed so hard that he was about to fall from his horse. *Virtue?* "Oh." She felt the heat rise to her face and knew once more that her coloring gave away her embarrassment. "You have no doubts . . ." She could not bear to look at him, so she turned away. The humiliation of their wedding night was fresh in her mind, along with her failure.

"Nay!" Rhys grasped her arms, forcing her to look at him. His dark eyes were earnest as he gazed upon her. Implored her. "The proof was there and I would slay any who says otherwise."

She searched his face, gazed into eyes that were like windows to his soul. Did his grandmother think the devil resided there because his eyes were as black as sin? Why did she not see the goodness within him and the need?

He has never known love. . . . His parents chose death over life when he was born. His grandmother chose God over him. The story was well known throughout the length and breadth of England, but none had ever spoken of the result those actions had on the boy who was abandoned. The boy who was not loved. He had built a wall around his heart, yet he had allowed her a few small glimpses.

I want more. . . . She had known nothing but love and found that she was greedy for it. She'd lost her mother at a very young age, yet remembered her well. It seemed as if everyone at Aubregate had tried to make up for the loss of her mother's love by bestowing more upon her. There was not a memory of her childhood that did not include love.

For someone like Rhys love was a mystery. Had he ever felt love at all? Was he even capable of it?

"I would not bring shame to you," Eliane said. She would ride sidesaddle if it would spare him embarrassment. The words she spoke promised more. She would have more. She would have his heart.

If only she knew how to get it.

Chapter Eighteen

$\mathcal{I}$t seemed that everyone at court was awaiting their arrival. Even Peter decided to go within the great hall to greet the king instead of escaping to the comfort of his wife. Pages rushed about, carrying messages to and fro. The entire castle was abuzz with the arrival of Rhys de Remy's mysterious wife. The objects of all the speculation were told to wait in the antechamber for the king's summons. *He wants all the players in place.* Rhys could only hope that Marcella would not create a fuss and Jane not resort to hysterics, although he was certain the king would find it most amusing if they did.

"Knowing Lydia, she is inside already, where she can see all," Peter assured them when Rhys bade him go on to his wife instead of waiting with them. Peter had proved to be a stalwart friend through everything.

"See all?" Eliane arched a delicate brow at Peter, then turned to Rhys. "Is there something else you should make me aware of? Are there more than two women who expected to marry you? I have a knife in my boot. Mayhap I should hide it within my sleeve so as to be prepared in case one seeks to bury a blade in my back?" Her tone was as frigid as the air outside the castle.

As they'd traveled the road to London, Rhys had told her of the king's edict that he marry as soon as possible. He'd explained that the edict had made it easier for him to agree to their marriage. One of the things he found he valued most in Eliane was her intelligence. However, it had proved to be a problem when she'd asked him why the king had made such a demand in the first place. It was when he found himself confessing why he'd been given such a choice that he suddenly realized he had lost what little favor he'd held in her eyes.

How is it that I told her those sordid details about Jane and Marcella? It is not as if I meant to. The words seemed to come out of his mouth of their own accord when she turned her lovely emerald eyes upon him. And she'd reacted as a jealous wife would. Even now she caressed the hilt of her jeweled dagger as if she would use it on anyone who might gaze his way.

Or does she seek to use it on me? Once more Peter's words about marriage and Lydia's promise to remove a certain part of his anatomy should he misuse it came back to haunt him. *I have much to learn about marriage.* It was a complete mystery to him how a husband should act or what he should confide in his wife, if anything.

"Wait . . . you have a dagger in your boot?" Her words suddenly sank into his addled brain.

"Yes, milord," she replied breezily. "One on my hip and one in my boot. You did say there were two women under your consideration?" Peter laughed and the men who attended the doors to the hall could not suppress their grins.

"Eliane," Rhys said firmly. He could not let it be known that he had a rebellious wife. That would certainly be the subject of gossip.

Eliane gazed at him with her emerald eyes and he could not be angry with her. Not after all that he had done to hurt her. *That damn thing on her head . . .* It might hide her ears, but it did nothing to hide the beauty of her face, or the great green depths of her eyes. There was not a man within who would not be smitten with her, including the king. Her natural beauty, along with the mystery of her rumored deformity, would make her the center of attention. If he had to, he would prostrate himself before the king and beg so that he could keep her away from court. He was certain there were many who would enjoy seeing him on his knees.

When he did not speak, she arched her brow at him in obvious impatience. "If the king desired our presence so desperately, why does he bid us wait now?"

"He wants to make sure all those involved are in place," Peter said. "You will find that the court thrives on intrigue and gossip. When Rhys left he was the center of much speculation. Which would he choose? Marcella or Jane? Now that you have arrived, the situation will be all the more interesting."

The door opened and a messenger declared the king was ready to receive them. Rhys took a deep breath and extended his arm. "Are you ready, wife?"

She looked at him, her emerald eyes darting over his face. She lifted her hand to his brow and smoothed back the hair that fell across his forehead. *How tenderly she touches me, even though I did nothing but violence to her in our marriage bed.* "I am ready, husband." She placed her hand on his arm and they entered the hall. He savored her touch and the trust that went with it. He had sworn to protect her and her lands. The first test of his merit was here.

All eyes were upon them. He could count three people who wanted him dead. Marcella, Jane, and the dastardly Renauld Vannoy.

They walked forward as the page announced their titles and their lands. Eliane kept her hand on his arm, and her stride matched his, her legs almost as long as his own. He was grateful that he did not have to mince his steps for her. It would only serve to show weakness if he did so. He saw curiosity on the faces of those gathered, their eyes searching her face and her limbs for any sign of her reported deformity. They would find none. She was perfect up to the tips of her pointed ears.

The king's eyes were steady upon them also. An indulgent smile split his face as he studied Eliane. "You are most definitely your father's daughter," he said when they bowed low before him. Rhys shifted his arm and took her hand into his so there would be no doubt as to his claim on her. No doubt that he was content with his choice. The gossips might say it was thus or so, but those who were present would know the truth of the matter.

"Thank you, Your Majesty." Eliane's voice rang clear and true in the hushed silence. "I can think of no higher praise."

"I was saddened to hear of his passing," Henry added. "He was a good man and served me well."

"He gave that same dedication to his lands and his daughter," Eliane replied. "There was no other like him."

Henry smiled obligingly. "Are you certain, my dear? Though Edward was a great man, there are those here who would claim that their own fathers were just as great."

Rhys squeezed her fingers in warning. Henry baited her. There was an undercurrent to his voice that bespoke a warning.

Eliane dipped her head prettily. "I admit my opinion of my father is somewhat biased, Your Majesty," she said humbly. "And I lack the experience or knowledge to know of any other man's greatness save your own."

Well done. . . . Even though she'd been sheltered from the intrigues of court, she was a natural at playing the game. Edward had trained her well.

"What of your husband?" Henry asked. "Have you knowledge of his greatness?"

Eliane tilted her head as if she needed a moment to consider the question. "If you mean his greatness on the battlefield, then I can say yes, he is great, for I have witnessed it myself when bandits sought to take me on the day after our engagement."

She was a wonder. She'd managed to reveal the reason for the hastening of their vows with her answer.

"If you mean his greatness in . . . other areas . . ." She blushed prettily. "I can only say that he is everything he is rumored to be, and I have no complaints, nor will I hear any against my husband."

If he could have kissed her, he would have. With that sentence she'd disarmed the gossipmongers. She'd announced to the court that she knew of his liaisons and would not put up with any who chose to malign him in her presence. She was content with the arrangement of their marriage and would not be pleased to have it put aside. She squeezed his fingers in return as the king looked at them meaningfully and the entire court held its breath.

"If only there were no doubts as to the legality of your marriage," Henry sighed.

Vannoy . . . Eliane's grip on his hand tightened and he saw the color leave her cheeks. Renauld Vannoy moved into their line of sight, to the left of Henry.

"Sire," Peter offered. "Though I was not present at the ceremony, I have seen the documents and can attest to their validity and legality. I can say without a doubt that Lord Edward's daughter has been wedded and bedded." A few guffaws were heard at Peter's proclamation. Eliane's cheeks flushed red, yet she held her head high. *She is strong, my warrior woman.*

"Yes, yes," Henry said. "I am certain it all happened just as you say. But why did you not wait for the banns?"

Eliane opened her mouth to speak. She faltered. Her courage, so strong for herself, failed while she still grieved for her father. Was it Henry's intent to cast their marriage in a bad light? After Edward had done everything in his faltering power to protect his daughter? Surely Henry's greed was not so great that he desired Aubregate. Yet there were those rumors of a treasure that Rhys had yet to see. Were they as distorted as the rumors of her deformity?

"It was Edward's last wish that he see his daughter legally wed," Rhys said. "He died within a few hours of our speaking the vows. Would you have been able to deny him this when it was only a matter of half a day standing in his way?" Rhys looked earnestly at his king. He could not believe that Henry would put the marriage aside, especially after all his problems with Beckett and the church. "We had the Church's blessing," he added to remind Henry that there was more involved here than just a few hours of time.

"Did you bring the documents?" Henry asked.

"Yes, sire," Eliane replied. "Our good Father Timothy made a copy for you." Rhys had not known that, yet his wife had seen the need. "They are with our man Cedric, who comes behind. I was so anxious to meet you that we traveled ahead of our household."

Once more he marveled at her ingenuity. She'd given him the opportunity to ask about living away from court.

"With your permission, sire." Rhys dropped her hand and stepped forward. Henry motioned him closer so that their words would only be heard by those close around, including Vannoy. "I have the responsibility of not only a wife, but also an entire household of people and animals to care for. With your permission, we will seek our lodging elsewhere lest our numbers become a burden on those who are already in residence."

"Do you have doubts as to my ability to provide for your care?" Henry challenged Rhys quietly. *There is something going on.* Rhys stole a quick look at Vannoy. He had a smug look on his face and his eyes were on Eliane. As if he knew something Rhys did not. *He has something on the king . . . something the king does not want known. . . .* The realization frightened him more than he cared to admit. Vannoy's desire for Aubregate was well known, and the only way to gain the lands was through Eliane. Would the king give her to him? Even though she was legally Rhys's wife?

"Nay, sire." Rhys glanced over his shoulder at Eliane. She stood next to Peter and kept her eyes on him and the king, even though everyone in the hall stared at her. Her great beast of a dog would be growling at the curious looks. *Llyr* . . . An idea came to him. He leaned closer to the king. "She has this dog . . . a huge beast. The only way I got her to leave him today was by tying him to the cart. I fear that he would be quite a nuisance in the castle, and I'm afraid that she will not sleep without him."

Henry's grin was delicious. "So if given a choice between you and the dog?"

"The dog would win. Even if it meant she must sleep in the stables."

Henry burst into laughter. "I give you leave to find a house for your menagerie. On the condition that you, your wife, and her beast of a dog will join us for dinner tomorrow eve."

"Thank you, sire." Rhys bowed and backed away.

Henry hooked a finger at Eliane, summoning her forward. "I would have a closer look at you."

She dipped into a low curtsey and then stepped close to Henry.

"It seems as if the rumors about you are not true," Henry said.

Rhys stood to the side, keeping Henry, Eliane, and Vannoy in his view.

"Rumors?" Eliane replied softly "None here know me."

There was one who knew her. Vannoy could not take his eyes from her. Rhys recognized that look. Vannoy wanted her, and not just because of her lands. He lusted after her. *I will kill him. . . .*

"Lord de Remy." The king spoke his name.

Vannoy arched an eyebrow in Rhys's direction. Then he looked at Eliane and licked his lips.

I have not forgotten that you tried to kill me. . . .

"Husband." Eliane took his arm. "I would see this house you speak of." The pressure of her hand on his arm made him finally turn his head away from Vannoy. Her emerald eyes captured him once more. "Please," she added silently, only moving her lips.

Rhys released his breath and bowed to the king. Instead of offering his arm, he took her hand in his. *Mine.* They left the hall with Peter trailing behind them. Rhys heard the buzz of the crowd behind them as they moved away. The gossips would have plenty to keep them busy tonight.

"Peter!" Rhys recognized Lydia as she pressed through the crowd with her maid on her heels. William and Mathias were with her also. Peter embraced his wife and gave her a kiss that would have been more suitable behind closed doors.

Will Eliane kiss me like that someday? It was his greatest desire that she would. She still held on to his hand as people moved about their group and cast inquisitive glances their way.

"This is Eliane," Peter said. "You are acquainted with Rhys."

"You are as lovely as Peter said you were," Lydia said. She folded Eliane into an embrace.

"I never said she was lovely," Peter said. "I said she was as skinny as a fence post and she once shot me with her bow."

"Peter!" Lydia appeared to be shocked.

"Beware lest I shoot you again," Eliane teased back. "And my aim might be truer this time."

"He would deserve it," Lydia said. "However, I must

ask that you don't, as I am not through with him yet."
Peter and Eliane grinned wickedly at each other, and
Rhys found he was envious of their camaraderie. *They
are like family. As if they were brother and sister. . . .*

"Come," Lydia continued. "You can stay with me
while Rhys procures the house for you. I have already
found one available; he simply needs to go meet with
the owner."

"You've done that already?" Rhys asked. "How did
you know?"

"Though you do foolish things at times, you are also
most practical," Lydia said. "It would only make sense
that you would want your wife away from . . . er . . . this
place." She was suddenly at a loss for words.

"I know what Rhys wishes to protect me from,"
Eliane said. "He told me of his dilemma this morning.
And how I saved him from having to choose."

"For which I am eternally in your debt," Rhys
replied in the same dry tone she used.

"William will take you to the house," Lydia said, in
total control of the situation. "Mathias can wait for
your men and follow after." She took Eliane's arm.
"You will find your wife in our chambers when you
have the house ready for her."

"I should go with my husband," Eliane protested.

*Yes . . . I want her with me. I can't leave her here, not
when Vannoy is so close.*

"No," Lydia said. "You are tired and you should
rest."

Peter shook his head. "You cannot fight Lydia," he
told Eliane. "She is determined to have you to herself
and will not cease until she has her way."

"Rhys?" Eliane turned to him.

He took her hand and pulled her aside. Peter and Lydia turned to each other, giving them some privacy. "Stay or go," Rhys said. "I will leave it to you."

She gave him a slight smile. "I find that I feel a need for the companionship of a woman."

"You miss Madwyn."

She nodded. "I do." She looked at Lydia. "I think she would be my friend, and I believe I will need one."

"Please take care," Rhys said. "I do not trust Vannoy."

"I have never trusted him," she assured him. "And if you recall, I do have a knife in my boot."

"This is not the forest of Aubregate," he reminded her. "The king will not look kindly on your stabbing his vassals."

"I will keep that in mind, husband." She reached up and kissed his cheek. "I hope that the house has a bath."

He felt like clay in her hands. "I will make sure that it does," he said. Even if he had to search every house in London to find one and give over every coin he possessed. He watched her go, hand in hand with Lydia.

Marcella . . . She approached Eliane and Lydia as they made for the stairs. He took a step.

"She is most capable of fighting her own battles." Peter put a hand on his arm. "You cannot protect her from all, so choose to protect her from those that are most dangerous." With his chin he pointed to the side, where Vannoy stood watching.

"I will kill him."

"Yes, you will. But not this day." Peter clasped an arm over his shoulder. "It seems Lydia has forgotten all about me. Let us go see this house she has found. I am certain it will be expensive, but worth every coin you are about to part with."

Renauld couldn't care less that Rhys de Remy looked at him as if he wanted to kill him.

At the moment Renauld only had eyes for one thing, and that was Eliane of Aubregate, who now happened to be the wife of Rhys de Remy.

Enjoy it while you can. . . . It had taken every bit of forebearance he possessed to keep from pulling his sword and plunging it through de Remy's heart when he'd walked into the great hall with Eliane on his arm. It would be a much quicker means to his ends than waiting for the king to take care of it.

He watched Eliane walk away with Salisbury's pregnant cow of a wife. Mayhap he could get her alone. De Remy and Salisbury left, along with their squires, and he turned to see that Eliane and Salisbury's wife were talking with a woman.

He moved toward them. *Not talking . . . arguing?* A crowd gathered around the three women. It enabled him to get close enough to hear what was being discussed.

"He will return to me," the blonde said with a toss of her head. She barely came to Eliane's breastbone. *Eliane is of a size with me, if not taller . . . not that it will matter when I'm done with her. I will take off her feet and make her crawl.* His plans for Eliane consumed his thoughts of late. Renauld moved about the crowd so he could see who it was that challenged his intended bride.

"Why should he, Marcella?" Salisbury's wife asked.

"He had an opportunity to choose you as a wife and still he sought one elsewhere."

"'Twas a trick played on him. By her father. Or mayhap by her." Marcella stared at Eliane. "She cast a spell on him. One that hides her true self so that none may see her deformity."

"I assure you, I am no different from anyone here." Eliane's voice was calm, but Renauld could not help noticing how her fingers caressed the hilt of the ornamental dagger she wore on her hip. Was she as skilled in its use as she was with her bow? That would make things even more interesting once she came into his . . . care.

"I have no desire to war with you, especially over things that came to pass before I even met my husband," Eliane continued. "Peace be with you. I will pray that someday you find the same contentment in marriage as I."

Eliane and Salisbury's wife moved to the wide staircase. The blonde remained behind, seething with anger. Renauld tried to recall what he knew about her.

She likes it rough. . . . That was the rumor he'd heard. Renauld was certain her idea of rough was much milder than his, but there could be a connection to build on. Quickly he moved around until he stood behind her.

"Mayhap what she hides is beneath her headpiece," he whispered into Marcella's ear, then moved on before she could turn and identify him.

With a determined step, Marcella flew up the stairs after the two women and wrenched the linen from Eliane's head with a shriek. She held it up as if she'd won a token on the field.

Eliane's hair, which had been in a single braid down

her back, came loose and flew about her head as she turned with her knife now in hand. She held it to Marcella's chin and backed the woman against the banister.

Look at her ears. . . . He saw the peaks of them peeping through her hair, but no one was looking there. Instead they watched the point of the blade as it moved to Marcella's neck. The woman whimpered as she leaned as far away from the threat as the banister would allow.

"Touch me again and you will not live long enough to regret it," Eliane said. "And the same goes for my husband. As for that thing—" She looked in disdain at the headpiece, which Marcella held clutched to her breast like a shield. "I have no further use for it. Consider it a gift."

"Magnificent!" he said as she continued up the staircase arm in arm with Salisbury's wife. A maid followed them. She would fight him to the end when he finally bedded her. Breaking her would be . . . *magnificent . . .* His cock surged upward at the thought of it.

Marcella burst into tears and ran from the hall. Renauld looked after her. She could prove to be of further use if the king did not cooperate. It was difficult to walk with his cock as swollen as it was, but still, he went after her. The woman needed consoling. Renauld was certain he had just the thing to help her past her anger.

Chapter Nineteen

As it turned out, Eliane's worry over the discovery of her ears was groundless. They were a curiosity, and nothing more. The king took the time to inspect them before dinner the next evening.

"They are quite exquisite, my dear," he commented after he ran his fingers over the peaks. Eliane did her best not to flinch at his touch. Lydia held her hair back so it would not hinder his examination. She kept her eyes on Rhys, who stood across from her. His face remained impassive, but she could tell by the way his fingers handled the hilt of his dress sword that his anger simmered beneath the surface. *Is he jealous of the king?* Llyr, who was another novelty as far as the king was concerned, lay at Rhys's feet, placed there by a word from her. He watched the proceedings carefully, his dark eyes following the king's hands to make sure there was no threat to his mistress.

"And you were born with them?"

"Yes, sire," she said.

"Did your mother have ears such as these?"

"Nay, sire, nor did her mother before her." She did not lie, nor did she volunteer any information. As long as Henry thought she was the exception, there would be no reason for anyone to investigate the people of the forest of Aubregate. She was most grateful that

Rhys had seen fit to send Jess home with a message for Madwyn. The king had bade them to stay in London until he dismissed them, so stay they must.

"I will summon my physicians to examine them," Henry declared. Rhys took a step in her direction and Llyr rose to his feet.

Eliane put protective hands over her ears. "I assure you there is nothing unusual about my ears other than their shape. If they bother Your Majesty, I will keep them covered."

Lydia dropped her hair into place and summoned her maid to replace her circlet and veil. "She is not an exhibit in the royal menagerie, Your Majesty." Lydia dared much. But her father, husband, and father-in-law all held great riches and power, so she was able to dare much. She dipped in a curtsey as if to say the matter was closed.

Henry arched an eyebrow at Peter, who merely grinned and shrugged. Lydia had turned out to be a wonderful friend.

"I find in this case I am in agreement with you," Henry said. He offered his arm to Eliane to escort her in to dinner.

Rhys followed, with Llyr, then Peter and Lydia. The tables were arranged in a huge square with the lower table pulled back to allow entertainers and servers to enter. As they were of lesser rank than most of the nobles, Rhys and Eliane were sent to a side table while Peter and Lydia joined the king at the main table. She commanded Llyr to lie beneath and he took up a position at her feet.

To her dismay, Eliane found herself sitting opposite Renauld Vannoy. Marcella was seated to his right and

Eliane noticed her upper lip was cut and swollen. Both stared at her. Marcella's gaze was venomous, but Renauld's look was strangely curious. As if she were a feast and he was about to eat.

"It seems as if Marcella has found someone to ease her pain at your loss," Eliane said as Rhys took his seat beside her on the bench.

"Yes, I noticed," Rhys growled. "I am certain that alliance does not bode well for either of us." He leaned over and whispered in her ear, "I do not like the way he looks at you." The low timbre of his voice sent a shiver down her spine. She looked sideways at him from beneath her lashes and saw him return Renauld's intense stare. They dared not risk a confrontation here.

Eliane touched his arm. "Rest assured, husband, she will not bother either of us after yesterday."

"She's more likely to slip a knife between your ribs in a dark corner than she is to come at you directly as she did yesterday."

Eliane arched an eyebrow at him. "I am glad to see that your taste in women has improved considerably since we met." A servant held a platter of meat between them. Rhys selected portions for both of them and placed the food on the trencher they were to share. A succinct glance across the way showed that Renauld did the same for Marcella. "At least they are well matched," she added.

Rhys gave her a lopsided grin. "Indeed," he said. "Perhaps we will get lucky and they will kill each other with passion."

She grinned back. "One can only hope." She let her eyes flick past him, up the table to where Peter and

Lydia sat. She was glad to see that Lydia had noticed the pairing of Renauld and Marcella also.

The woman on Rhys's other side asked him a question and he politely answered. Eliane took the opportunity to look around at those who were gathered for the feast. Lydia had carefully instructed her on who held important roles in the ruling of the country and described them to her. Richard de Clare, the Earl of Pembrooke, sat to Henry's left. Raymond de Gros was farther down the table. On the king's right was his son, Prince Henry, a younger version of his father. Beyond him sat Dermot, the King of Leinster, who had recently been deposed in Ireland. Lydia said he was here to raise troops to reclaim his lands and had Henry's support, along with Pembrooke's.

The chatter that greeted her ears was of Ireland, and the fire that had recently destroyed the roof of Norwich Cathedral. She was grateful that none of it was about her or her ears. They were a passing curiosity, nothing more. All that worry over nothing. She was of little consequence when it came to the machinations of court.

She turned to glance down the table and could not help noticing a sad, dark-haired woman close to her age at the lower table who was staring in her direction. Her look was not full of venom, like Marcella's, but one of loss. *Jane* . . .

"That would be Jane," Rhys confirmed.

Eliane turned back to him. "She seems sad."

"Life has not been fair to Jane," Rhys said. "I suddenly find I regret my part in that. Hopefully things will be better for her now. The man she is with is Robert Rochelle, the young Lord of Temersea. They are to be wed, or so the king informed me earlier today. It is a good match for both of them, and he appears to be in excellent health, unlike her last two matches."

Eliane looked at the plain-looking young man next to Jane. Her earthy beauty made him seem rather drab in comparison. Robert Rochelle was no match for Rhys, at least not in her opinion. In her two days at court, she'd found none that compared.

If only she knew how to break through the barriers he'd erected since their wedding. She was a complete failure as a wife. Yet he was patient with her and most attentive. Any who observed them would not know that they did not share a bed.

Eliane looked once more at Marcella, and then at Jane. Something had attracted her husband to these women. What was it they possessed that had caused him to seek them out and bed them? What was it about bedding that was so enjoyable they would risk shame and punishment to do so? Was it because it was forbidden or was there something in the act itself? She would ask Lydia. Lydia would not laugh or gossip about her. Lydia would tell her what she should do. *"I will not touch you again unless you desire it."* Lydia would tell her what it was she should desire.

"What of our match? How long will we have to wait for the king's blessing?" With all the commotion of settling into their new house, they had had little opportunity to talk since their arrival the day before. She could tell something about their audience with the king troubled Rhys.

"I do not know what he plans for us, only that he plans something."

"It has something to do with Renauld," Eliane

observed. "Vannoy has no claim to me. Yet I can think of no other reason for the king to detain us."

"We have both come to the same conclusion." His eyes showed his approval of her observation. "You will do well here at court."

"I would rather do well at Aubregate." Eliane resisted the urge to place her hand on his cheek. To push back the hair that brushed across his forehead. "Thank you for your belief in me."

"My wife pulled a knife on a woman who insulted her. I have absolutely nothing to worry about." He raised his chalice in a toast to her.

"From your tone, I would surmise that it is not a usual occurrence," she teased.

He smiled at her, and then suddenly turned serious. His eyes upon her were dark and deep, like a moonless night sky. His one arm was around her back, and the other on the table before her. Eliane held her hands in her lap and returned his look, trying to read his mood. He licked his lips and the possibility that he would kiss her right here in front of the king and everyone flew through her head.

"My loyal subjects—" Henry stood with his chalice in hand. "A toast. To Dermot of Leinster."

All raised their wine and toasted Dermot.

Raymond de Gros rose also. "Who here will go with me to retake Dermot's lands as decreed by our king?"

Rhys groaned beside her. "What?" Eliane asked. "What is wrong?"

"The king has neatly trapped everyone here," Rhys said as he slowly stood. Eliane looked around the table. Every able-bodied man stood in his place. Including Renauld Vannoy. They drew forth their short ceremonial swords and raised them high. "Long live King Henry!" they shouted. "Long live King Dermot! Long live England!"

Eliane looked at Lydia. Her face was set, and showed no emotion, even though Peter stood beside her with his sword in hand. At the lower table, Robert Rochelle stood also and Jane's face held a look of horror. Marcella, however, looked quite happy. She clapped her hands together.

Eliane gripped the edge of the table. "You are leaving me?"

"I must," Rhys said. "It seems I am going to war in Ireland whether I want to or not."

Eliane found herself at a loss as to what she should do. She had never been one to find enjoyment in sewing or weaving, nor did she take an interest in cooking. She had forever been a creature of the forest, exploring its depths and finding a kinship with the animals that dwelled within. Unfortunately for her, the forest was far, far away.

In the waning days of winter and early spring, Rhys was gone far more than he was at home. First the days were filled with preparations for the invasion in Ireland. Then he had to go to his lands and gather men-at-arms and funds for the coming siege. Armor had to be fitted to Mathias and the squire instructed in what was expected of him. The horses must have new shoes and the saddles and bridles be inspected for wear. Then Rhys's armor underwent inspection by both him and Cedric, who polished it all until it was blindingly bright.

Eliane felt like a prisoner. The king would not let

her go to Myrddin with Rhys, nor would he let her return home to Aubregate. She was under his most generous protection.

In the meantime, Renauld seemed to be quite taken with Marcella. Eliane hoped Marcella's lands were richer than Aubregate and he would forget about her. Still, they both seemed to watch her whenever they were summoned to court dinners.

During these times Eliane found that she was grateful the king allowed her to stay in a house rather than at court. She was not under the constant scrutiny of anyone, save Khati. At times she was even able to get out and ride Aletha, but only as long as her men-at-arms were present.

When Rhys was in residence, he was so busy with preparations that he left before she rose in the morning and fell asleep as soon as he'd had his evening meal. Eliane found herself exhausted at the end of the day too. The endless days wearied her more than any hunt or harvest had in the past.

Her only escape was Lydia, who grew large with the child that she hoped would be born before Peter departed for Ireland with the rest of the army. Peter was as busy as Rhys, so Eliane kept Lydia company and her friend taught her to sew the painstakingly small stitches that were needed for tiny garments.

"The men talk as if the siege will be nothing more than a lark," Eliane said as they sat sewing in Lydia's quarters at the castle. It was the middle of April and the men were scheduled to depart in a week. Eliane dropped the piece she was working on and went to the window that overlooked the large courtyard. The weather was fine and dry for once, and the air was fresh from recent rain. Several squires were training below, Mathias among them, with Rhys watching and giving instruction. Llyr had taken to following him, much as he used to do with her. It was something to be grateful for. He could have kept growling whenever her husband came near. Not that *that* was a common-place occurrence.

"It is true that the Irish warriors are not as well armed as our own," Lydia said. "Their fortifications are weak also. Peter thinks it will simply be a matter of showing up to force Ruairc to surrender."

"If it is so simple, then why do they carry on as if they are going off to the Holy Land for a crusade?"

"God save us from that," Lydia said. "It is the way of men. They live for war. It is the women who suffer at home without news and wonder each day what is happening and whether they are coming home."

"Madwyn once told me that men embrace war as they embrace their wives."

"Madwyn is a very wise woman," Lydia commented. "You must miss her."

Eliane leaned her forehead against the pane of glass, hoping it would cool her body. Not only did she sleep most of the time, but she seemed to be perpetually warm. "I do . . . I miss everything about home." She was so lonely at times, she felt as if her heart would break. She had turned into a weakling since leaving Aubregate. She needed the forest to restore her soul.

"Does it affect your hunger?" Lydia asked.

Eliane turned, curious at the strange question. "What do you mean?"

"You are sick for home." Lydia put her sewing aside, pushed her heavy bulk out of the chair, and waddled most ungracefully to Elaine. "Are you having trouble eating?"

"Only in the morning. I can't keep anything down. But come evening, I make up for it."

Lydia placed a hand on Eliane's forehead. "Sleeping during the day, unnaturally warm, and losing your breakfast?"

"Yes." Eliane looked intently at her friend.

"How are your breasts?"

"My breasts?"

"Are they tender when Rhys . . ."

Eliane felt her skin turn bright red and Lydia stopped.

"I am sorry if talk about the marriage bed embarrasses you. I forget that some women do not enjoy it as much as I. Although with Rhys de Remy beside you, it would have to be delightful. Unless all the rumors I've heard are lies," she teased.

Eliane dropped into a chair by the small table that held Lydia's sewing and covered her face with her hands. "I fear there is nothing to enjoy," she cried.

"What?" Lydia's tone and face showed her disbelief. "How can this be?"

"It is simple." Eliane lowered one hand and peered at Lydia through the other. "My husband does not share my bed."

Lydia dropped heavily into the chair opposite. "That was the last bit of news I ever expected to hear." She fanned her face with her hand, her body flushed from the exertion of walking across the room. "I've seen how he looks at you. He has the look of a man who desires his wife." Lydia laughed. "The look of a man who desires his wife most desperately." She clapped her hands in glee. "Oh, you are a most cunning woman, Eliane."

"Cunning? How am I cunning when my husband chooses to sleep by himself?"

"Because he desperately wants what he cannot have. . . . No . . . wait. Did you say he chose to sleep by himself?"

"I did not banish him from my bed. He said he would not touch me unless I desired it."

Lydia took Eliane's hands in hers. "It is obvious you desired it one time. On your wedding night, I would say. The proof of the taking was there for all to see, was it not?"

"Our wedding night was a disaster that I do not wish to revisit," Eliane confessed. She stretched her arms onto the table and pillowed her head upon them. "What do you mean that it is obvious I desired it one time?"

Lydia smiled at her. "You are with child, Eliane. The signs are all there. Unless you've had your courses. Have you?"

Eliane sat up suddenly, her mind reeling. She counted the days, the weeks, the months. "So much has happened since then. . . . I have not." Her mouth flew open and she clapped her hand over it. "No wonder Khati has been watching me so carefully. She knows." Eliane put her hands over her stomach in wonder. The thought of a baby had been the last thing on her mind.

"Maids usually are the first to know everything."

"But how?" Surely she could not be breeding. After one time that had been so . . . lacking?

"Eliane!"

"I know how it happens—I'm just not certain of

how it happened with us. As I said before, it was a disaster."

"Tell me about it, Eliane. You've kept this inside all
these months. Tell me what happened between you
and Rhys and mayhap we can fix it before he goes to
war."

"I don't know what happened," Eliane wailed. She
dropped her head onto the table with a klunk and it
rattled unsteadily.

"Tell me," Lydia insisted.

Eliane sat up with a sigh and told her everything
except for the part about meeting Rhys in the forest
before their betrothal. She ended with a brief descrip-
tion of how Rhys had bedded her after Peter's warning
that Renauld was on his way. She watched carefully
for Lydia's reaction when she was done with the story.

"I have to agree with you," she said. "Your wedding
night was a disaster." Lydia chewed on the end of her
finger. "Yet it seems as if Rhys enjoyed it, if your de-
scription of his actions is true."

Eliane made a face. "Why would I lie?"

Lydia laughed again. "I'm not saying that you lie,
I'm just trying to gather my thoughts." She let out a
squeak and put her hand over her massive stomach.
"The babe must agree with me. She kicked. Would
you like to feel it?" She grabbed Eliane's hand before
she had a chance to answer. Eliane knelt on the floor
before her and let Lydia guide her hand to the baby's
movement. "Do you feel it?"

She did. A ripple like a stone dropping in a pond.
Then a thrust of a hand or a foot, she could not tell
which.

A baby . . . a daughter born of this marriage . . . What

would she look like? Would her hair be flame-colored like hers or would it be dark like her father's? Would her eyes have the color of the forest or be as dark as the night? She rocked back on her heels and once more put her hands over her stomach.

"I'm going to have a baby."

"Yes. You are. And now you must tell your husband the news."

"Do you think he will be happy? Do you think it will change the way things are? What if he doesn't want a baby? What if this makes it worse? How can I have a baby when things are not right between us?"

Lydia grabbed her hands. "Hush, child. Rhys well knows that babies come after marriage and has been wise enough to make sure none has come before."

That thought had never occurred to Eliane, and she opened her mouth to speak, but Lydia stopped her with a finger to her lips.

"Do not go seeking trouble, Eliane. Tell him he's to be a father and see what happens. My guess is he will be as dumbfounded as you are."

"And what of the rest?"

"All you can do is follow your heart. It will show you your desire when you are ready. And I promise you this. Your one time was not as it should have been and Rhys knows it. What comes next must be decided between the two of you. I've seen the way he looks at you. He is a man who desires his wife."

Eliane's teeth found her lower lip as she listened to Lydia's words. He might have desired her before. But would he now that she had a babe inside her?

If only Madwyn were here. She would tell her what to do. But Madwyn, like Aubregate, was far, far away.

Chapter Twenty

*R*hys stared at his wife. She was waiting for a reaction. *A baby?* He blinked. "How?" Anger and pain flared in her emerald eyes and she turned to leave him. *I am a fool.* He reached for her and took her arm to stop her. "Elaine . . . wait . . . I am sorry . . . 'Tis not news I was expecting."

She wrenched away from his grasp. She drew her fist back, and he thought she might hit him. Rhys looked around the courtyard to see if anyone was watching them. The only one in sight was Khati, who was carrying a basket into the house. Rhys had been currying Yorath when she'd told him the news. The horse tossed his head at the interruption while Llyr, Rhys's constant companion, yawned lazily, disturbed from his nap in the sun.

Rhys stepped away from the steed, to protect both horse and wife her anger. Elaine took a deep breath and her eyes flashed beneath her dark lashes. He was very glad she was not wearing her sword or carrying her bow. He watched her hands carefully lest she pull a dagger from her sleeve. "What news did you expect to hear? That I was tired of waiting here for the king to make up his mind? That I was leaving and returning to Aubregate?"

"Nay." He held out his hand. "'Tis a surprise. That's all." *A baby?* "Are you certain?"

This time she did hit him. She used her fist against his jaw and it jolted his head. "Do not mistake me for a fool, *husband*." There was a note of disgust in her voice that angered him more than her blow.

He picked her up by her waist, no easy feat as she was nearly as tall as he. He pushed her against the stable wall and pinned her arms to her side. She tried to kick him but her legs caught in her skirt. He pushed his leg between them, effectively pinning her. She seethed, her eyes shooting emerald daggers at his face.

"Do not mistake me for a fool, *wife*." She turned her head away as if she could not stand to look at him. "Is it mine?"

"Ohhhhhh." She jerked her knee upward but he was too fast for her. He expected it. She jerked and she squirmed until he had to lean his entire body against her to keep her still.

"Is it?" His mouth was right next to the delicate peak of her ear and, as always, he wanted to kiss it.

"You must have doubts as to your prowess, *husband*, if you have to ask."

Rage, red, hot, and blinding, washed over him. Through all this time he'd been patient with her, waiting for her to seek him out, and she'd chosen another to bed while he was running about the country preparing to go to war?

"I will show you my prowess," he growled into her ear, then nipped it with his teeth. He found her skirts, raised them, grasped at the long length of her thighs and then her rounded cheeks. His erection pressed between them, and he released one of her hands to lower his chausses. He heard a growl, then felt a stinging pain in his backside. Llyr. He spun and knocked the dog away. Llyr quickly regained his feet and lowered his stance, his hackles raised.

"Is this how you wait for me to desire you, *husband*?" Once more disgust sounded in her voice. "What happened to your promise?"

My promise . . . Would he take her in anger? Against her will once more? With a curse he struck his fist on the stable wall. She sidled away, jerking her skirts into place. With a snap of her fingers, Llyr moved to her side and once more took up a protective stance.

"Wait!" He commanded her as he would Yorath or Mathias. He took a deep breath. Yorath pulled at his lead and pawed the ground in agitation and Eliane put a calming hand on his neck. The horse immediately settled. "Eliane. Please wait."

"Why should I?"

"Because I am a fool." *She drives me mad with desire. How much longer must I wait for her?*

"I can now say we've found common ground in our marriage as I agree with you on that subject." She folded her arms across her chest and looked at him with disgust.

"I will give you a whip and let you beat me," he said. "It is what I deserve."

"I would not mind the task." A slight smile curved her lips and was gone as quickly as it came.

"Eliane . . ." Rhys ran his hand through his hair and grimaced. Splinters showed on his knuckles, along with blood.

"You have injured yourself."

"I would rather cut off my hand than cause you pain."

"You are maddening."

"As are you." He gave her a lopsided smile. "Something else we agree on."

"I have not played you false." Her eyes dazzled him as they did every time she looked at him.

"I know." He studied her earnestly. "I know." Rhys rubbed his forehead. His cock throbbed and it took every bit of his willpower not to throw her down on the ground and have his way with her. "Believe me when I say I have not played you false either. I will honor our vows until the day I die."

She nodded and turned to go. "As the news of this baby is a shock to you, I will give you time to think about it before we talk again." Her voice broke. "You leave in a few short days. I would have this matter resolved between us before you go lest I go mad during your absence." She left him, and he could do nothing but watch her go. He looked at his hand and the damage caused by his impatience.

"I fear her wounds may be much deeper than mine," he said to Yorath. He returned the steed to its stall and bellowed for Mathias. He needed a release; perhaps training with his squire would provide it.

Mathias came at a run, through the gate that led to the river. He was soaking wet; no doubt the lazy git had been swimming instead of seeing to his chores. "Tend my hand!" Rhys stuck out his fist. "And see that you do not pain me when you do it, for I will surely beat you this day."

Chapter Twenty-one

Why am I so afraid? Why do I continually push him away? Eliane might not know much about being a wife, but she knew enough to know that Rhys's outburst was caused more by frustration than jealousy. He had no reason to mistrust her any more than she did him. Still . . . she fingered the hilt of her jeweled dagger . . . let him even think about bedding another . . .

She shook her head at Llyr, who sought a sunny spot on the balcony that overlooked the back of the house and the river beyond. "I speak bravely when it comes to using my weapons, but when it comes time to follow my heart, I am the biggest coward in the land."

She was hot. Unbearably so. She removed her bliaut and shoes. She placed her leg on a stool and rolled down the long stockings that covered her knees. The touch of her hands brought back the touch of another and she saw the imprint of his fingers on the back of one thigh. *Would he have taken me against the wall if not for Llyr?* She looked at the dog, who had stretched lazily upon the warm stone. "I have not decided if you did me a favor this day." She attacked the other stocking and wondered how many more weeks it would be before the babe inside her grew too big for her to perform this simple task on her own. Barefoot, and clad only in her yellow kirtle, she went to the balcony, hoping for a cool breeze from the river. She flipped her hair over her shoulder to cool her neck and looked beyond the wall to the boats that skimmed over the water.

The clash of swords brought her gaze from the river to the yard below. Rhys and Mathias were training. His attention had quickly turned from her to his squire. *Mathias will have the worst of it....* Both had stripped down to their chausses. The sweat dripped from them and droplets flew as they raised their arms and shook the hair out of their eyes. They used swords made from wood so that Mathias could hold his broadsword and his movements would be quick.

Rhys was glorious. Her eyes drank him in from the top of his damp dark hair to his leather boots. There was power beneath that sweat-soaked skin. He moved gracefully as he showed Mathias the proper way to block and thrust. He held the weight of the wooden sword easily whereas Mathias struggled to keep his aloft long enough to block. Rhys was patient with him, taking the time to adjust his sword grip or move his feet into a better stance. Would he be so with their child?

"I will not touch you unless you desire it."

How do I make him love me? I know he desires me, but I want more. Is that what frightens me so? Do I fear giving him my heart and not getting his in return? Will it be enough that I am his wife and carry his child? Is it enough that I have told the king I am content with him? Will this thing that we have, whatever it is, be enough to get us through the rest of our days?

I think not.... There must be more. There must be love between us. I do not know how to find it. I do not know what it is he wants of me. How will I know desire if he will not show me?

There were nights when he came to her room and looked down at her as she slept. At times she thought if she would just reach out to him, everything would fall into place. It felt as if a wall had been placed between them and she did not know how to remove it.

If only she had not failed him so miserably on their wedding night. There were those who would say she had not. She was with child. That was her duty. But she had not pleased him. Too much had happened too fast . . . there had been no time for anything beyond accomplishing the deed.

But before . . . before her father's summons to his deathbed, there had been something extraordinary. What would have happened if she had not been called away? Where would Rhys's touch, his kisses, and his hands upon her body have taken her?

The gentle warmth of the day was suddenly more than she could stand. The pale yellow kirtle she wore had a tie at the neck and she loosened it, opened the fabric, and lifted her hair from her shoulders so the breeze from the river would cool the sudden heat that came over her.

" 'Tis the babe. . . ." She knew it was not.

"Damn!" Rhys swore. When she looked down to the garden, she saw Rhys shaking his hand as if he'd jammed it. Mathias was bent over double with laughter.

"Do not give me an excuse to beat you," Rhys growled at the squire.

"Did you not say that the first rule of any battle was to keep your eyes upon your opponent?" Mathias asked.

Rhys looked up to where she leaned on the balustrade, and returned his grip to his sword. "That only works when one's wife is not sunning herself on the field of battle," he said.

He watches me. . . . As she watched him. He raised the broadsword over his head, and his chausses slipped down onto his hips, revealing the curve of his buttocks and a reddening of the skin from Llyr's attack. He was sleek with sweat. And most likely thirsty. Did he desire water? Was there something else he might desire? If only she knew what it was *she* should desire. *His touch?* There was only one way for her to find out. She would ask him. Llyr rose from his spot and followed. Eliane's bare feet flew down the stairs and she went to the well to draw a bucket of water.

They were talking when she came into the yard. Rhys had his hand on Mathias's shoulder and his head was bent to the boy as he gave him instructions. Mathias looked her way when she approached, carrying the bucket.

"You should not carry that." Rhys rushed to her side and took the bucket. "We have servants for that."

"Our servants are about their jobs as they should be," she replied. "The women of Aubregate manage to work the fields and care for their families until their time comes upon them. Look at me, husband. Am I so frail that I cannot carry a pail of water to relieve your thirst?"

His dark eyes moved over her from head to toe. She should have checked her appearance before she left her rooms. His gaze upon her was hot and piercing and she knew she appeared a mess, wearing nothing but her yellow kirtle with her hair falling around her hips.

"You look as if you just came from the fields." Rhys handed the dipper to Mathias, who took it and drank greedily. "A field full of wildflowers in bloom." He picked up a lock of her hair and rubbed it between his fingers. It had been a long while since he'd done so.

"If only I had." She stood perfectly still, enjoying his touch. She kept her eyes upon his face, losing herself in the depths of his gaze. "I find that I miss . . . them." She almost said him. Should she have?

Rhys dropped her hair and looked around the walled yard as if it were a prison. Llyr, with his tongue lolling, moved out of the sun to lie beneath a small willow.

"I will return you to Aubregate as soon as the king releases us."

"Will he ever release us?"

With a nod of his head, Rhys bade Mathias leave them. The boy went off gratefully to jump in the river. Rhys took the dipper dropped by Mathias and raised it to drink. He dumped the rest on his forehead and let it run down his face. "The king plays maneuvers for power with the Church." He picked up the bucket once more. "We are naught but pawns."

"And Renauld?"

"He is biding his time. I shall have to kill him before it comes."

Without thinking, she grabbed his forearm. It was slick with sweat and as hard as stone. His veins and tendons stood out from the weight of the bucket. She felt the faint beat of his pulse. "This game is dangerous for us, Rhys. I fear its outcome."

"What outcome do you fear?" He raised the bucket over his head and poured the water over himself. Eliane jumped back as it sluiced over his shoulders and downward, washing away the sweat and the grit from his exertions. He dropped the bucket and wiped the water from his eyes with the back of his arm. Droplets clung to the shadow of his beard and to his dark lashes like tiny stars. He blinked them away.

"I fear losing you."

He tilted his head to one side as if it would help him see her better. His eyes burned over her, hot, scorching. The heat of the sun was nothing by comparison. Her breath caught in her throat and she felt her skin flush, giving proof to the fire he'd started inside her. She was not brave enough to look into the flames of his eyes, so she cast her gaze on his chest, only to find there was no escape from the inferno. She stared at the silver cross that rested in the hollow beneath his throat. She wanted to touch the damp skin, to marvel at the smoothness of it. To trail her hand down the ridges of his stomach into the dark hair around his navel and beyond. His chausses, loose and wet, dipped dangerously low. Her eyes widened. He grew hard beneath her gaze. Was that possible? Could her look have the same effect on him as his had on her?

"Rhys." Eliane swallowed. "I desire."

"Don't say it unless you mean it." His voice was full of pain.

"I know not what else to say." Tears came unbidden to her eyes. "I only know that I desire . . ."

"Eliane." He whispered her name. Placed his fingers on her cheek, then trailed them down her hair, until he reached her trembling hand. "Let me show you what it is you desire. Let me kiss you and touch you as we did at first. Let me take away the pain of our joining." His hand moved to her stomach. "I want it to be right between us." He swallowed hard and there were shadows of pain in his eyes. The lonely boy he'd been was now showing his soul because he feared for the child she bore. His mouth brushed against her ear. "Let me love you."

She swayed against him. His hands gripped her face and he kissed her as he had the day they were attacked. He claimed her for his own, demanding her body and capturing her soul.

"Love me, Rhys." He pulled away so they could take a breath. He leaned his forehead against hers and she clung to him, her knees weak from his kiss. "Show me my desire." He nodded his head against hers and then bent to scoop her up in his arms. He moved into the house quickly, surprising Cedric and Khati.

"Milord?" Cedric asked, his brow arched in question.

"Milady?" Khati turned from the table where she worked.

Eliane buried her face in Rhys's shoulder. She could not look at them.

"Leave us!" Rhys roared. "Do not come unless I call." He rushed to the stairs and took them two at a time. Eliane saw Llyr about to follow, saw Cedric catch his collar, saw Khati stuff her knuckle into her mouth to keep from laughing out loud as Rhys carried her up the stairs. She saw it all as if in a dream.

He kicked open the door of her chamber. He placed her on the bed, then went back and barred the door. He pulled off his boots as he returned to her. Eliane watched him as if hypnotized. She could not tear her eyes from his face, from the burning look that scorched her. He knelt beside her on the bed, putting one arm over her hip to brace his body, while she leaned against the pillows.

Another scorching look went from the top of her head to the tips of her toes, which peeked out beneath the hem of her kirtle. He touched her neck where the fabric lay open, then moved his hand down to her belly and splayed his hand over it.

"Will it be safe for her? I do not wish to hurt—"

Eliane did not let him finish. She took his head in her hands and pulled him to her. Her lips found his and demanded what he'd promised. He groaned deep in his throat and rolled them both to their sides. His pulled the hem of her kirtle up her leg, and his hand followed, resting on the bare skin of her hip. She threw her leg over his and pressed against him.

"The babe?" he asked again as he moved his mouth to her throat.

"Yes," was all she managed to gasp. His mouth and his tongue moved down her neck and into the space between her breasts and she arched against him. The heat that flushed her body settled between her legs. *This is desire. . . . I want more.*

Her kirtle was hot and heavy between them. She wanted to feel his skin on hers. She ran her hands over the dampened smoothness of his back and downward until she felt the powerful muscles of his buttocks beneath his chausses. She squeezed and flattened her hands, which pushed his hips closer to hers. She could feel his shaft, hard and heavy between them.

Rhys growled low, deep in his throat, and turned them over so she was on her back. He kneeled over her, his legs straddling her. He grasped the hem of her kirtle and she held on to his shoulders so he could pull it from beneath her. He flung it aside and she pulled at the waist of his chausses.

He grabbed her hands. "Let me look at you." His voice was husky with desire and his eyes black as night. Eliane fell back against the pillows once more. Her hair was wild and spilled over her, tangling about her waist. He pushed it aside, trailing his hands over her skin as he moved it, exposing her breasts and the slight curve of her belly.

"You are beautiful." He kissed her stomach, then moved upward. His hand found one breast and she arched again against the rough feel of his palm. His mouth found the other and she moaned. *Desire* . . .

"Rhys . . ." She twisted her hands into his hair, holding him close against her breast yet squirming beneath him. The bristle on his cheek was rough, and the small silver cross that hung at his neck tickled. That combination, along with his lips and tongue, drove her wild with something she could not name . . . *want* . . . *need* . . . *desire*. Rhys raised his head, and she reached for him. He merely smiled and moved down her body. He put his arms beneath her thighs and pulled them upward and apart.

"What . . ." she gasped, alarmed, yet curious. His lips touched her knee, then his tongue. The bristle of his beard burned the tender skin of her inner thigh, then his tongue cooled it as it followed.

She felt the heat of his mouth move to the place that she should not touch. She put her hands over her face, embarrassed, yet fascinated. *Oh . . . my . . .* She could never confess this thing that he did. . . . Then all conscious thought left her. She grasped the sheets, twisting the fabric in her hands as her hips moved of their own accord. Something was happening. Something was coming. Something was pushing her and pulling her and she did not want it to stop, yet she feared what was to come.

"Rhys." Her voice cracked on his name and then she screamed as a tide of stars poured over her. Her body rose from the bed and sailed outward into millions of pieces, scattering into the air like ash. Rhys pulled her up, into his arms, cradled her against him as her body shuddered and screamed and throbbed. He pushed her hair away from her face and kissed her cheek and the peak of her ear.

"That was desire," he whispered. As her senses returned, she heard Llyr barking, but she did not care why. Something much more important pulled at her.

"More," she gasped. She was empty and needed to be filled. She felt his hardness beneath her. He still wore his chausses and she pushed them down, freeing him. His breath caught and she took him in her hand. His head fell against hers. "Fill me, Rhys. Fill me with desire."

She was boneless as he pushed her back, yet she managed to twist her legs around his hips when he raised himself on his arms over her. "This time will be different," he said. "There will be pleasure."

She knew it as surely as she breathed. He slid inside her, so very slowly, until he was buried deep inside. She felt her passage mold around him. *Yes . . . this is . . . Rhys . . .* Felt the size of him and the power that he held back because he still feared hurting her or the babe. *This is desire. This filling of one's body and soul.* He propped his upper body on his elbows, put his hands in her hair, and gazed down at her with his soul plainly showing on his face.

"This is what I wanted to give you on our wedding night. This pleasure."

She moved her hips, adjusting her body to the feel of him, to his weight, to the fullness, and he closed his eyes, every muscle of his body drawn taut.

"Show me, Rhys," she said. "Show me before I die of want."

He smiled and opened his eyes. "You are greedy, wife." He pulled out, teasing her, and she gripped him tighter with her legs, showing him the strength born from years of riding.

"Only for my husband, who has been most selfish."

He plunged back into her once more and she gasped, her eyes widening as he filled her even more. He moved and she found his rhythm. Once more she felt the pressure she'd known before, the reaching, and the wanting. She arched toward it, seeing it, feeling it build with each thrust as he moved against her, faster and faster. She kept her eyes on his face, marveling at the intensity of his gaze, and at the fire that burned in his dark eyes. Then his focus went beyond her, to a point far away, and she saw what he saw, joined him in reaching for it. She felt her bones turn to ash once more as he carried her into the sky.

Chapter Twenty-two

Rhys put both hands on her stomach and held his breath. Eliane said the babe moved when she was still and he wanted to feel it. He still could not wrap his mind around the truth. Their first time together he'd put a babe inside her. He wished the child was a result of today's union, but he was not one to question God's handiwork. The fact that she was breeding would surely be enough for the king to give his blessing to their union. Renauld would be gone from their lives forever.

How did Eliane feel about the babe? Did she welcome it? Or would she feel as his mother had, that she was trapped? He would need to watch her carefully for any sign of sadness or anger, anything that would indicate she was the same as his mother. He could only pray she would not seek death as his mother had. He would do everything in his power to stop such a thing.

This would worry him every day he was gone. It would gnaw at his insides in the same way Edward's illness had gnawed at him. Killing him on the inside. Rhys de Remy, who gave not a thought to anything outside of his control, would be in constant agony over his wife's pregnancy.

He looked at her face, so beautiful, and saw peace within her emerald eyes. She glowed. His conceit said it was because of the hour just past but he knew better. She glowed because the babe grew inside her. He felt it then . . . a flutter, as if a butterfly had landed on his palm. He looked at her stomach, then back at Eliane and the smile that lit her face.

"How did you know that we would not hurt her?" It had to be a girl that grew inside her womb. It was the way of the women of Aubregate to breed only daughters. *My daughter . . .*

"Lydia assured me it would be safe."

He was surprised. "You talked to Lydia about this?"

"Lydia is the one who told me I was breeding." Her skin turned as fiery as her hair. Rhys laughed when she began worrying her bottom lip with her teeth. She cuffed his head. "Do not laugh at me. I wanted to know . . . how to please you . . . since the first time was . . ." She turned away. The shame he'd felt at his actions on their wedding night came flooding back. He should have found another way and waited until she was ready. Yet if he had, it would have been easy for Henry to put aside their vows. The fact that she was bearing his child was the only reason the king would allow them to remain together.

He placed a hand on her chin and turned her face back to him. "You have done nothing but please me Eliane." Her emerald eyes stared up at him, but he was not sure of their expression. Was it hope? "Since the first time I saw you in the forest, I wanted you. I hate that I caused you so much pain when you were grieving for your father, but it was the only way."

"You put me aside because of your guilt over our wedding night?" She sat up and pulled the sheet around her naked body, once more becoming the warrior woman of the forest. Her anger flashed in her eyes.

"Eliane . . ." He pulled her into his arms, yet she remained stiff and unyielding. "I never put you aside." He kissed the top of her tousled hair. "Do not think such thoughts." It was hard being a husband, treading carefully lest you close off the very thing you sought to open. "I have ached for you every single moment since we met. I did not want to frighten you or force you again."

She softened and leaned her head back against his arm to see him better. "Is that why you have not shared my bed?"

He smiled at her. Took her hand in his and put it between his legs. "Do you feel that? Already it swells from want. It seems that my cock has a mind of its own where you are concerned. Sometimes it does the thinking for both of us. I always wanted you, but I wanted you to enjoy it also."

Eliane grabbed hold of his cock, and he grunted as she tightened her grip slighty. "Be careful, husband, that this does not lead you astray. I do not mean to share you with anyone."

He gritted his teeth and took her hand away. She raised an eyebrow, taunting him. "Why would I search elsewhere when everything I desire is right here in my arms?"

"Truly?"

He pushed her back onto the bed once more. *Mine.* . . . "Truly," he said, and showed her the strength of his desire.

She fell asleep soon after as she did most afternoons. The babe tired her. He watched her sleep, enjoyed the rise and fall of her breasts, her soft sigh as she turned toward him. He felt the press of her belly against him and held perfectly still at the chance that there would be movement within her womb.

The afternoon sun danced across the bed and turned her hair into molten copper. It was everywhere, twisted about her arm and her waist and spread upon the pillows. He lifted a long tendril, rubbed it between his fingers, and inhaled. As always, the scent took him back to the forest and the first time he saw her. When they returned to Aubregate and the babe was born, he would take her to the forest and make love to her beneath the dancing trees.

Make love . . . Now I understand why it is considered so. This thing we have, it is more than sex. With the others it was a way to seek a pleasurable release, but with her . . . with Eliane . . .

Rhys sat up, quickly, quietly. He moved to the doors that opened onto the balcony. He cared not that he was naked. None could see him. He sucked in the warm air and gripped the balustrade with both hands.

Is this love? He put a hand over his heart. Surely it would break into a thousand pieces if he lost her. He looked over his shoulder at Eliane. A frown creased her forehead and she turned away from him, giving him a view of her spine and the curve of her buttocks as they disappeared beneath the sheet.

Was this what his father had felt as he watched his mother sleep? Did he wonder about the child and the future and his ability to provide and protect? Did he worry that she did not love him back, because he'd forced her into marriage after he forced his way into her bed? Did his heart shatter that day she jumped from the tower window and left both of them behind? Was this why he chose death over life with his son?

His hand moved to the tiny silver cross. He held it between his fingers. Prayed. *God, spare us that pain . . . spare this child . . . my daughter. . . .*

Eliane wrapped her arms around his waist and placed her cheek against his spine. "You are cold," she said. "What is it?"

Rhys turned, gathered her into his arms. " 'Tis nothing," he said. "The wind . . ." There was none, but she did not seem to notice.

"I am hungry." Her face was almost on a level with his. Her eyes were right at his nose, so she leaned back a bit. "Starving actually. Your daughter wants food. And I want a bath. Can you make it so, husband?"

"I can." He kissed the tip of her nose. "All that you desire and more."

"My desire is right here. I found it at last." She went to the bed once more and pulled the sheets over herself. Rhys found his chausses and she studied him as he pulled them on.

"Is something amiss?"

"Nay, husband," she said. "I was thinking how convenient it would be if you were to give up your chamber and move in here with me."

It had been his intention, but he loved to tease her. "Convenient for whom?"

"You, milord." She stretched a long, lissome leg out from beneath the sheet and drew it back as if he were a fish and she held the line. "As this is where your dreams seem to bring you."

"You knew I watched you at night?"

"I did," she admitted. "There were times when I

wanted to ask you why, but I was afraid of the anger that stood between us."

"It stands between us no more. 'Twas a wall that came down with a mighty crash and is gone."

"Oh . . ." Her eyes widened in her face and her face turned the color of her hair. "Oh no . . ." Eliane slid beneath the sheets, turned her back to him, and covered her head.

"What it is?" Rhys went to her side and put a hand on her hip. He could not lose her again. Not when they had just discovered what they could share.

"I screamed." Her voice was muffled beneath the sheet. "The servants must have heard me. I am certain all of London heard me." She moaned her despair. "How will I ever be able to look at Cedric or Mathias or even Khati again?"

"I'm fairly certain they knew what we were about when I carried you up the stairs."

"Rhys . . ." she moaned again.

"Eliane. They are more than likely celebrating now. Servants know more about things than they let on. And while it is not their place to give us advice, they do what they can to make things better."

"But I screamed."

"Which means I pleased you well." He slapped her hip with the palm of his hand. "I took it as a compliment."

She flipped the sheets off and bounced upward. She grabbed his arm and pulled him close. "Instead of a compliment, see it as a challenge." Her emerald eyes dazzled him. "What must you do now to please me better?"

He had thought his body too weary for more after two bouts of lovemaking. Yet his cock jerked upward at her words. "I am certain I will be able to think of something."

"Not until I've had a bath."

The former owner of the house was a portly man who'd indulged in many luxuries, one of them being a rather large copper tub for bathing. It was big enough for the two of them. He had never imagined that one of the benefits of marriage would be sharing a bath with one's wife. Eliane leaned against his chest, her body between his thighs and their long legs propped together on the opposite end.

He circled her with his arms and placed his hands on her stomach, where he traced lazy circles with his thumbs. Her hair had been braided and pinned up by a grinning Khati and it cushioned her head upon his shoulder.

Eliane placed her hands over his. "Does it bother you overmuch that you are to be a father so soon?"

He laughed. " 'Twas to be expected, although it was the last thing on my mind that night." He stretched his hands over her stomach. *What will it be like when your belly swells with our child?* "My ego is large enough to be flattered that I put a child in you the first time we were together."

Eliane squeezed his thumbs. "Methinks it will take most of my waking hours to keep your head from swelling beyond the size of your helm."

"What of the other part of me that swells?" He nipped at her ear.

"Is that the only thought that fills your swollen head?" She teased him mercilessly but he found that he enjoyed it.

"I am a man with the most beautiful wife in the

kingdom. What else should I think on?" He nuzzled her neck and thrilled at the shiver that rippled down her spine.

"Think on this, husband. Do you believe the king will be tempted to put aside our marriage now that I am breeding?"

Rhys moved his hands up and circled his arms around her breasts. "I think the king plays a game of chess and we are his pawns."

"You said that before. I don't understand why we are of such importance to him. Our estates combined are still minor compared to others. We have no connections save Peter and no enemies save Renauld."

"I believe that Renauld has something on the king. Something that Henry does not want revealed."

"What could it be?"

"It would have to be something that would affect his standing with the Church. He and Becket are battling for control of England. The king would willingly sacrifice us to gain what he wants."

"In the time we've been here, it seems as if he's given no thought to us at all."

"Henry did not win his power by being foolish. He's a patient man. He's waiting for someone else to make a move. To set aside our marriage, especially when it is most obvious you carry my child, would risk excommunication. So he waits for one of us to make a move."

Eliane turned to him and took his hand. "That is why he sends you and Renauld to Ireland. He hopes that one of you will die there."

"I have thought the same thing many times."

"Be careful, Rhys. Renauld is not above sticking a knife in your back or paying someone to do it for him.

Think of how easily it could be done, especially during a battle."

"Peter and I have talked of the same thing. And Mathias has been instructed on what to do. Renauld tried to kill me once; I will not let him try again."

"What happens if you both come back safe and sound? What then? Can you challenge Renauld? Could we not just go home once you've fulfilled your obligation?"

"Nay, if we were to leave without the king's blessing, we would forfeit our lands and possibly our lives. Mine most certainly. If I attack Renauld and lose, then Renauld will get you, Aubregate, and Myrddin by default. If Renauld attacks me and I lose, then you will go into the king's custody along with the daughter you carry in your womb."

Eliane sat up and turned in the tub. She drew her legs up and wrapped her arms around them. She rested her chin upon her knees and studied him with her emerald eyes. Llyr, who lay beside the bed, sat up at her movement and watched to see what she would do. The fire, just large enough to take the chill off the evening, lit her profile. "Then do not lose," she said carefully.

"As much as I appreciate your confidence, winning is not something I can guarantee."

"Things would be much simpler if we were at Aubregate and he could simply disappear. Could we not make the same thing happen here?" Eliane suggested.

Rhys leaned forward to face her. "Eliane. I will not do anything without honor. When I face Renauld, it will be face-to-face and with honor. I will not lower myself to loiter in some dark place where a knife could be slipped into his back." He took her hands in his. "Do you understand?"

She smiled. "I do." She reached for a towel. "I regret that I did not kill him years ago. I could have spared us this trouble."

"When could you have killed him? And why?"

She rose from the tub, wrapped herself in a towel, and handed him one. "Should I summon Mathias and Khati?"

He wrapped the towel round his waist. "Tell me of Renauld first."

"It was right after Peter left. Right before his knighting. And Renauld's too. He was at Chasmore for some reason. He had not been there in years. It was the first and only time I saw him. Han and I were in the forest and I wanted to see what was on the other side. So he took me to the edge that borders Chasmore lands. There was a field, and a crofter's hut that had a wall caved in. We heard the most pitiful cries, and Han and I both went because we knew some creature was in pain. Renauld was there and he had a puppy with him. A tiny thing, like one of the lapdogs that Lady Longsmere carries about. He had his knife and he . . ." Eliane covered her mouth with her hand and a tear coursed down her cheek. Her emerald eyes were full of pain as she recalled the events long past. He could not bear it. He pulled her into his arms. "He was torturing it . . . cutting it . . . I killed it with my bow." She cried into his chest. "If only I had killed him too. But Han would not let me. Renauld chased us, threatening us. He called me an ugly freak because of my ears."

"And now he sees your beauty and curses himself for a fool because he did not try to win you sooner."

"I will kill him, if given the chance." Her tears were gone and steely resolve took their place. "We have been forever at war with Chasmore. Since before the Normans came." Eliane slipped on her robe and sat on the bed. Llyr jumped up beside her and lay down with his head next to her hip. She rubbed his huge head. Rhys knew it would have pained her greatly to see an animal suffer. She had a way with them. Even his great Yorath was captured by her charm.

Rhys went to the door, summoned Mathias, and told him to bring their meal up to the chamber. It was long past time for them to eat.

"Aubregate has been in your family since before William's time?" he asked when he'd sent the boy to his task.

"Through my mother's line to the time before the Romans came. Since before such events were recorded."

Rhys shook his head. It was beyond his comprehension.

"If something were to happen to you, the king would keep me hostage and never let me remarry because of the rumors of Aubregate's secret treasure."

"Is there a treasure hidden in the forest?"

She looked at him quizzically.

"Your father bade me not go in unless you were with me. And when I asked you about it the day of the attack, you would not answer. If I am to die to protect this treasure, shouldn't I know what it is?"

"There is no treasure, Rhys. No gold, or silver, or jewels. The treasure is a rumor, nothing more."

"Nay, there is a treasure." He sat down beside her. Llyr groaned in protest. Rhys shoved his head away and placed a hand on Eliane's cheek. "It is you." He put his hand on her stomach once more. "And her." He kissed her. "You are my treasures."

Chapter Twenty-three

Finally, home. Before when he said the word, it meant nothing to him beyond the name of the place that was the seat of his power. There was no emotion attached to it, no happy memories, nothing beyond a sense of duty. Now the word had meaning. Home was Eliane. Throughout the long summer in Ireland, home was all he thought about.

They'd arrived in Ireland in May and immediately built a fortification so that they would have a safe place to wait for Pembrooke's arrival. Some of the knights, Vannoy among them, chose to spend their time raiding the countryside and taking what riches could be found. Rhys knew his greatest treasure was in London. He could not wait to see Eliane again and his mind raced to that sweet moment when once more they would be together.

"Is your mind on what is behind us or what is before us?" Peter asked as they rode toward London.

"I am certain my mind is on the same thing as yours," Rhys replied. The two had grown close through the summer, finding they had much in common beyond their mutual admiration and love for Edward.

"Here's hoping the king will release us to our respective homes. I have no desire to be in the pot he currently stirs."

While they'd been in Ireland, Henry had once more

tweaked the nose of the Church by using the Archbishop of York for his son's coronation instead of
Thomas Beckett, whose right it was as the Archbishop
of Canterbury. In July, the two men had met and Henry
had given Beckett a partial forgiveness. But things remained unsettled between the state and the Church.

"I can only hope that his current schemes will cause
him to lose interest in Eliane and me," Rhys said.

"Eliane bears your child, Rhys. The king may dare
much, but even he would not separate you now."

"He hoped that by sending us to Ireland, either
Vannoy would kill me or I him, and his problem would
be resolved."

"Henry either underestimated us or overestimated
the Irish," Peter observed. "I am certain we could have
sent William and Mathias to do the job on their own."

Rhys nodded in agreement, but his mind was not on
the battle just recently fought. It was on the victories he
soon hoped to win. He was going to approach Henry
and demand that he give his blessing on the marriage
so he and Eliane could leave London. Eliane wanted to
be home when the babe was born and he would do
everything in his power to make sure she was.

"Do you still stand by your belief that Vannoy has
something on the king?" Peter asked.

"I do," Rhys said. "Why else would he give the man
such consideration? Vannoy has made no secret of the
fact that he desires Aubregate. He believes there is a
treasure hidden within the forest."

"I too heard rumors of a treasure, although I never
saw any proof of it in my years there."

"The treasure of Aubregate is Eliane. None other
matters."

Peter grinned widely. "It seems that marriage does finally agree with you."

"Only this marriage, with this wife. Any other would be lacking."

"You love her?"

"I do."

"Then I am most happy for you, my friend." Peter reached out and clasped a hand on his shoulder. There was value in having a friend. One you could talk with freely. Still, Rhys did not confess to Peter his deepest fear. That once he told Eliane of his love for her, she would not return it.

"A rider comes," William said. Peter held up his hand to stop the group. They were a large troop. Rhys had left those men-at-arms with families at Myrddin as they passed through. He had also retrieved the emeralds kept there. Emeralds that he planned to give to Eliane.

The rest of his men had chosen to come to London to experience the sights and sounds of the big city. Combined with Peter's group, they were still an impressive number. They pulled off to the side to let the rider pass by.

Instead he pulled up when he saw their colors. "Lord de Remy?" he questioned. The rider wore the colors of the king.

"I am he." A million thoughts tumbled through his mind, the first and foremost being the welfare of his wife.

"The king bids you come straightaway to the castle."

Rhys nodded in agreement. He dared not speak. A

cold, dark fear spread outward from his gut. What did the king want of him now?

Summer was nearly gone. The fields at home would be thick with crops. The hay long ago harvested. Apples bending the branches of the trees. Eliane loved this time of year; she loved going among her people and seeing the pride on their faces at their successes. The lambs would play in the tall grass, and the foals would run just for the sheer joy of it. The mill would grind from daylight until dark and the people would gather together for meals. Come September there would be a fair in the town with vendors and tricksters and musicians. The latest message brought by Jess from home did not say these things, yet Eliane knew them in her heart. She could close her eyes and see it all.

"And I am stuck in London still. . . ." Why wouldn't the king release them? Rhys had done his duty to the king in Ireland. She had stayed put in deference to the king's wishes even though there were times when she thought she would pull her hair from her head and scream out of frustration and sheer boredom with her life. She was not one to simply sit and wait. She needed to be active. She needed Aubregate just as she needed air to breathe and water and food to sustain her. Surely she would die if she did not return soon.

If only Madwyn were here. But neither Madwyn nor Han would leave Aubregate with their mistress gone. Their duty lay within its borders. Eliane splayed her palms upon the mound of her stomach. "I promise you, little one. Madwyn will be the one to bring you into this world. Even if I have to deny the king."

What will Rhys have to say about that? His letters bade
her to be patient. Easy enough for him to say. He was
off fighting a war while she was stuck in London, getting fatter every day. She looked down toward her
feet. They were lost to her, gone beneath the round
mass of her stomach. She wiggled her toes against the
stone floor of the balcony just to make sure they still
existed. She could no longer stand to wear shoes; her
feet had swollen in the intense late-summer heat that
had settled over the city.

The streams of Aubregate would be cool. As would
the water from the well. The spring next to Madwyn's
cottage would do wonders to relieve the aches and
pains that had settled into her back. Eliane placed her
hands in the small of her back and arched against
them. She closed her eyes and imagined Rhys's hands
there. Rubbing away the aches and pains. She could
see him, placing his big hands on her stomach and his
dark eyes widening in wonder at the antics of their
babe. Their daughter. She kicked lustily as if she heard
Eliane's thoughts.

"Soon, little one, soon. Your father will be here to
regale you with tales of his battles." *Soon* . . . His last
letter had said as much. He'd told her to watch for him
in the coming days. That he could not wait to see her
and his babe. That he had much to tell her. *And I
him.* . . . The first being that she would not be parted
from him again. As much as she missed Aubregate,
she missed Rhys more.

She missed the way he casually threatened to beat
Mathias each and every day. She missed the way he
teased her by turning her own words upon her.
She missed the way he slipped food to Llyr beneath

the table when he thought no one was watching. She missed watching him train Mathias, the way his back moved, the long length of his stride, the strength of his arm as he held his sword aloft. She missed the way his hair fell across his forehead and how he seemed to stop breathing when she pushed it back into place. She missed the way he looked at her with his dark, fathomless eyes as if he could see into her very soul. Sometimes when he looked at her, it took her breath away.

She missed him so much that she felt as if her heart had been ripped from her body and thrown into the sea that separated them. She loved him and she would do anything to make him love her back. But she could do nothing until he returned home.

The heat on the balcony became unbearable, and as always she was restless. Llyr had abandoned her long ago and sought shelter beneath the weeping willow in the corner of the yard. The branches moved lazily in the slight breeze that came from the river. Mayhap she would see for herself if it were cooler there.

Eliane gathered up the skirts of her pale blue kirtle and walked barefoot through the house. Cedric and Khati had gone to market, and only a few men-at-arms were about. The bell at the front gate tolled and she went to see who it could be.

There was no man-at-arms at the door as there should be. The bell rang again, and again, most insistently. Indeed she feared the rope would come off. Llyr trotted through the house and went to the door. He snuffed around at the door frame and whined. Eliane opened the view port.

"Mathias!" Eliane heaved up the bar and flung the door open. She threw her arms around a grinning

Mathias. Llyr stood on his hind legs and pawed at Mathias, causing them both to stagger. They crashed into the open door and Mathias stuck out an arm to steady them.

"What—" Eliane looked beyond him in hopes that Rhys was hiding outside, but Mathias was alone.

Mathias interrupted her before she could go any further. "Milord bade me come and tell you he is here in London. The king summoned him before he could come to you." He bent to rub Llyr's head, and the dog slurped his tongue across his face. They both laughed at Llyr's welcome.

He's here. Joy and feared gripped Eliane at the same time. Rhys was home. The king had summoned him. Why?

"Milady, he is most anxious to see you and will be here as soon as possible."

"I too am anxious." She threw her arms around Mathias once more. "Oh, Mathias, it is so good to see you."

The clatter of horse's hooves drowned out her words. "Rhys?" Eliane turned from Mathias. Went out to the street. A troop of men bore down on her. But they did not wear the burgundy and gray of Rhys de Remy. They wore the black and gold of Renauld Vannoy.

Chapter Twenty-four

You have my blessing on your marriage."

Rhys bowed before his king.

"Now take your bride home so that she may deliver your child in peace."

"Thank you." Rhys hoped his sigh of relief was not evident to those present. After a long wait, which had nearly driven him mad, he'd been ushered into a private room where Henry and his closest advisers were waiting. Pembrooke smiled benevolently at him, along with Peter's father. He had served king and country well in Ireland and deserved his prize.

Henry smiled his approval, but his eyes held a warning. *Beware of Vannoy.* He expected Rhys to solve the problem of Renauld Vannoy for him. *What does Vannoy know about Henry that gives him this power?*

He decided he did not want to know. He wanted nothing to do with the intrigues of court. His sincere desire was to live his life in peace somewhere he would not have to answer to the whims of others.

"I will be like Edward and stay far away from court," Rhys said to himself as he left Henry's chambers. "I will take Eliane to Aubregate and raise our daughter and keep her free from these games of strategy."

Rhys hurried to make his way from the castle. The woman he desired most awaited him. He needed only to claim her. Worrying about what might happen was nothing more than a waste of time. He would meet whatever was to come bravely, content in the knowledge that Eliane was by his side. An image of her face came to mind and the joy on it when he told her they could return to Aubregate. He could only hope that her joy would be the same when he told her he loved her.

"Rhys!" The voice stopped him just short of freedom. Marcella must have known of his summons and been waiting for him to appear. To leave without a word would be an insult, and the last thing he needed was someone else holding a grudge against him. He could not help recalling that the last time he'd seen her, she'd been in the company of Vannoy. It would be best to hear her out, even though he longed for nothing more than to escape Henry's court, never to return.

She came to him, wearing a gown of pale pink that enhanced the delicacy of her face. "I am most gladdened to see you safe."

"Our losses were slight," Rhys said politely. "The battle no more than an exercise."

"Modesty does not become you, Rhys." She placed a fingernail against her lip, and then trailed it down his chest. Rhys recognized the gesture for the invitation it was. "I would welcome you as the hero you are."

"You are mistaken if you believe my feelings for my wife have lessened in the time we were apart." He grabbed her wrist and held it tightly between them. He well knew her penchant for striking out. The last thing he wanted was to greet Eliane with Marcella's mark upon him.

"Wives come and go in these times." Her pale blue eyes were like ice. "But a liaison born of convenience can be of great comfort." She jerked her wrist from his

grip. "Remember me, Rhys, in your time of need."
She gathered her skirts and walked away, leaving him
with a feeling of dread. First the delay of waiting upon
the king and now this. Was it all part of Vannoy's last
desperate attempt to take Eliane?

He could chase after Marcella and find out what she
knew, if anything, or he could gather his wife and his
household and make for Aubregate with as much haste
as Eliane's pregnancy would allow.

"Wives come and go...." Rhys touched his silver
cross and said a quick prayer. He had a sinking feeling
that it was too little and too late.

The streets were crowded and his patience was thin.
He had lost hours waiting on the king. He had no regard for the commoners who scattered before him as
Yorath pounded through the streets. There was only
one thought in his mind. *Eliane* ... The men-at-arms
who'd followed him tried their best to keep up. They
had no idea where the house was, and Mathias had
gone on, at his bidding, to tell Eliane of his delay.
Rhys did not care. He just knew he must get to his
wife, and as soon as possible.

When he turned onto the street, his heart leapt into
his throat. There was a crowd gathered before his
gate. He jumped from Yorath's back before the horse
could fully stop and the crowd parted. Mathias lay in
the street, his head in Khati's lap, his hand still wrapped
around his sword.

"What happened?" Rhys fought the urge to lift
Mathias by his jerkin and shake the answer from him.
There was a lump the size of a fist on the boy's temple,
and blood mixed with tears streaked his face.

"He took milady," Mathias said. "Vannoy and his

troop." Mathias grasped at his arm as Rhys knelt by his side. "I fear the time has come for you to beat me, milord. I have failed you greatly this day."

The words penetrated the red haze of panic and fear that surrounded Rhys. He placed a hand on the boy's cheek. "Your sword is bloodied, and you gave your all."

Mathias swallowed and nodded. "I fear it was not enough."

"Take care of him," Rhys commanded, and Khati nodded. Tears rolled down her face, but her resolve showed in her eyes. "Where is Cedric?"

"He went after them," Mathias gasped.

Rhys turned to his men-at-arms. "I know you are tired and weary of battle. Milady . . ." He stopped and swallowed back his fear. "Our lady has been taken. I need two of you to protect our home and people. The rest of us will pursue those who dared to take her."

He swung onto Yorath's back. His steed and his men needed a rest. In his eagerness to see Eliane, he had pushed them hard since returning to England. Now he had to ask for more.

"For our lady and for Mathias," they said as one.

Fear and rage combined in Rhys's soul. He saw not the road ahead, only his purpose and the pain he would inflict upon Vannoy if he harmed a hair upon her head. *What of the babe?* It was close to Eliane's time. Vannoy would not have mercy upon her because of her pregnancy. If anything, he would use it against her. Rhys could only hope that Eliane would do what she could to delay Vannoy. Once they were behind the walls of Chasmore, it would be almost impossible to rescue her.

"Be strong, be brave, but above all, be wise and do not make decisions in haste." His fingers touched the silver cross around his neck as he prayed for guidance for both of them.

It was not until he saw Cedric coming toward him that his fear really took hold. Llyr lay bloody and boneless across the saddle before him and Cedric's face was grief-stricken. Without a word Rhys halted his troop beside Cedric's mount and reached out a hand to Eliane's protector.

"He lives," Cedric said. "Barely. He was spared the fate of our men."

"Eliane?"

"She is gone, milord. He rode ahead while his men stayed to slay us. I fear she is lost to us forever."

Eliane could not move. Her hands and feet were bound and she rode in the saddle before Vannoy. He held her tightly clamped against him, with his thighs beneath her, helping to cushion the impact of the saddle against her spine. There was no doubt in her mind that he did not know holding her thus protected her. He did it to annoy her, because he knew she could not stand his touch. She would bide her time and let him think her weakened because of her condition. He did not know that it only strengthened her resolve to escape him. She had no doubt of his intentions for her babe.

"I will cut it from your womb and leave you bleeding in the road for him to find," he'd threatened.

"By doing so you will ensure that you never possess Aubregate," she'd replied. They'd stared daggers at each other then, each one taking the measure of the other. Eliane knew that he needed her alive or he would never achieve his goal. He could only take Aubregate through her, or through the daughter she carried. So for now he must wait and Eliane prayed that somehow Rhys would catch up to them before they reached the walls of Chasmore.

"He will kill you."

"He is a coward, or he would have done it sooner."

"He is a man of honor."

"His honor can comfort him in the grave."

"He would never stoop to attack an unarmed boy as you did."

Vannoy laughed. "I should have finished the job, just as I should have paid more attention to you, my sweet." His tongue roamed over her cheek and into her hair. "Little did I know that the ugly child would turn into a beautiful woman. And you were right beneath my nose all this time."

"Rhys will not have to kill you." Eliane suppressed a shiver of disgust. "I will do it myself."

He threw back his head and laughed. She wanted his laughter. She wanted his antagonism. They kept the fear from coming over her. Fear for the babe, fear for herself, fear for Llyr and Mathias and the men who'd tried to save her. Were they dead? She'd seen them fall, first Mathias before the gate, then Llyr as he gave chase. After that she'd seen nothing as Vannoy's men-at-arms turned round to face her defenders. Vannoy, coward that he was, rode on, with her in his arms, knowing that they would not risk a bow shot when there was a chance she could be harmed.

"I need to stop," she said finally. The babe constantly pressed on her bladder. She was already soaked with sweat from the heat of the day, the heat of his body, and the lathering of the horse that labored beneath them.

"So you can escape?" he asked. His breath on her

face was foul and her stomach weak from hunger. She did not know how much longer she could hang on. Her head swam from the heat. She needed water, but more importantly she needed to relieve the pressure on her bladder. Her back was clenched in a spasm that was nearly unbearable.

"I have needs, as does your horse." She clenched her teeth against the pain. "Or do you want my husband to find you on foot? It should make for an easy killing then. Unless you plan to use me as your shield."

They were near a copse where a trio of huts was scattered. Vannoy roughly pulled his mount to a stop among a flock of geese. The horse blew heavily as Vannoy dropped Eliane to the ground. Her legs, numb from the ride, gave way and she fell into a heap in the dirt, catching herself with her hands. Before she had a chance to gather herself, he yanked her up by the hair, cut the bindings around her ankles, and dragged her to the door of one of the huts.

He shoved her inside without ceremony. The family, who had been eating, stood against the back wall. The man grabbed a shovel and attempted to swing at Vannoy. He pushed Eliane at the man and she stumbled heavily against him. Vannoy grabbed a small girl and held his knife to her throat. The women sobbed and screamed as the man sought to untangle himself from Eliane.

"Stop before he kills you," Eliane said. "You see what he has done to me. Do you think he will feel compassion for you?"

The man looked at her, let out a deep breath, and dropped the shovel. Eliane saw the smile of contempt and satisfaction that covered Vannoy's hawkish face.

"See to her needs," he commanded the two women. "If she escapes, I will kill all of you." Both women shrieked and reached for the little girl, who cried silently.

"Fear not," Eliane said calmly to the women. "I will not put you in danger to seek my own safety."

"Is it your time?" the older woman asked.

"Nay." Eliane pressed her hands into the small of her back to relieve the cramp. "Although this fool will hurry it upon me."

"Go!" Vannoy barked, and the women jumped. As they led Eliane out to the privy, he commanded the man to see to his horse.

The old woman pulled a small knife from her apron and cut Eliane's bonds before she entered the privy. When she was done, the woman pressed it into her hands. "I have no way to conceal it," Eliane said. Her pale blue kirtle, which was soaking wet with sweat, had no pockets. "I will take some water and a bite of food if you can spare it."

"Fetch water," the older woman said to the daughter. She sat Eliane down on a stump and knelt before her. They heard Vannoy shouting at the man, but the woman ignored it. The woman slit the hem of the kirtle and slipped the knife inside. The daughter came back with a pail of water and an apple.

"Eat this," the old woman urged. Eliane quickly took a bite. She was so thirsty and the apple so tart. The old woman quickly wiped her face, neck, and arms with a square dipped in the bucket as the other gave her a dipper to drink.

Then the young woman gasped. "Your ears!"

Eliane's hands went to her ears. They were the least of her concerns now.

"Fool," the old woman said. "Do ye not see what she is? She is of the fey."

The young woman crossed herself and looked nervously over her shoulder. They could hear the little girl's sobs and Vannoy's shouts for Eliane.

"Take my ring." Eliane slid the band from her finger and pressed it into the old woman's hands. "My husband will be looking for me. Give it to him and tell him . . ." There were so many things she wanted to say. *I love you . . . I am frightened . . . I will try to be strong for our daughter . . . I am sorry for the time we lost . . . I believe in you.*

"I will tell him," the old woman said. Her eyes held the sorrow of things lost and the memories of things missed.

"Give him the ring and he will reward you," Eliane said. "Tell him I will do what I can to delay." They hurried back around the hut as the sobs grew louder.

"Have a care for your babe, milady."

As soon as they rounded the hut, Vannoy pushed the little girl at the women and grabbed Eliane. "Ah, there you are, my sweet," he said as he twisted his hand into her hair. "I was worried about you." He hoisted her into the saddle and jumped up behind her. She gritted her teeth against the pain. She wanted nothing more than to lie down and be left alone. Her body screamed out for rest and her back cramped against the abuse.

"If you have a need, it will be met at Aubregate," Eliane called out to the family.

"Yes, do come to Aubregate," Vannoy said. "I will have need of vassals when I take control." He dug his spurs into his horse's flanks and they were off once more.

Chapter Twenty-five

*R*hys stared up at the walls of Chasmore as he slowed Yorath to a cooling walk. He was too late. Vannoy was safely inside with Eliane as his prisoner. Rhys's eyes darted around the walls and towers, looking for any sign of weakness. There was none that he could see. He raised a hand to push his sweat-soaked hair from his forehead and could not help thinking of Eliane's touch. She would push it back for him when it fell in his eyes. It always made him feel like a small boy when she did so. A small boy who had someone to care for him as his grandmother never did. It made him want to be a better man. *I must save her. . . .*

Rhys patted the neck of his stallion in gratitude. Yorath was in much worse shape than he. Only the horse's great heart and love for his master had kept him going. Vannoy's horse had not fared so well. Rhys had come across the dying animal in the early morning hours and had mercifully cut its throat. Then he found the dead body of a merchant and knew that Vannoy had found another animal to take them onward.

"She is mine, de Remy!" Vannoy stood on the castle wall, surrounded by archers. "You are too late!"

"The king gave his blessing to our marriage, Vannoy!" He rode closer to the walls, daring the archers to shoot. "Are you willing to commit treason to have her? Let her go and we shall not speak of this again."

"It's too late for that," Vannoy said. "The king told me of his blessing. Why do you think he did that?"

"Because he wants me to kill you." Rhys did not have to raise his voice. He dismounted, pulled out his sword, and slapped Yorath on the flank to send him safely away. The horse stumbled off to the shelter of an oak tree. It was well out of reach of arrows, and a tiny stream ran by it. Rhys heard the horse bury his head in the stream and his own thirst haunted him. But he could not drink or eat or rest until he saw Eliane.

He gripped his sword and wished for his shield. "And kill you I will."

Vannoy spread his arms as if he were a willing target.

"Come out and face me with honor instead of hiding behind castle walls and the skirts of women." How did one fight a coward? Rhys's frustration and rage grew until he feared they would overtake him. He must not let them. He must remain clearheaded and calm before his enemy.

"Funny. My dear Eliane said the same thing." Vannoy baited him. He wanted Rhys to be foolish and hasty. He could not rise to the bait.

"She well knows your affinity for attacking the innocent. Puppies, boys, and pregnant women. Your courage is boundless."

Vannoy crossed his arms and tilted his head as if he could look into Rhys's mind. "It gladdens me to know I was the topic of so many conversations. Mayhap Eliane and I can return the favor."

"You. Will. Not. Have. Her." The words echoed off the walls.

"Yet I do." Vannoy turned and walked away, leaving

Rhys to stare in frustration at the dozen arrows that landed in the dirt before him.

Eliane could see the forest. It called to her. Tears rolled from her eyes as she stood in the high tower room that imprisoned her and gazed at the land that was in her blood. She felt her hope leaving her with each tear that she shed. Rhys had not stopped Vannoy.

Did he even come? Was he grateful to be rid of her? Her courage, so strong during the journey, left her and doubts filled her mind. Her hand went to her finger, but the ring was gone. All that remained was a white band where the ring had blocked the sun. How long before it was nothing more than a memory?

Her back clenched. The burden of the child was heavy. The hard and torturous journey had taken its toll. The babe would be born soon and there was nothing she could do to stop it, just as there was nothing she could do to keep Vannoy from killing the babe once it came.

A middle-aged woman brought her some food, a pail of water for washing and a fairly clean gown. Eliane tried to speak to her, but the woman covered her mouth and shook her head. She was mute and her eyes told the story of years of terror and mistreatment. This woman would not help her; nor would the guard at her door.

All was lost. . . . At least she had the small knife, now hidden beneath her mattress. If the need came, she would use it on herself. Vannoy had told her of his plans for her. Starting with her ears.

"You. Will. Not. Have. Her." The shout echoed against the stone and she turned to the narrow arrow slit that faced the castle gate. In the distance beneath a tree she saw Yorath.

"Rhys . . ."

He had come. She saw him, standing on the pathway to the gate with his broadsword in his hand. He was alone. He must have ridden through the night, just as Vannoy had.

From the shouts within the keep, she knew Vannoy was on his way to her. He would use her to bait Rhys. She had to make her move now, before the birth pains got worse.

She grabbed up the knife from its hiding place and put it in her sleeve. She moved to the table where other weapons would be readily available. A candlestick, the platter from her meal, even a small stool.

Vannoy burst through the door. The portal swung back and remained open. Eliane flicked her eyes over it, deciding whether she could make a run for it. She crossed her arms over her stomach as he came near, as much to protect the babe as to conceal the knife.

"Your *husband* seems to think that he can command *me* within my own keep," he said, sneering.

"My *husband* seeks to protect me as I am *his* wife."

"He will not want you for his wife when I am through with you."

"No wonder you are without a wife of your own." Eliane sneered. "Your words of courtship are enough to make any woman scream and run as far away from you as she can get."

He grabbed her neck so that he could turn her head to look at him. "Oh, I promise you will scream. They all scream."

Eliane sought the knife in her sleeve. "You disgust

me." She hoped his anger would distract him. Her words had the desired effect. He raised his hand to strike her and she used his movement against him, pulling the knife and slashing it across his upper arm. She let the impetous of her motion carry her toward the door. Vannoy caught her hair in his fist and brought her up short. Without a thought Eliane twisted and slashed at her hair with the knife, cutting the braid from her head. She kept moving and stumbled through the door, burying her knife in the guard's neck. She was going down the curving steps when another pain wrenched her and she slipped in the sudden rush of water that poured from her womb. She managed to grab on to a sconce mounted in the wall to keep from falling, but the delay gave Vannoy enough time to catch her.

He wrapped his hand in what was left of her hair and pulled her back. Another pain grabbed her spine.

"The babe is coming," she ground out between clenched teeth.

Vannoy pitched her back into the chamber. "Good," he said. "I will tell your *husband* to prepare the grave. He can bury his brat next to your father."

Eliane fell across the bed. "Send for a midwife or I will not survive the birth."

"Oh, do not worry." He stood at the door. "You will have the best of care."

Eliane put her face in her hands as she curled onto the bed. Her hair, now shorn, fell in curls about her face and brushed her shoulders. She heard the bar slam across the door and knew she would not have another chance.

"If only I had told Rhys I love him," she said.

There was no one to hear her words.

Han, Ammon the stable boy, and fifty men-at-arms joined Rhys beneath the oak tree.

"Rest assured, the forest is full of huntsmen, just waiting for our signal," Han informed Rhys.

Rhys nodded grimly and looked at the odd collection of armor that Ammon wore.

"She is not only milady, she is my friend," he said simply.

Rhys placed a hand on Ammon's bony shoulder. "I thank you."

"I will get my thanks from Eliane when we remove her from this place," Ammon said firmly.

The neighing of the horses alerted Rhys to more men coming. Cedric and his men-at-arms. Cedric drove a wagon with Khati sitting on the bench beside him. Mathias lay in the back with Llyr, their wounds carefully wrapped with bandages. The dog weakly thumped his tail when Rhys laid a hand upon his huge head.

"They would not stay behind," Cedric said.

"It seems as if I am besieged with those who care more for their lady's well-being than their own lives," Rhys observed as Cedric quickly went about the work of setting up camp. Khati carefully laid out Eliane's stash of weapons and picked up the short sword as if she would wield it herself. "The only one missing is Madwyn."

Han stood beside him, observing all in his quiet way. He wore his wool cap as usual, yet the heat of the day seemed not to bother him in the least. "Madwyn tends to a birthing. She will be here when it is over."

Rhys looked at the castle before him. Somewhere within was Eliane. How had she fared during the trip? Surely not well. It would suit Vannoy's intent if she went into labor and lost the babe.

Rhys desperately needed some sign of her. He needed to know that she was still alive, that there was still hope.

"De Remy!" Vannoy once more stood on the wall, only this time he was alone. There were no archers, no men-at-arms, only the man, holding a piece of white linen in one hand and what appeared to be a brown rope in the other. His upper arm was wrapped in a bandage, and Rhys could not help smiling.

"Eliane's work, no doubt," he said to Han, who nodded in agreement.

Vannoy waved the white linen and shouted once more. "A truce. For your lady."

"I can have the archers take him," Han murmured in his ear.

"Until we know Eliane is safe, we will do nothing," Rhys instructed. "I do not put it past him to hold a knife at her throat." He mounted Yorath. "Stay your hand until I have proof she is safe."

Rhys rode to the castle wall. Never, in all the battles he'd fought, had he felt such fear. How was she? He needed to see her face. He needed to know that she was, for the moment, unharmed. He needed her to know that he was here for her. That he would lay down his life to save her. He needed her to know that he loved her.

I should have told her before. . . .

"Do you surrender?" he asked Vannoy. He stopped before the wall, close enough that Vannoy could see the threat in his eyes.

"It seems that I have need of a midwife."

Rhys's heart jumped into his throat. He swallowed determinedly. He would not show fear to his enemy. It would only give Vannoy a measure of victory.

"Don't bother with your threats," Vannoy said when Rhys did not answer him. "I have heard them all. Your bastard is on its way. It is my desire that my sweet Eliane survive the birth, so that she can bear my child. Send in a midwife. I promise I will not kill her."

"I will send for one, if I can find any willing to enter." He knew Madwyn would gladly go in. But would Vannoy recognize her and know of her devotion to Eliane?

"As a promise for the midwife's safety, I send this token from your wife," Vannoy added. "She gave it up willingly." He pitched the rope over the wall and Rhys snatched it from the air.

It took a moment for him to realize what it was he held. *Her hair* . . . He knew the look he turned up to Vannoy was frightful. He could not control his face any more than he could control the pounding in his veins or the red haze that covered his eyes.

"Consider it the first of many pieces I will slowly return to you." Vannoy left the wall.

As Rhys turned and rode away, he held her hair to his face and inhaled her scent. The braid quickly grew damp with his tears.

Chapter Twenty-six

𝒟usk settled around the keep. From her tower, Eliane saw the fires of Rhys's camp as she paced about the room with her hands fisted against her back. The spasms were coming closer and closer together and she was trapped with no creature comforts except for a bit of water left in the pail. There wasn't even a candle to relieve the darkness of her prison. She had only the pain of the coming babe to keep her company.

She was so alone. Never had she felt this way. Was this what it had been like for Rhys as a boy? To have no one? Another contraction gripped her and she leaned against the wall, her hand braced against the arrow slit, her eyes on the camp below, hoping for some sign of Rhys. She'd kept quiet so far, but this pain was worse, and it finally tore a cry from her lips.

She leaned her head into the slit, hoping for a cool breeze to ease her. She caught a movement beneath the great oak tree and saw two tall forms step away from it and gaze toward the castle. The light of the full moon shone upon them and she quickly recognized Rhys. The taller form beside him was Han. She kept her eyes on Rhys, as if she could draw strength from him, until another spasm racked her body and sent her to her knees with the pain. When it passed she collapsed to the floor and lay there, letting the coolness of the stone soothe her.

A noise made her stir and she pushed against the floor to sit against the wall as she gathered her strength for the next contraction. A movement caught her eye, a flutter, and then she found herself staring into the great golden eyes of Madwyn's owl. It blinked, hopped to her outstretched arm, and bent its beak to touch its leg. There was a small piece of rolled parchment tied there with a piece of string.

Eliane's hands shook as she took the parchment and held it up to the shaft of moonlight that came into her chamber. *Be strong. I am coming.* There was no name, nor was there need for one. Madwyn would come. It also meant that Rhys had a plan for her release.

The owl hopped to the arrow slit and Eliane struggled to her feet. As the owl left, she saw Rhys and Han both follow its flight. They wanted to know where she was, and the owl showed them. Rhys stepped forward and stared up at her tower. She waved and was gladdened to see him raise his hand. He turned toward the path that led to the gate and she saw a bent figure wearing a heavy cloak and carrying a large basket. The woman limped heavily while using a stout stick for support. Eliane sank to the floor. Madwyn was coming.

The woman who entered her chamber was an old crone, with a humped back and gnarled hands. The serving woman who came with her was the one who could not speak. She carried two pails of water and a bundle of cloths. She set the things down, drew a candle from her pocket and placed it in the candlestick, then scurried out. Once more the bar was thrown over the door, leaving Eliane alone with the crone.

She sat on the floor and watched as the crone put down her basket and lit the candle. As she turned to look at Eliane, she threw off her cloak and her body straightened. Gone was the crone, replaced by Madwyn. The hump on her back was Eliane's bow and quiver.

"How did you do it?" Eliane gasped at the sudden change in her appearance.

"The fools see what they want to see." Madwyn gathered Eliane into her arms and another contraction took her.

" 'Tis too soon," Eliane cried.

"Just a few weeks," Madwyn soothed. She ran her hand over Eliane's shorn hair. "The fool will pay for this among other things."

Eliane shook her head. "I did it. He held me by my braid, so I cut if off to escape." She let the sobs come.

"Poor child of mine. So brave," Madwyn cooed.

"I don't want the babe to come," Eliane cried. "He will kill her."

"Do you trust me?"

"I do."

"Then you must do as I say and trust that all will be well in the end." Madwyn pulled Eliane to her feet and guided her to the bed. She removed the bow and quiver and shoved it beneath. "Let us take care of the babe," she said as she wiped the sweat from Eliane's brow. "Then we will take care of the rest."

Rhys kept his eyes on the tower. Now that he knew where she was, he felt a bit better, but not much. The babe was coming, and coming soon. Her cries rent the night air, causing him to wonder. How could something so wondrous cause so much pain? It was if she were being ripped into halves, and in a way she was. A piece of her, a piece of him, was becoming whole unto itself. A daughter was coming into this world.

"Please, God." He fingered the cross around his neck. "Let the plan work." It was dangerous. Especially for Eliane and Madwyn. But it was the only way. Their only chance.

A scream echoed off the walls.

"It will be soon," Han said. His pale blue eyes were fixed on the tower also.

Something bumped Rhys's hand and he saw Llyr, trembling beside him. Rhys blinked as if awakened from a deep sleep. He had not realized that everyone watched and waited with him. Khati, Cedric, Ammon, even Mathias, although he sat on a stool. The boy's face was pale in the coming dawn.

Behind them was nothing but silence. The men-at-arms were silent. Even the horses made no sound as they grazed behind the camp on Vannoy's grass.

Llyr whined and sniffed at the braid that Rhys wore wrapped about his waist. Rhys knelt beside him. He put his arm around the beast. There was another scream and Llyr tried to move forward. Rhys held him back. A shadow moved across the light in the tower room, and Rhys felt his body tense. He waited.

There was nothing. No sound, no word, not even the sounds of the night came to him. There was nothing but the small light that shone from the arrow slit above.

"It will soon be upon us," Han said. "You should rest."

Rhys did not hear him.

Madwyn stood with her back to Eliane. She held the babe in her arms. "Let me see," Eliane said. She felt as if she'd been torn asunder, yet she felt the relief of having completed a long journey. Her reward was within reach, yet Madwyn held it from her.

Madwyn shook her head. There was no sound from the babe. Why did it not cry out? Was that not the way of things?

Madwyn cleaned the babe and wrapped it in a square of linen. She placed it in the basket, then turned to Eliane.

"I want to see."

"Let me cleanse you first," Madwyn said. She washed Eliane's body and placed a kirtle on her. One of the ones left at Aubregate when Eliane went to London.

"Why doesn't she cry?"

"She is as tired as you are. There isn't much time. Vannoy will come as soon as he wakens. You must rest for what will happen next."

"Let me hold her."

Madwyn nodded. She went to the basket, moved things from within it while she held the babe. She kept her back to Eliane and still there was no sound.

"Let me see her," Eliane asked again.

Madwyn turned with the babe in her arms. "I am sorry, Eliane. It was too soon. She did not survive."

It was as if time stopped. When did Madwyn put the babe in her arms? When did she put on her cloak and pick up her basket? When did she turn once more into the old crone?

Eliane pushed back the blanket. The infant was tiny, yet perfectly formed, with delicate fingers and tiny nails. Her hair was dark and heavy on her brow. Her skin was so very cold and looked blue in the candlelight.

Eliane heard the bar being lifted from the door.

"Eliane. Look at me," Madwyn said.

Eliane tore her eyes from her daughter and stared into the face shadowed within the cloak.

"Be strong. It all depends upon you." Madwyn faded into the shadows behind the door.

Eliane nodded. This was her only chance. She must be ready, no matter that her heart was breaking. Mayhap it was better this way. Vannoy could not touch her daughter now. He would not have the joy of killing her.

Vannoy loomed over her. "I see she looks like her father," he said.

"You cannot hurt her." Eliane painfully rose from the bed, keeping it between them. "She is dead." Eliane wrapped the babe up and held her close.

Vannoy shrugged. "How disappointing for both of us," he said. "Still, de Remy does not know it. She can still serve my purpose." He made a move to take the child and Eliane turned and held her tighter. "Give her to me now," he said. "Or I will kill the midwife."

"Oh no, sir, please," the crone cried out as she bowed and bobbed before him. "I have done as ye asked." She looked at Eliane. "I am sorry, milady. It was too soon. Too soon." She said it over and over again and rocked as she repeated the words.

"What will you do with my babe?"

"I will return her to her father," Vannoy said. He held out his hands and bared his teeth in what he thought was a smile. Eliane looked at Madwyn, who still rocked and moaned as if her life depended upon it. It did. Eliane had no choice but to hand over the body of her daughter.

Vannoy looked at the babe closely as if he did not believe she was really dead. He lifted her by the arm and shook her roughly. Eliane wanted to shriek and cry at the abuse, but she remained quiet. She knew her protests would only encourage him.

"Is your job here done?" he asked the crone.

"Yes, milord, yes. I pray thee, sir, ye must give milady time to heal lest she take the sickness and die."

"How much time?" Vannoy's eyes upon Eliane were calculating.

"Until the moon is full again," the crone said.

"You may go," he said. "The man who summoned you will pay you."

The crone looked at Eliane and gave her a slight smile.

"Tell my husband that I would name her Arden, after my mother," Eliane said. Tears welled and she quickly dashed them away. "Tell him to baptize her with that name."

The crone nodded and left. Vannoy followed with the body of her daughter, and the bar slid home, once again leaving Eliane alone with nothing but her tears.

Rhys held his breath as Madwyn made her slow and painful way from the gate. The transformation was amazing. Just by wearing her cloak and adjusting her stance, she gave the illusion of age and a broken and twisted body. As she approached the trees, he and Han went out to escort her into the shelter of the camp. Han took the heavy basket from her as she threw back her hood and once again became the elegant and graceful lady of the forest.

"Hurry," she said. "He will need milk."

"He?" Rhys asked.

She lifted the babe from the basket and it stirred. "Fetch the woman. She may still give life to this child." She turned to Rhys and placed the babe in his startled arms. "You have a son, milord. I would not have believed it had I not seen him come forth from Eliane's womb."

Rhys looked down at the thatch of bright red hair over the tiny face while Madwyn adjusted his arms to better hold the babe. Tiny fists jerked and the arms and legs stretched. The eyes opened and stared at him with a deep intensity that reminded him of Eliane's emerald gaze; then the babe turned his head and with mouth open nudged the armor covering Rhy's chest. Rhys touched his finger to the tiny shell of his ear. It was rounded and quite normal looking.

"A son?" He looked at Madwyn with disbelief. "Eliane?"

"She is strong. She thinks the babe dead. I could not tell her otherwise, lest her hope give away our plan."

"Will she fight?"

"She will fight."

A young woman came forth. She was quite small, had long dark hair and great dark circles beneath her eyes. "This is Jodhi. It was her daughter who died and is sacrificed to Vannoy. She will nurse your son until his mother may do so."

Rhys placed his son into her willing arms. "You will never want for anything as long as you live," he promised her.

Jodhi dipped her head and gave him a sad smile. "My husband will fight for our lady," she said, and left with his son.

The top of the sun appeared among the trees to the east. Day was upon them. Rhys stepped out from the shelter of the oak once more and stared up at the tower room. If only he could see her. *A son . . . We have a son. There are only daughters born to the woman of Aubregate. Until now. Eliane . . .*

"De Remy!" Vannoy once more stood on the castle wall.

It was time.

Chapter Twenty-seven

*V*annoy stood on the walls again. His archers were in their place and his men-at-arms on horseback gathered in the outer bailey behind the gate. He was ready for battle and Eliane knew he planned to use their baby to enrage Rhys into doing something foolish.

As Rhys had hoped he would do.

She was so very tired. She had not slept for two days. The hard travel and the subsequent birth had drained her. She wanted nothing more than to lie down and sleep, but she could not. Her life and the lives of her people depended upon her.

She'd moved the small table before the door and used the stool to brace it against the bed so that none could enter. She pulled her leather gauntlets over her arms and placed the knife she'd found in her quiver on the sill. She positioned the quiver beside her and tested the tautness of the bow. Her head felt exceedingly light and her hand went self-consciously to the curls that teased her shoulders.

"De Remy!" Vannoy shouted. Dawn had broken over the land and it lit the field before the castle, although the oak tree still lay in shadow. To her surprise she saw an entire army of people gathered behind it. Tents, wagons, cook fires, and horses. It had sprung up during the night. Her eyes easily found Rhys as if there were a line strung between them. He stood before the tree looking up at the tower. She saw several others beneath the tree and wondered who they could be. Madwyn surely. Han? What of Cedric, Khati, and Mathias? She should have asked Madwyn about Mathias, but there had not been time. There had only been the pain of birthing and the pain of death. The pain that she could not give in to. Not yet.

Within a moment of Vannoy's shout, the group beneath the tree dispersed and Yorath was led forward. Her heart leapt with joy at the sight of Llyr walking back to the shelter of the camp with Mathias. She had feared them both dead. As the echo of Vannoy's shout faded into the morning sky, Rhys rode forth.

Eliane notched her bow.

Rhys wore full armor except for his helm. His head was bare and his dark hair fell over his forehead and curled haphazardly about his ears. Her fingers itched to touch it and she strummed them over the bow string as she watched.

"De Remy!" Vannoy shouted again. He lifted the body of the baby girl up and held it over his head. "Here is your daughter!"

Eliane drew the bowstring back. She could kill Vannoy now, easily. His back was within her sight line. But Vannoy was not the immediate danger. She pointed her arrow at the archer who stood next to him on the wall.

Vannoy threw the body out and over the wall. From the camp a woman screamed. Eliane bit her trembling lip to keep from crying out and kept her bowstring taut. Rhys disappeared from her view as he rode within the shadow of the castle wall. Vannoy shouted down to him, but his words were lost to her.

As Rhys rode back to the camp with the body, a flash of white flew across the sky. Madwyn's owl, a signal to her and the archers in the woods. The owl flew straight to her tower and landed inside just as the sky filled with arrows. The great longbows of the Aubregate huntsmen were loosed. Eliane added hers to the assault. As the arrows came in from the side, she fired from behind, picking Vannoy's archers from the wall as easily as when she shot apples from a tree.

Rhys turned Yorath as he entered the camp, and the men-at-arms joined him. The army rode out, shielding the men who rode in tandem with a battering ram between them.

The confusion on the wall grew as those beneath the assault of arrows tried to decide where to take shelter. Eliane turned her attention to the gate. Vannoy stood on the wall beside it and shouted down instructions to the men gathered below. He had hoped to send them out to attack. Instead the attack was coming to him.

She only had a handful of arrows left. She rapidly shot them, targeting the enemy. Men fell, horses reared, and the ram pounded on the gate. The archers from the forest ran to the walls and rained arrows into the outer bailey.

Vannoy ran across the bridge that connected the outer wall to the inner. Eliane only had one arrow left and her knife. Vannoy would come for her, if only to use her as a shield to make his escape. This time he would not surprise her. This time she was more than ready for him.

She heard the gate splinter. She heard the battle

cries of the men as they met. She staggered to the
middle of the room with her bow. She was weak and
her arms and shoulders trembled from the effort of
firing the arrows. Her back and legs ached from the
delivery and she felt the blood that still seeped from
her womb.

Madwyn's owl blinked at her from its perch upon
the bed frame.

"Go," she said. "Fly to the forest and to home." He
hopped to the slit and swiveled his head around for
one last look as she heard the pounding of Vannoy's
boots on the stairs.

The bar was thrown. The door moved slightly, and
then stopped as it came up against the table. He pounded
against it. Eliane notched the arrow and raised her bow.
Her shoulder cramped and she blinked as the door
seemed to waver before her. Lightning flashed across
her eyelids.

Be strong . . . stay strong . . . you cannot fail now. . . .

With each blow, the table moved until finally the
leg splintered and it broke against the bed. With one
last kick Vannoy pushed the door open and strode into
the room.

Eliane took a deep breath against the cramp that
shot across her back and let the arrow fly. For the first
time in her life she missed. Instead of his heart, the
arrow pierced his shoulder. Vannoy snarled at her and
jerked the arrow loose. He threw it to the side as
Eliane snatched up the knife. Her hands shook and
her legs felt like stalks of grass. She had no more
strength to fight him.

"Rhys will kill you," she said. "He is within your
walls."

"You will not live to see it," Vannoy said. "If I cannot have you, then neither shall he."

"Your hatred will be a sorry companion in hell."

"Then I shall have to take you with me for company." He came at her. Eliane held the knife close in as Han had taught her and waited for him to strike. She saw an opening in his belly and made to swing upward, but she was too weak, and he too strong. He struck her across the face and she spun round. The knife fell from her grip. Eliane collapsed against the wall and slid to the floor. Vannoy wrapped his hands around her neck and pulled her up. He pinned her against the wall and he squeezed. Eliane kicked at him, but she had no strength. She was weak and exhausted and she had nothing left to fight with. She gripped his arms, trying to pull them away, and then clawed at his face. Blackness overwhelmed her. She could not draw a breath. She could not make a sound. Her heart pounded and she felt herself sliding away. *Rhys . . .*

He was here. He kicked aside the door and the table. He held his sword in one hand and with the other he grabbed Vannoy by the shoulder. Vannoy's eyes widened and his grip relaxed as Rhys buried his sword in Vannoy's stomach and thrust upward. Blood gurgled from his lips. Rhys turned them both so he stood next to Eliane. Vannoy faced them with his eyes wide in disbelief.

"You. Will. Not. Have. Her," Rhys said, and he yanked his sword free. Vannoy crumpled to the floor.

Eliane felt herself falling, but Rhys grabbed her with his free arm and pulled her against his hip. "Can you walk? I fear we may still have to fight."

"With your help I can fly," Eliane said.

He was right. Men-at-arms charged up the steps toward them. Rhys pushed Eliane behind him and stood with his sword in the ready position.

"Your master is dead," he said. "Do you still wish to fight?"

The men shook their heads and backed away. They had no love for their master, and with his death there would be no payment for their services. Han and Ammon came up behind them, along with some of the men-at-arms from Aubregate. Ammon grinned up at her.

"You are saved, milady," he said.

"I am . . ."

The world swirled around her and Rhys caught her as she fainted dead away.

When she woke, she was on a pallet beneath the limbs of the oak. Llyr lay beside her, and the cries of a babe caused a spasm of pain in her breasts.

"Why is there a babe here?" she asked Madwyn, who rushed to her side.

"He was born here," she said. "His father kept him close at hand so that he may meet his mother."

Eliane looked at Madwyn, who smiled a beautiful smile at her. "Would you like to sit?" she asked. She pulled Eliane up and Khati put pillows behind her, using the tree as a backrest. Llyr once more settled against her side and she twined her fingers into the hair at his neck. A bandage was around his middle, but his eyes were clear and his nose cool to the touch. He would recover, as would she. Once they returned to Aubregate. Once they returned home.

"Here comes the father now," Madwyn said.

Eliane looked up and saw Rhys coming to her with a babe in his arms. The smile on his face was broad and his dark eyes shone with something she'd never seen before.

"I do not understand," Eliane said. "What has happened?"

Rhys knelt beside her and laid the babe in her arms. "We have a son," he said. Eliane looked down at the babe and saw a thatch of red hair and a strong brow, much like his father's. Her heart swelled as the child nudged her breast.

"We have a son?" she asked. She looked from Rhys to Madwyn.

"He is yours. I gave him mandrake to make him sleep so I could carry him out. The child you saw died yestermorn in birth. 'Twas Jodhi and Peter's. Jodhi has nursed your babe 'til your return."

"But a son." She still could not believe it. For as long as history was written, there had only been daughters born to the women of Aubregate. The babe whimpered in protest at not being fed. Madwyn nodded encouragement and Eliane loosened the tie on her kirtle and put the child to her breast. He latched on with a determined ferocity that made her gasp. Rhys laughed and placed his hand around the back of his son's head. His other hand found the end of her hair and he pulled the curl straight, watching with a rueful smile as it bounced back. Eliane tore her eyes from the babe to watch Rhys's reaction to her hair.

"Madwyn told me you did this," he said.

"I am sorry." She was suddenly self-conscious of her looks. She had not seen him for months and knew she was not the same wife he'd left behind.

"It will grow."

She nodded and ran her finger down the soft cheek of her son. He raised his arm and placed his tiny fist against her breast.

"I would have cut off my arm to get you back," Rhys said, and she knew he meant it.

She looked at him once more. His eyes upon her were deep and dark, haunted by the lonely little boy he had once been. While her son nursed at her breast, her blood quickened with want and need for her husband.

"I love you, Eliane."

Her eyes filled with tears and she blinked them back. "As I love you."

He slowly bent his head to hers. "You are the treasure of Aubregate," he said as his lips found hers in the gentlest of kisses.

Later, when they were in the keep at Aubregate and once more clean and well fed, Rhys realized that what he felt was contentment. He gazed at Eliane from his chair by the fire. Llyr felt it too. His tail thumped against the floor as Rhys gave his huge head a rub.

Eliane sat on the bed, playing with their son. Her hair was freshly washed and had quickly dried into a riot of curls that bounced around her shoulders as she laughed at a face the babe made. Her countenance glowed and he knew in his heart that she would never regret giving birth. That she would never abandon their son or willingly leave his side.

At last he had a home. As if she knew he watched her, she lifted her face and her emerald eyes dazzled him as they always did.

"We must have a name for him," she said as he joined her on the bed. Rhys put his finger in the babe's palm, and his fist closed over it in a tight grip.

"He will do well with a sword," he said.

"Already training him to fight, are you?"

"I have enough trouble training Mathias." The babe's eyes shifted between their faces, and once more he was struck by how much his gaze resembled Eliane's. "We will give him plenty of time to play boyish games and learn the ways of the land before putting a sword in his hand." Feeling a bit foolish, he added, "Mayhap I can learn these things as well."

"You will be a good father, Rhys." He was once more caught by her emerald gaze. "I know it in my heart." She smiled sweetly and he could not help kissing her. The babe pushed at them with his legs and thrust his arms out, causing them both to laugh at his antics.

"We could name him Edward after your father."

"I would like to use Edward, but there is also another name I like. Since he is a male child and the first in more years than I can count, I thought we might give him a name of the forest also."

"Do you have one in mind?"

"Yes. I would like to call our son Duncan. After Han's father."

"Duncan," Rhys said. "I like the sound of it." He raised an eyebrow and looked at Eliane skeptically. "Are you sure Han has a father? I had always thought Edward kept him in a box and only brought him out to deliver messages."

Eliane laughed at his joke, and then turned serious once more. "Truly? You like Duncan for our son?"

"Duncan Edward de Remy. 'Tis a fine name."

Eliane moved their son from the bed to her lap and cooed down at him. "Duncan is your name. 'Tis a fine name indeed and one you will do justice to."

"If Duncan was Han's father, then who was his mother?"

"Madwyn, of course."

Rhys shook his head in disbelief. "It seems to make sense, now that you've told me." He watched in fascination as Duncan latched on to Eliane's breast. "The people of the forest are a kingdom unto themselves."

"Oh, dear husband, you have no idea."

A knock on the door interrupted his question. "Come," he commanded, and Mathias came in, walking slowly became of the wound in his side.

"We have visitors," he said.

"Please tell me they are not from the king," Rhys groaned. He'd sent a message by Jess to Henry, telling him of Vannoy's actions and his death. Now there was the wait to see who would claim Chasmore. Rhys chose not to worry over it. He had more important things to fill his mind.

"Nay, milord," Mathias said. "'Tis a family of crofters. They said milady bade them come here if they were in need." Mathias placed his ring in his hand. Rhys had noticed it was gone from Eliane's hand but had not had time to ask about it. He held it up for her to see.

"My ring!" she exclaimed, and a look of sheer joy came over her lovely face. "They cared for me when I begged Vannoy to stop. They were most kind and gracious to me even though their own lives were at risk. I told them they would always have a home at Aubregate."

"Indeed they will," Rhys said. "Give them shelter and tell them I will meet with them on the morrow."

"Yes, milord," Mathias said, and made to shut the door.

"Mathias," Rhys called out. The boy looked at him expectantly. "It pleases me to say that of late, I have no cause to beat you."

Mathias grinned. "It pleases me to hear so, milord."

They both laughed as Mathias closed the door.

Contentment . . . If every day could have moments such as these . . . Rhys took Eliane's hand in his, and slid the ring back where it belonged. Her fingers closed over his. He put his arm around her and pulled her and Duncan against him, while placing his cheek against the satiny softness of her curls. He pulled a curl straight and watched in fascination as it bounced back into place. It was a simple pleasure. One that he would never tire of.

Epilogue

"We must walk from here," Eliane said. They dismounted in a small glade that was barely big enough for their horses. The small game trail they'd followed had gone up and down and twisted upon itself until he had no clue at to where he was within the forest of Aubregate. It seemed much bigger once one was in it than it did when one rode around it.

It came to him as they rode that he had now seen Eliane in every season. He'd met her in the dead of winter, within the forest. He'd lusted after her through the spring, missed her during the heat of summer, and realized he could not live a day without her when the leaves blazed bright as her hair. Love, once discovered, was something he desired more than anything.

Eliane was sad and his heart ached for her. He could tell her mood by the way her fingers twisted in the hair at Llyr's neck. It was the first time they had left Duncan for more than a few hours, but it was not missing the child that caused her mood. Duncan was well cared for by Khati and Jodhi. It was Madwyn's imminent departure that caused her sadness.

As they followed the nearly invisible trail deeper into the forest, Madwyn carried her basket and Han carried a blanket wrapped with her other things. Her snowy owl landed in a branch overhead and watched them with its golden eyes before taking off again to lead the way.

A heavy frost had come the night before and the air was thick with cold; his lungs hurt with the effort to breathe, and the air fogged with each exhalation. The thick carpet of leaves crunched heavily under his boots as he followed Madwyn, Han, and Eliane down the trail between the twisting roots of the oaks.

They walked in silence, Llyr, Han, Madwyn, and Eliane before him. They knew they were safe here. There was none from the outside world who could survive coming in this deep. Rhys felt as if he'd gone into another world. They walked on, the only sounds the chirping of the birds and the occasional flutter of wings, and the crunch of the frozen leaves.

The air felt suddenly warmer. The sharp bite of the frost was gone. A breeze that felt like summer touched his cheek and Eliane turned and graced him with a smile. The smells changed also. No longer was there the forest smell of decay and rotten wood. Instead he smelled something fresh and clean, like newly cut grass.

The trail spiraled downward again. Through the trees he saw a glimmer of water. The leaves that still hung on the trees overhead sighed with the breeze and he looked up. He saw the owl again, a flash of white against the bronzes, reds, and golds of autumn.

The trail widened and thick grass edged the trail. They moved into a glade bisected by a wide stream. Llyr bounded down to the water's edge and drank. The glade was so large that it was hard to see into the trees opposite. Even though it was fall, flowers bloomed brightly in patches and butterflies skimmed over their tops. It was so warm that he could remove his cloak.

Rhys stepped out into the open and turned in a circle with his eyes on the sky. It was the same bright blue as before and scattered with a few fluffy clouds. He could not count the miles they had ridden, or walked.

"What is this place?" he asked Eliane.

"This way," she said with a mysterious smile.

They followed after Han and Madwyn, who had disappeared around a huge pine with branches that swept the ground. When he came round it, he stopped in his tracks. Two stone columns stood before him. The warm breeze he felt upon his face came from between, yet the grass beyond did not move.

Madwyn dropped her basket next to the things Han had carried. Her son bent to her, took her in his arms, and hugged her tight.

"I will miss you, Mother," he said.

"It is time for me to go," she said as Eliane went to her.

"You can stay," she said. A tear rolled down her cheek and she wiped it away. "I don't know if I can do this without you."

Madwyn took Eliane's hands into hers. "Nonsense. My duty was to show you the way and help you raise your daughter." She ran a hand through Eliane's curls and smiled her approval. "But you have a *son*. It is up to Han to show him the way."

"But what if we have a daughter someday? What then?" Eliane asked tearfully.

"Then there will be someone for her as I was there for you, your mother, and her mother before her." She hugged Eliane to her breast. "More of your mothers than you will know, Eliane. They wait for me inside. As I will wait for you." She looked at Rhys and she suddenly seemed younger and more beautiful than ever. "And you."

"What is this place?" Rhys asked. "Where are you going?"

"It is the passageway to our world," Han said. "We are the guardians of this gate."

"Your world?" Rhys asked.

"You know of Merlin and Arthur?" Madwyn asked.

"Yes. Camelot." Rhys knew the legend.

"Merlin was one of us. We are the fey. Long ago this land was ours, but men and their wars drove us from it. This is the only place that remains where our kind can cross over into our paradise. We leave it open for those who are still lost."

"It is my duty to protect it," Eliane said. "As long as the portal remains open, Aubregate will prosper. This is the treasure."

"If a mortal passes through, it will be destroyed," Han said.

"But you said you will wait for Eliane . . . and me."

"Eliane may come when it is her time. She may bring you if her heart desires it."

Eliane took his hand. "My heart will always desire it."

"But what of your mother? And Edward?"

"We may only die in battle," Han said. "Arden died fighting to protect the keep."

"Therefore Edward could not go with her," Rhys surmised.

"A good reason to keep me safe," Eliane teased.

"Always," he promised. "No matter the cost."

They stood hand in hand as Madwyn waved good-bye

and stepped through the portal. The breeze quickened, and blew across them, throwing Eliane's curls
into wild disarray around her. Rhys watched Madwyn
fade into the distance and heard a soft whinny. A white
horse, nay, not a horse, for it had a horn upon its
forehead . . . Eliane squeezed his hand.

"Yes. 'Tis what you think," she said. "Someday I
will show you."

"I can wait," he said. "For my heaven is right here,
beside you."

✂

☐ **YES!**

Sign me up for the Historical Romance Book Club and send my FREE BOOKS! If I choose to stay in the club, I will pay only $8.50* each month, a savings of $6.48!

NAME: _____

ADDRESS: _____

TELEPHONE: _____

EMAIL: _____

☐ I want to pay by credit card.

☐ **VISA**　　☐ **MasterCard.**　　☐ **DISCOVER**

ACCOUNT #: _____

EXPIRATION DATE: _____

SIGNATURE: _____

Mail this page along with $2.00 shipping and handling to:
Historical Romance Book Club
PO Box 6640
Wayne, PA 19087
Or fax (must include credit card information) to:
610-995-9274

You can also sign up online at **www.dorchesterpub.com**.
*Plus $2.00 for shipping. Offer open to residents of the U.S. and Canada only.
Canadian residents please call 1-800-481-9191 for pricing information.
If under 18, a parent or guardian must sign. Terms, prices and conditions subject to change. Subscription subject to acceptance. Dorchester Publishing reserves the right to reject any order or cancel any subscription.